D0901282

My Heart Belongs

in *Gettysburg,*
PENNSYLVANIA

DISCARDED

My Heart Belongs

in *Gettysburg,* PENNSYLVANIA

*Clarissa's
Conflict*

MURRAY PURA

BARBOUR BOOKS

An Imprint of Barbour Publishing, Inc.

© 2018 by Murray Pura

ISBN 978-1-68322-740-3

Adobe Digital Edition (.epub) 978-1-68322-742-7
Kindle and MobiPocket Edition (.prc) 978-1-68322-741-0

All rights reserved. No part of this publication may be reproduced or
transmitted in any form or by any means without written permission of the
publisher.

This book is a work of fiction. Names, characters, places, and incidents are
either products of the author's imagination or used fictitiously. Any similar-
ity to actual people, organizations, and/or events is purely coincidental.

Scripture quotations are taken from the King James Version of the Bible.

Series Design: Kirk DouPonce, DogEared Design
Model Photo: Ilina Simeonova/Trevillion Images

Published by Barbour Books, an imprint of Barbour Publishing, Inc., 1810
Barbour Drive, Uhrichsville, OH 44683, www.barbourbooks.com

Our mission is to inspire the world with the life-changing message of the Bible.

 Member of the
Evangelical Christian
Publishers Association

Printed in the United States of America.

Dedication

This novel is for Bob and Jennifer and Emma—
an amazing family that has been with my stories for a lifetime.

Chapter One

Saturday night, early December 1860
Adams County, Commonwealth of Pennsylvania
Five miles north of Gettysburg

*J*t was so black she could not see her hand even if she held it so close it touched her face.

To the left and right she could not even pick out the trees on either side of the forest path.

It did not matter.

Overhead, where tree branches were not closing together to form a canopy, she could see the stars burning and recognized every one of them—she knew the constellations well and where the North Star blazed, no matter what season of the year it was.

Under her boots was the deer trail she had walked many times, day and night, so how dark it was did not concern her—her feet knew the way, and she never had a misstep. Even if her eyes had been blinded and her legs shackled, she would not have lost her sense of direction. The path to freedom was carved in her heart.

No snow on the trail, but the cold bit. Never mind. They were dressed for it.

"Mizz Clarissa," whispered a woman behind her. "Ain't we ought to have got there yet?"

But the whisper was too loud.

Clarissa turned swiftly.

"Hush!" Her whisper was low but sharp as a musket shot. "It is only another mile. But this is the most dangerous stretch. Slave catchers are aware the Underground Railroad has a track that runs through this region. Not another word. If you must talk, talk to God in your soul."

Dark as it was, she could just make out the five faces behind her: two older women, two children, and one young man. She felt their fear. But she also sensed the courage that would not let the fear overtake them. Doubting they could see the smile that was famous with friends and acquaintances, she let it part her lips anyway.

" 'Behold, I go forward, but he is not there,'" she recited softly, " 'and backward, but I cannot perceive him: on the left hand, where he doth work, but I cannot behold him: he hideth himself on the right hand, that I cannot see him: but he knoweth the way that I take: when he has tried me, I shall come forth as gold. My foot hath held his steps, his way have I kept, and not declined. Neither have I gone back from the commandment of his lips; I have esteemed the words of his mouth more than my necessary food.'"

She could barely see their faces in the pitch dark, but she felt the smiles form that matched her own.

"Amen," said the two women and the young man together.

Clarissa resumed her cautious but persistent pace along the trail.

She had not gone more than seven steps before someone seized her and yanked her off the path.

Her wide-brimmed hat flew off her head and into the trees.

A hand clamped over her mouth.

Startled and frightened, she still managed to fight back by biting down as hard as she could on the hand and delivering a strong kick to her attacker's knee. He grunted in pain, and she felt his leg buckle. Thrusting a hand under the ragged men's coat she was wearing, which was three sizes too large, she gripped the butt of the revolver tucked under the wide leather belt that held up her men's pants, also three sizes too large, and began to tug it free, cocking back the hammer.

But a large hand closed over hers and practically crushed it. She screamed her agony into the flesh of the hand over her mouth and was unable to push the revolver into her assailant's stomach or squeeze the trigger.

"For an itty-bitty scrap of nothing," hissed a man's voice in her ear, "you sure put up a heck of a fight, little missy. Now stop struggling and be still before I take your head off."

She screamed into his hand, this time in rage and fury, bit into his flesh even harder, and kicked his knee twice more, so that his leg gave way and they both crashed to the earth.

Trying to roll over and scratch out his eyes, she was prevented from doing so by two things—the man's hand closed over her nose as well as her mouth and began to choke out her breath. And he whispered several Bible verses quickly into her ear.

" 'How sweet are thy words unto my taste! yea, sweeter than honey to my mouth! Through thy precepts I get understanding: therefore I hate every false way. Thy word is a lamp unto my feet, and a light unto my path. I have sworn, and I will perform it, that I will keep thy righteous judgments.' "

Clarissa immediately went rigid.

It was the night's password for the Underground Railroad.

Either her attacker was a slave catcher who had learned the password, which was entirely possible, or he was an operator with the Railroad who was doing what he was doing because of an emergency. Not entirely sure what he was or wasn't, but needing to breathe again, Clarissa ceased struggling, and he gradually loosened his hand so that she could take in air.

But her left hand slipped slowly toward a bayonet tucked away in a concealed scabbard in her boot, a men's boot that, unlike her clothing, actually fit her perfectly because her father, a shoemaker in Gettysburg, had made them just for her.

"Walk your ten thousand miles to freedom," he'd told her the day he gifted her with the sturdy black boots, "and, God willing, take ten thousand souls with you, my girl."

Now her attacker was pointing her Navy Six revolver at the five people she had been guiding through the forest.

"Get into the woods," he growled in a low voice.

They did.

"Stay put and don't move," he growled again. "Or I'll shoot every last one of you."

No one moved.

Clarissa remained motionless. Except for her left hand, which was curled around the bayonet.

Harriet Tubman had threatened men twice her size with her revolver. Clarissa reckoned she could do the same thing with the bayonet. She was certain she'd have no problem thrusting it into her assailant's leg. Or even his stomach. It meant saving her passengers' lives, and any one of theirs was worth ten of his.

The blackguard, she seethed.

Or maybe not a blackguard. But she wasn't going to wait much longer to find out. If he was a slave catcher, he'd sell her passengers back into bondage. And skin her alive. She began to count to one hundred.

Lord Jesus, she prayed, *if he is an angel from heaven, let me know right quick. If he is an angel from hell, let me dispatch him right quick. Just let me know. Right quick.*

Despite the circumstances, she half smiled to herself. She could imagine her mother shaking her head and saying, "And you call that a serious prayer to God Almighty?" And she would reply, "Well, it is mighty serious, ma'am, and it sure isn't a prayer to the mayor of Gettysburg, is it?"

"Stop muttering to yourself." The hand closed tightly over her mouth once again. "Do you want to be killed?"

Her anger boiled up in her. *Do you?*

Her grip tightened on the bayonet.

And her count reached eighty-seven.

God forgive me, she prayed as she slowly brought the bayonet free of her boot. *And God let my hand strike swift and sure.*

Ninety-two. . .ninety-three. . .ninety-four. . .

Then everything in her stopped cold.

Men's voices, low but distinct, came along the trail in the direction she and the others had been heading.

She made out two, three, four bodies moving stealthily through the darkness.

Carrying guns and whips and clubs.

And chains.

"I thought you said Bobby would bring the hounds," grumbled one voice, and the voice was loud.

"That's right, Billy," snapped another man, "tell the whole county we're here. That oughta help us catch those runaways real easy, huh?"

The reply was still grumbly but too low for Clarissa to make out.

The four reached the spot where the man had her pinned in his arms and her passengers crouched in the trees.

"My spy in Gettysburg said they'd be in this forest tonight and pushing for a hiding place north of town," one whispered.

"It's a big forest," another whispered back.

"Not that big. And we got men on the other trails."

"A three-hundred-dollar reward for all five. I can pretty much taste it."

"Taste is all you're gonna get if we don't get the chains on 'em."

"We need those hounds!"

"Shut yer mouth about the hounds! We're the hounds! Now sniff 'em out!"

"I can't believe a little scrap of a girl is capable of running us in circles."

"She ain't no girl. She's the devil. A Yankee's devil."

It was the second time that night Clarissa had been referred to as a "scrap." If she had been free to do so, she would have pounced on all four men and kicked their legs out from under them. Then turned on her attacker and dealt with him as well. All she could do was grit her teeth. And clench her bayonet until she was sure her knuckles were white.

The men lingered nearby for several minutes, arguing among themselves.

Her attacker's revolver, which was her revolver—something else that annoyed her in the moment, doubly annoying because she could not immediately do anything about it—was now pointing at the slave catchers. Which counted for something.

Or maybe not.

He could be a rival slave catcher who wanted the three-hundred-dollar reward all to himself.

Or he might have plans to sell them off for double that.

And then string her up from a tall oak tree as a warning to other do-gooders and slave lovers.

"Standing here ain't helping none." It was the grumbling whisperer again.

"Then let's keep going, smart-mouth. And you can lead the way." A snort. "I hear tell she has a Navy Six. And that she is a devil of a shot to go along with that devil of a heart. Why, Billy, it could be that little scrap of nothing is what'll put you in the ground permanent-like."

Three times she had been called that!

With the grumbler still grumbling and growling, the men continued their creep along the forest path.

A minute went by without Clarissa or her attacker or her passengers moving.

Then the man said, "Let us get the passengers to safety. The catchers don't know it's Prickert's barn. If they did, they'd have men there. I am going to release you, *Joshua*." He had used Clarissa's secret name. "No screeching or hollering or they'll come back for us. I'm sorry I was so rough. I didn't have time to explain. They were almost on top of us. Are you going to make a fuss?"

Clarissa shook her head.

Not much!

"All right," the man whispered. "Now please put your bayonet back in your boot."

Clarissa made a face of acute irritation he could not see and shoved the bayonet back in its scabbard.

"Now I am going to let go of you and climb to my feet. I'd rather not receive another boot to my knee. You kick like a Missouri mule. And we are on the same side, even if I did have to manhandle you. For which I apologize again."

Apologize all you like, Clarissa growled to herself, *it won't save you.*

"And in case all of that is not enough to assuage your spitfire temper —your reputation precedes you, missy—you should know my code name is Liberty. I'm sure you've heard of me."

Clarissa had indeed been planning a kick to his leg, both of them, when he used his code name.

That can't be! she almost shouted out loud—except his hand was still on her mouth. *Liberty runs the whole Railroad to Prickert's barn and Methuselah's tavern. He's guided runaways to New York and the Great Lakes. The Amish in Lancaster know about him. Even Harriet Tubman knows about him. He's ferried passengers across Lake Erie into Canada. He's been shot and whipped.*

His hand came off her mouth.

They both got to their feet together.

He was considerably taller than her. Which fit the description she'd heard about him.

He wore the kind of long, heavy coat a sailor shipping out of port in Philadelphia might wear. What they called a peacoat or pilot jacket. Which was also right.

And a black hood covered his head. With two slashes for the eyes and no openings for the nose or mouth. Which also was part of Liberty's look.

He handed back her revolver.

She took it and tucked it in her belt.

And slapped him as hard as she could across the face.

"Don't ever try that on me again, mister!" she snapped, and not in a whisper. "I don't care if Lucifer himself is on the path! Understood?"

"Joshua—"

"Understood?"

Liberty nodded. "I do understand."

She poked around in the undergrowth for her hat, found it, reshaped the brim, and planted it back on a head of tightly pinned-up hair.

"And another thing," she snarled, lowering her voice. "Don't call me an itty-bitty scrap of nothing ever again. I don't care if Harriet Tubman thinks you're the cat's cream and the hero of the commonwealth. I don't. So never call me a scrap again."

She thought she detected a smile under the hood.

Which did nothing to calm her down.

"I assure you I won't," Liberty responded.

He bowed to the five passengers. "I am sorry for my rough-and-ready actions. But you were all in danger of being captured." He glanced at Clarissa. "And one of you was in danger of being flayed alive."

Clarissa narrowed her eyes. "I can take care of myself."

"What are you? All of sixteen?"

She flared up. "None of your business! And I'm nineteen, sir! Nineteen!"

"Are you? With a mop of red hair to go with your temper! It must take a thousand pins to keep it from tumbling down like the walls of Jericho."

Oh, the man infuriated her! Was he capable of doing nothing else but bring the blood to her face and murder to her heart?

"My pins and my hair are also none of your business, sir! And God has taught me how to control my temper!"

"Until tonight," he added.

"Until tonight!" she spat. "And until you!"

Once again she was sure she detected a smile under the hood and wanted to smack him a second time.

But he was beginning to move off quickly through the woods.

"We can't use the trail anymore tonight," he said, looking back over his shoulder at Clarissa and the five runaways. "We may never be able to use it again. Follow me. We'll cut a new path through this scrap of forest and be at Prickert's in less than an hour. You have no objections if I call this part of the forest a scrap, do you, Joshua?"

Clarissa continued to boil. "Be my guest, sir."

She gestured to her five passengers, and the seven of them began to pick their way through the trees.

Ten minutes later it began to snow. For which Clarissa thanked God. Since they were no longer on the path, the slave catchers would not be able to track their footprints in the fresh snowfall. And the snowflakes falling faster and faster would make visibility difficult for their hunters. Especially once she and Liberty had to guide their passengers across open ground. There was the additional hope that if the flurries turned into a storm, it might discourage the slave catchers and make them seek out their lodgings, a warm fire, and a glass of brandy. And bed.

No one spoke. They moved, thought Clarissa, like dark ghosts through a forest that was turning increasingly white. Or like gray wolves. Fast, silent, a mystery to anyone who caught a glimpse of them, and, with her bayonet and revolver, lethal to anyone who got in their way.

She found herself wondering about Liberty as she followed his back through the snowfall and past hundreds of tree trunks. It was an irritating line of thought, but she couldn't help herself. Who was under that hood? Did he carry a gun or knife like she did? Where did he live? What did he do when he wasn't an agent or conductor working the Freedom Train? How many times had he taken baggage right into Canaan or Heaven or the Promised Land—into Canada? How long had he been an operator and a conductor? And how old was he anyway? It bothered her that now he knew her age and she didn't know his. It bothered her that he knew what she looked like (hair pinned up, thank goodness!) but she had no idea what he looked like. In fact, everything about him bothered her. If only she could hear his voice properly she might be able to identify his age or even, if he was a resident of Gettysburg, who he was. But the black hood muffled everything he said.

As if he'd been reading her mind, he glanced back at her through the swirling snowflakes. "I wouldn't trouble myself too much if I were you, Miss Clarissa Avery Ross. If I want you to know who I am, I'll tell you. If I don't, it will be the secret I take to my grave."

Oh, how did he know what I was thinking? And who told him my real name? I could strangle the man! Speaking of graves!

"Don't flatter yourself, sir!" snapped Clarissa, unafraid of how loud her voice was, since the rising wind was even louder. "No man on earth could be farther from my mind. I would prefer to memorize Greek verb conjugations than dwell on any aspect of your unfortunate existence."

"I know Greek," Liberty responded quickly.

Perhaps too quickly. For Clarissa sensed that he regretted he had told her even that much about himself. When she pressed him for more information on his linguistic abilities or urged him to say something in Greek from the New Testament, he remained silent as if he had not heard her voice through the noise of the growing storm. She was certain he had heard but had no intention of letting anything else about himself slip from his lips.

"There!" Liberty stopped and pointed. "The station!"

Prickert's farm did not look like much, Clarissa reflected, not for the first time or the last. It was small and, so far as Pennsylvania farms went, down in the mouth. But it was a safe haven. And with its lights all out but one ("One if by land, two if by sea" after the poem by Henry Wadsworth Longfellow that had been published earlier that year, which she knew served as a signal that all was well) and a column of smoke rising as straight as a pencil from one of its two chimneys, it was a place of refuge for the five passengers until another conductor guided them to the next station on the Freedom Train to Canaan.

"*Run!*" ordered Liberty.

It was dark and stormy, and everything was obscured by the heavy snowfall, but still they ran across the open ground. They ran at a crouch, like they always did, and Clarissa half expected a musket shot to ring out, like she always did, because conductors on the Railroad had been shot and killed before.

But they reached the barn and slipped inside, and the stationmaster, the perpetually smiling Brian Prickert, met them with thick woolen blankets, hot stew thick with chunks of potato, and mugs of steaming coffee. She helped him brush the snow off the runaways and get the blankets around their shoulders and the bowls of stew in their hands. Liberty stood back and watched but didn't lift a finger. He merely turned up the lantern so that it was a bit brighter and a bit warmer in the barn.

"Thanks for all your help," snipped Clarissa.

"You're welcome," Liberty responded.

She kissed the older women on their cheeks, the boy and girl on their foreheads, and gave the young man her best smile. They all found places to sit, using stools or settling onto mounds of hay. Liberty was the only one who remained on his feet while he ate and drank.

"Will ye stay the night then?" Prickert asked Liberty and Clarissa.

Liberty had already wolfed down his stew and drained his coffee mug. He shook his head.

"Joshua may," he said, "but it wouldn't do for me not to be present in Gettysburg as usual come Sunday morning. It might give rise to unfortunate suspicions considering the dangerous times we live in."

Clarissa ignited like powder in her Navy Six revolver. *Joshua may?*

"But the storm is fierce," protested Prickert.

"I am fiercer. Ask the slave catchers who thought they had me in their grips last fall." Liberty turned to Clarissa. "You can stay until the storm blows itself out. Your family knows what you're doing, and you won't be missed by anyone else."

The powder flashed. "I beg your pardon?"

"It is snowing quite hard and—"

"And what? I'm a damsel in distress? I most certainly will be missed, and I have no intention of waking up in any other bed than my own in the morning. And be sitting in my pew at church by eleven."

Prickert was staring at her.

She could only imagine the sort of carriage wreck she'd present to the world after a night in the winter woods, and she knew very well how wild and blazing her green eyes appeared when she had her "Avery Ross" up. But no way on God's green earth, or His snow-covered one for that matter, was she going to let Liberty play the man and return through storm and ice to Gettysburg while she cowered in a barn like Little Miss Mousy, too afraid of snow and cold to venture out till all the world was sunny and bright and safe. Is that what Harriet Tubman—Moses— is that what Harriet Tubman would do?

She turned to the five passengers and hugged each one. "You will get to Heaven. You will reach Canada. I am sure of it. My prayers will be constant and fervent." She took Brian Prickert's hand in both of hers. "Thank you again for your courage and your faith. Until the next time."

Then she brushed past Liberty and stormed out the barn door.

"You may follow my lead, sir!" She bit out the words. "That way you will be sure to end up in Gettysburg before dawn rather than miss your road and wake up in Philadelphia or Pittsburgh."

Chapter Two

Sunday morning
Gettysburg

I hate the man! I absolutely detest him! From the bottom of his ugly booted feet to the top of his silly hooded head!"

Stormier than the storm, her mother thought as Clarissa blasted into the house with the wind and snow at her back.

Clarissa threw her snow-covered hat into one corner and ripped off her scarf, almost hitting her father as she hurled it into another corner where he happened to be standing.

"I try to be polite. I try to be kind. I try to be gracious. But he's enough to make a saint drink hemlock. Twice."

"We're glad to see you back safe, dear," her mother interjected, helping her daughter with her snowy coat. "Did you have trouble with slave catchers?"

"Slave catchers?" Clarissa gave her mother a wild-eyed look. "Slave catchers would be a treat compared to him. At least I could shoot them." She pulled off her boots with a savage fury, one after the other. "Seven miles from the Mason-Dixon Line here and you'd think I could get a few of them to use my Navy Six on. But no. I get him."

"Who, dear?"

"Liberty. The great and mighty Liberty."

"Liberty?" Her father repeated the name, setting Clarissa's wet, muddy, and icy boots on a straw mat by the door. "Not Harriet Tubman's Liberty?"

"Oh yes indeed, Father, Harriet Tubman's Liberty. And she can have him. I'll send him to her in a gift box. A pine box would be best."

"Clarissa Avery!" Her mother put a hand on her daughter's arm. "Hush!"

"Oh, but no, we can't harm our precious Liberty. He's too important to the Railroad." Clarissa jabbed a finger at her mother and father. "I have to go all the way to Prickert's with him and all the way back. I'm trying to be a Christian woman. Trying to carry on a conversation with the man. And all the time he's letting me be the one who breaks trail. What sort of gentleman does that? I'm jabbering away about who knows what, hoping to get some sort of response from a fellow human being, tramping through the snow and muck, leading the way, thank you very much, sir. . .and then I spot Gettysburg through the storm and I turn to him to tell him we've made it, and what do I see?"

Her parents waited several long moments, staring at her white face and her freckles and the wet hair unraveling about her head, but it was clear she wasn't going to say another word until she was prompted. So her mother supplied the necessary words—"What did you see, dear?"

"Nothing!" Clarissa exploded. "Absolutely nothing! Heaven knows how long I'd been talking to myself. Miles. I couldn't even see boot prints. Why, he'd abandoned me long before we reached Gettysburg. Of course, anything could have happened to me. A branch heavy with ice might have fallen on my head and rendered me unconscious, and there I'd be, lying in a snowdrift, freezing to death, and him not caring one whit whether I might get to town alive. Not one whit. Slave catchers could have surrounded me. I might have fallen through the ice of one of our creeks. But where was the hero of the Underground Railroad? At home by then, no doubt, and soaking in a hot bath. I hate the man. I'm sorry to be so unchristian, but there is nothing worth saving in him. And I haven't even told you the half of it. The first thing he did when he met up with us was throw me to the ground."

"Oh my," her mother responded. "And why would he do that?"

"Oh, to save me from slave catchers, apparently. He thought I might talk too much and give us away, and so he clamped a hand over my mouth too."

"Oh no."

"Can you imagine? The blackguard."

"Were there slave catchers?" asked her father carefully.

Her green eyes blazed at him. "What?"

"Were there slave catchers, my dear?"

"I don't see what that has to do with it, but yes, yes there were. They came down the trail looking for us. No hounds, thank goodness." Clarissa jabbed her finger at her parents again. "Do you know why he wears that ridiculous black hood? He does it because he thinks he's important. Well, he's not important. Just ugly. I swear that's why he wears the hood—he's as ugly as a wild pig."

"Clarissa!"

"I'm sorry, Mother, but what's ugly inside is bound to show up outside. You've told me that many times yourself. A person's soul leaks into their face. And his soul is rotten to the core."

Suddenly she slumped into a chair. "I'm exhausted."

Her mother rushed to throw a thick woolen blanket around her daughter. "Of course you are. It's four in the morning. You've been up all night. I have some hot soup and a mug of hot cider for you."

Clarissa finally smiled a smile, the kind of smile that made her parents still marvel at how beautiful their only child was. "Oh, that would be marvelous. That would be top of the mountain."

"And your father is going to put a hot brick in bed with you."

The smile broadened. "Oh thank you, thank you. I'm going to sleep like a brick myself. Even my little toe on my left foot aches." She laughed. "When that aches, it means the carriage called Clarissa is about to have a crash."

21

"You can sleep until we're back from church. We'll wake you at noon and—"

"Noon!" Clarissa sat up straight. "No, I must be at church. I can't have people asking questions about my absence."

"Why, we'll just tell them you're under the weather, dear. Which is true enough."

"Oh no, no, thank you, but no. I have to be at Christ's Church. I absolutely must be there. I must be seen."

"You must be seen? By whom?"

"Everyone. Anyone. I must be seen."

"Oh. Well. Kyle Forrester has been out of town. I believe he was in Philadelphia on business. I'm not sure he's back."

Red sprang into Clarissa's face. "It doesn't matter if. . .if Mr. Forrester is at church or not. I must. . .I must be seen. . .by all the others."

"So, I'll wake you at ten?"

"Ten?"

"The service is at eleven o'clock and it's only a five-minute walk to the church for us."

"Ten o'clock?" Clarissa had gone from red to white. "I can't get ready if I'm not awake till ten. Nine, Mother, nine o'clock. I don't want to show up at church looking as if I spent the night tramping around the woods in a blizzard."

"Why, you'll get less than five hours sleep."

"That's enough. I don't need more than that. I'm young." She suddenly scowled. "He thought I was sixteen. Sixteen. Can you imagine? What a blackguard."

She wolfed down the soup and cider and was up the two flights of stairs to her bedroom in six or seven minutes with a candle in its holder. After placing it on a nightstand and changing into a green flannel nightgown, one that was a match for her eyes when she was in a gentle mood, she stepped to the window and pulled back the curtain just enough to look out. It was still black as a pot of tar, but the white snowflakes pierced the dark like needles. She had insisted on having a bedroom in the highest part of the house since she'd been nine, but her parents had been reluctant to put her in the garret. Eventually, as in most things, she had gotten her way, and her father had fixed up what until then had been no more than a storage attic, including the pasting up of wallpaper with a variety of colored birds on it, and had also made a new bed in the shape of a sleigh for her.

Clarissa loved the privacy and seclusion of the garret. It helped her gather new strength and direction after long nights of rushing escaped slaves across the roughest regions of the Commonwealth of Pennsylvania. Lingering at the window, she made out various houses and buildings and could see the cupola of her Lutheran church, swirling with flakes of snow as if they were wildly spinning moths and the cupola a flame. It was exactly like the cupola on the nearby Lutheran seminary except it was a lot smaller. Watching the cupola in its whirlwind of snow and darkness, her mind remained with the Lutheran seminary's cupola and then shifted to the students who had rooms in the building beneath it. Kyle Forrester took front and center stage. Tall, strong, dark brown hair, a trim beard and mustache, lovely gray eyes, a smile that made her weak—and no one ever made her weak. She looked out the window, no longer seeing the storm or the cupola, and savored her memories of Kyle the way she would savor a Scotch mint in her mouth.

"Oh Kyle," she whispered, still standing at the window. "Be there, please, be at the church. God, Father, I need him there. I need him at the worship service tomorrow."

Clarissa's eyes and mind returned to the streets, to the carriage and furniture shops, the banks, the law offices, to the tanneries of the town she loved, so sweet and cozy and happily nestled into the ten roads that ran into it. As if the town were the center of all local existence. *And it is,* she thought, *and so is he, so far as I'm concerned.* Finally, she eased herself under the sheets and under the quilt the Amish had gifted her with for her work on what they called the Freedom Train. She loved the pattern of stars and locomotives. The quilt was heavy and snug, and her eyelids immediately began to droop. Her feet touched a thick blanket under the sheets that was wrapped around a hard and hot object. She smiled and pressed her toes into it, and her whole body quivered with delight. The brick her father had promised her. She would be fast asleep before it lost its heat from the stove.

A train was gliding along smooth steel tracks. Its smoke puffed gray and dark over the stars in the night sky. There was Ursa Major. And there was the North Star. It was stitched into her quilt too. Impossible to miss. She slipped like a shadow through the woods. But she was so tired. Eventually, she called for a stop and told the escaped slaves with her to sit and catch their breath and eat some of the bread and bacon she'd given them. Except she never thought of them as slaves and always referred to them as freedmen, pointing out that in the Genesis account in the Bible, man meant both male and female: " 'So God created man in his own image, in the image of God created he him; male and female created he them.'"

Her lips moved in the dark, reciting the verse.

"You are all *freedmen*." She spoke out loud, eyes closed, half-asleep. "Each one of you. And you always were. No matter what others say or do. You are as free as the birds. Free as the sea. Free as the north wind. As free as me."

And she slept under the tree in the woods, and the snow covered her like a blanket, and she felt warm, not cold, and her feet found the brick in the snow, and she purred like a cat and was content and never dreamed anymore after that.

True to her promise, although she performed her task reluctantly, Clarissa's mother woke her at nine and poured hot water into the basin on her daughter's washstand. Clarissa was up in an instant, tugged aside the curtain, saw a white street and white rooftops sparkling in the sun under a sky as blue as a gemstone, grinned like a twelve-year-old, skipped to the washstand, and began to clean her face and hands.

"There is a bowl of oats for you downstairs," her mother announced. "Good morning, my dear."

"Good morning." Clarissa splashed. "With walnuts? And demerara sugar?"

"Yes."

"I won't be a minute."

"Would you like me to brush out your hair?"

"Yes. After I eat."

"And what dress can I get ready for you?" her mother asked.

"Oh, the jade one," Clarissa responded, wiping her face with a towel. "It goes with my mood, and it only has six hoops. Which also goes with my mood."

"Six hoops always go with your moods, any mood, Clarissa Avery."

Clarissa laughed. "Well, that's because I'm not a lady. I prefer riding pants."

"But you *can* be a lady when you put your mind to it."

Clarissa made a sour face. "It takes too much of my mind. And then there's nothing left for any other thoughts."

"Nevertheless, you play the lady in church."

Clarissa nodded. "That's true. I'm happy to do it there. For God. For you. For the other parishioners."

"For young Mr. Forrester."

Again, blood rushed to Clarissa's white face, framed in a tangle of flaming red hair, at the mention of his name. "You said he might not be there."

"He might not."

"So, I'll still play the Pennsylvania lady even if he isn't."

A half hour later, Clarissa was soaking in a tub. The steam made her crimson hair curl even more, if that were possible. Her mother began to brush it out the minute her daughter had toweled herself dry.

"Look at those curls." Her mother smiled as she plied the hairbrush vigorously. "No wonder heads turn when you walk through Gettysburg."

"Oh Mother, heads do not turn."

"Yes they do. You never notice because your own head is in the clouds. But, I swear, we could start a windmill to grind grain with all those spinning heads."

"Ouch. Not so hard. My head is not in the clouds."

"Don't you want your hair to shine like red gold? Or like fire? What chance will Kyle Forrester have then?"

Clarissa blushed and laughed. "Oh stop it, Mother. You're being so silly about he and me. As if my hair color or how it shines makes a difference to him."

"Many a man has met his match with green eyes gazing into his. And surrendered. Imagine the effect of scarlet hair and emerald-green eyes in one pretty face. The poor man. All the poor men."

Clarissa laughed again. "You're being ridiculous."

"I'm not. I know what my red hair and green eyes did to your father."

"And what was that?"

"Brought the poor, proud man to his knees. Everyone said he wouldn't make up his mind about me in a year. Well, he proposed in less than a month."

Clarissa giggled. "Poor, poor Father."

Her mother giggled too. "Yes, poor, poor Father."

"He still worships you."

"He does, doesn't he? I like it that way."

"First God, then thee."

"First God, then me."

Clarissa sighed. "I wish it would happen that way for me."

"Oh my, I don't know a single man in town who wouldn't go to his knees for you."

"Well, I mean, a man I want."

"Yes, even the man you want."

Clarissa shook her head and looked at herself critically in the mirror. "He's too proud. And too caught up in his seminary studies. Him and his Greek verb conjugations. And he's always off to Philadelphia or Harrisburg. He scarcely notices me."

Her mother stopped brushing and looked at her daughter's reflection in the mirror. "Is that what you think?"

"It's what I know."

"Then you don't know much about men. His eyes never leave you when you two are in the same room."

"That's not true. . .is it?"

The brushing resumed. "Oh yes, it's true. But your mind is always elsewhere. That's why you don't notice. A young lady knows it when a young man is admiring her from afar. But you are planning your next escape route out of Gettysburg for your friends."

"My freedmen. Well, maybe. That's entirely possible."

"Let's see if we can't get you to direct your thoughts Godward this morning. And Kyle-ward."

Clarissa rolled her eyes. "Oh, all right. I will go to heaven for God and try to come down to earth for Kyle."

"Good."

"If he's even there."

Her mother nodded and put down the hairbrush. "If he's even there. Now let's get you into that six-hoop wonder. The clock is moving right along without paying any attention to us."

Not for the first time, as she strode along the snowy street toward Christ's Church on Chambersburg, Clarissa reflected on her good fortune in having a father who made boots and shoes. His craftsmanship was solid and always in demand, and he also had a contract with the army in Harrisburg. His was a lucrative business that blessed the three of them and the church that received their tithe, and especially her, for she went through a good pair of boots every month it seemed. Except for the ones she wore to church. She'd had them for three years, and she never failed to polish them to a shine. She knew she looked good in them, and it pleased her when she saw eyes wander to her feet. It was so comfortable going on long walks in town with them, and they had a wonderful grip in snow and ice.

And now they propelled her toward the four white pillars, the brick facade, the wide steps, the two large trees on either side of the steps, and the small white cupola of the English-speaking Lutheran church in Gettysburg. Though she had always said she could learn German in two weeks if they chose to attend St. James, the German-speaking Lutheran church. With its tall tower and its three medieval-looking doors, it looked like a European castle. When she was a girl, she'd often linger at the steps when they went along York Street because she half expected Martin Luther to emerge from one of the old doors.

"My goodness, Clarissa Avery." Her mother had laughed. *"Why, the man's been dead for three hundred years."*

"You didn't see him die," Clarissa had asserted, *"so you can't say for sure."*

"Miss Clarissa Avery. Good Sabbath to you."

She actually responded to the unexpected greeting with a *huh?* For which she kicked herself a thousand times over.

Lost in her thoughts—*My head really was in the clouds,* she thought ruefully—she hadn't even noticed Kyle Forrester's approach from a side street. Now he was walking right beside her, turning his head briefly to greet her parents who were walking at her back, and then telling her how handsome her green woolen coat and cape and winter bonnet were.

"You look fetching, Miss Clarissa Avery. If I may be so bold."

"Uh. . .well. . ." Her tongue would not work. "An early Christmas present. . .the outfit is. . .early. . .an early Christmas present from my mother's parents in. . .in. . .uh. . .They are in New York."

"They have remarkable taste."

"So do you. No, I mean, yes, yes they do, thank you very much. Thank you, sir."

Her father rescued her.

"How was your trip to Philadelphia, Mr. Forrester?" he asked. "Did everything go smoothly?"

Her father and mother came up beside her and Kyle, her mother by her shoulder and her father by his. Clarissa felt a squeeze on her arm from her mother that was unobserved by anyone else. Meanwhile, her father was smiling and chatting with Kyle, and she was surprised to see that her father was at least half a head taller than him.

"I apologize if the matter of your business trip is confidential," her father went on.

"No, no, but it was as you know, church business, Mr. Ross," Kyle replied. Clarissa saw regret in his handsome face, and that made her feel wonderful. He'd rather be talking alone with her, she was certain of it. "It is all about the issues we struggle with here at the seminary and, I suppose, among our two Lutheran churches in town. Should our faith be expressed in German or English, especially our deeper theology and philosophies? In addition to that, should ours remain a confessional faith, going back to the earliest Confessions of the Lutheran Reformation?"

"Especially the Augsburg Confession of 1530."

"Especially that, yes. It was written in Latin and, of course, German. Certain people think much is lost in translation when it is recited in English. And then there is the whole matter of what some refer to as the Americanizing of the Lutheran faith. Where the debate is not only about the use of English in place of German, but a move away from the Confessions toward an expression of our faith that is more. . .well, accommodating to the American people."

"I believe our professors are not all in agreement about these things."

"No, they are not, Mr. Ross. In one case, as you're probably aware, a professor's son disagrees with his father about the use of the confessions in our churches."

"Yes."

"His father wants their role diminished, while the son wishes them to be at the forefront."

"Yes."

"So, as you can appreciate, sir, an uncomfortable situation."

Clarissa's father nodded. "Compounded by the fact that certain professors and other church leaders feel the Confessions are not without error."

"Yes, sir. Some want them treated as if they are sacred scripture. Others feel that while important and historical so far as our faith is concerned, they are in no way on the same level as the Gospels of our Lord Jesus Christ."

"So long as they keep all this wrangling out of the pulpit," Clarissa's mother interrupted. "I simply want to worship God."

"Amen," responded Kyle. "I'm sorry, Mrs. Ross, I didn't mean to go on and on."

"Not at all. I'm glad young men like yourself, with level heads on their shoulders, are the ones handling all this. I trust you will be certain to ensure everything works out admirably. To a different matter, Mr. Forrester—do you enjoy Cornish hens?"

"Uh, Cornish hens? Yes, yes I do."

"Then will you join us for lunch after church and see if you like them baked with gravy and potatoes?"

"Why. . .certainly, certainly, Mrs. Ross. I should like nothing better."

"And we can then discuss the matter of the Southern states," added Mr. Ross, "and if you believe they are going to part ways with our republic and form their own nation."

Clarissa's heart sank like a stone in a deep, dark pond.

She would have Kyle Forrester in her house for the first time, but her father would first command the conversation at the table and then drag Kyle off into the parlor for coffee and politics for the rest of the afternoon. While she cleaned up. And helped her mother mend clothing. She would hardly see Kyle. And she had done her hair up under her bonnet perfectly. And her jade-green dress was just right. It wasn't fair.

"Mrs. Ross?" asked Kyle as they began to mount the steps to the church, all cleared of snow, and to the large white doors, firmly shut against the cold.

"Yes, Mr. Forrester?"

"Would it be possible. . .would you mind. . .do you think there is time before lunch. . .if I asked your daughter to take a stroll with me before we sat down to the meal?"

Mrs. Ross smiled. "Oh, I'm certain there is, Mr. Forrester. Ample time. And if you took her for another stroll after lunch, a long one, why, there might just be a warm supper waiting for you both at the end of that one too."

"Truly?" responded Kyle.

Clarissa watched Kyle's face light up as if someone had ignited a candle. Seeing his delight, she knew her face lit up too, and she felt warmth rush through her blood.

"Truly?" he said again.

"Truly," Mrs. Ross replied. "Though I suppose you had better get around to asking Clarissa what she thinks about all this."

"Yes, yes, oh yes, you're right."

Clarissa watched him blush. Oh my, she had never seen strong, tall, dashing Kyle Forrester blush. And over her. Now the stone that had dropped in the deep, dark pond was sending wonderful and beautiful ripples through her spirit.

"Miss Ross." Kyle opened the door to the church for her and her parents. "Clarissa Avery. Would you. . .could you. . .might you like to take the long way back to your house after church?"

She smiled. It was nice to see him get tongue-tied too. "By myself?"

"Oh. . .no, no. I meant in my company, Miss Ross. I meant accompanied by me."

Her smile widened. "In your company, Mr. Forrester, and yours alone?"

"Yes, yes, but only if you. . ."

"I should like nothing better, Mr. Forrester."

Now the smile became what her mother called her daughter's impish and devilish grin. "I should like nothing better," she repeated.

She swept past him and into the warm church but then glanced back over her shoulder and gave him an even larger version of her impish and devilish grin. "Please sit with me at our family pew, Mr. Forrester. . .if you'd like."

Chapter Three

Sunday afternoon
Gettysburg

Clarissa was in high spirits.

She'd enjoyed the hymn singing even more than she usually did. The sermon, encouraging people to find heart and hope in their faith, had been particularly inspiring. The men and women who had greeted her that morning—and the children—had been particularly kind. One of the professors who worked with the Underground Railroad and had assisted her on several occasions gave her a meaningful handshake and a nod.

Something was up. But she wanted something to be up. She wanted to help people get free of slavery and tyranny whether they lived in the North or the South or any of the states in between. Would she like to be trapped or chained or whipped or sold to someone as if she were a cow or a goat? No, and she didn't think anyone else liked to be in that situation either. So she hoped she would soon be contacted to help on the Freedom Train again, even though she'd just had a long and exhausting night ferrying her passengers through Adams County. True to form, she had bounced back and was ready for more.

Her faith and her youth and her red hair—she smiled to herself—they all combined in one fiery mix to keep her engine running day and night.

"I said, don't you think so, Clarissa Avery?"

She blinked. "What?"

She looked up at Kyle Forrester.

"Where have you disappeared to?" he asked, smiling a small smile she liked.

"I was. . .um. . .I was thinking about Christmas."

"Christmas. About presents?"

"No, not about presents. About how the church might be decorated. And my room up on the third floor. And what I'd wear to the Christmas Eve service." She glanced around her. "Where have you brought me?"

"Well, you said you wanted to stretch your legs." He pointed. "The snow is already melting on the fields."

"And the barn roof." Clarissa stared. "Doesn't that land belong to one of your professors?"

"It's Samuel Saxon's all right. He helped found our church too."

"I know that. I didn't see him at the service this morning."

"He was at the back and on the left. I think he has begun to rent that pew now."

"I don't walk this way very often, I'll admit."

Which was a lie. *I should blush,* Clarissa thought to herself. She had been to Professor Saxon's barn and house many times. He was an outspoken abolitionist who gave shelter to runaway slaves, and she had often gone there to gather up passengers for the Railroad. She knew she shouldn't bring up the question of slavery, or about getting slaves safely through Adams County and Pennsylvania across the border into Ontario, but now that she finally had Kyle Forrester at her side to converse with at length, well, she wanted to know what he thought about a thousand things, especially what her Amish friends called the Freedom Train.

"Professor Saxon is quite adamant about putting an end to slavery in America," she said, gazing at the barn.

"Yes. Yes he is, Clarissa."

"What do you think about all that, Mr. Forrester?"

"What do I—" Kyle was surprised.

"It's not a difficult question I've put to you, is it?"

"No. I'm just not used to discussing the matter with a woman. The fact is, I never have."

"Well, so this is your opportunity."

"I. . .well, I approve of the stand Professor Saxon takes against slavery. Indeed, I applaud him for it. I believe it is not only a proper Lutheran thing to do, but a proper Christian thing to do. . .even a proper human thing to do, whether you are a churchgoer or a Jew or an atheist or whatever your religion or creed happens to be. The Dred Scott decision was, if I may be so blunt, a sin against humanity and against the Republic. Imagine saying people with black skin have no protection under our constitution, not even those who have received their freedom or been born free. Imagine how they have added that to the odious Fugitive Slave Law of 1850—permitting slave catchers to cross the Mason-Dixon Line and capture men and women up here and drag them back to cotton plantations in chains."

Clarissa liked what she was hearing but decided to prod him further. "The Dred Scott case was a majority decision by our Supreme Court, Mr. Forrester, a seven-to-two decision, if I'm not mistaken."

"It was."

"You speak as if you would flout the highest law of the land. I'm surprised."

"Are you, Miss Ross?"

"Almost shocked, sir." She was deliberately stoking a fire inside him. *I'm a devil, but I have to know how he really feels about all this, how far he would go.* "Isn't it your plan to become a Lutheran pastor?"

"It is."

"Perhaps a leader in the Lutheran Church in America?"

"If that's where prayer takes me."

"Yet you speak poorly of our Supreme Court."

Kyle did not respond.

Clarissa pushed further. "I've heard it said around town that your Professor Saxon harbors fugitive slaves."

Kyle's face and body seemed to grow rigid and cold. "I have no knowledge of that."

"That he is. . .what they call *an operator* on this so-called Underground Railroad that ferries slaves across our northern border."

"I've heard of the Railroad, of course."

"That slaves hide in his house and barn."

"That's ridiculous."

"Well, sir, I have it on good authority."

Kyle snorted. "It's nonsense."

"You don't think Professor Saxon is part of the Underground Railroad?"

"No. No I do not. Nor do I think much of the Railroad."

"You don't?"

The stone dropped into the deep, dark pond of her heart again.

Kyle shook his head vigorously. "Such matters are for the judges and courts and Congress to decide. If we do not like their judgments—and no, I do not approve of the Dred Scott decision—then we appeal. We try new cases to get different results that overturn the old ones. We bring new bills into Washington that create new laws. We debate, we argue, we filibuster, we vote, and then we start debating all over again, if we must. We alter things within the framework of the laws and constitution of the Republic, Miss Ross, not outside of them. Do we need a secret and illegal operation like the Underground Railroad? No, we do not. Should Christian ministers, let alone Lutheran ministers, aid and abet such enterprises, no matter how well-meaning? They should not. But ought there to be prayers lifted up for the end of slavery in our republic? Yes. Ought there to be prayers against the slave trade and the slave drivers and the slave catchers and their ilk? Most assuredly. Ought there to be sermons from our pulpits condemning the scourge of human enslavement and echoing Saint Paul's words 'If you can gain your freedom, then gain it'? Yes, yes, and yes. But there is no need to break our laws, Miss Ross. We can change them from within in a good Christian manner." He suddenly smiled. "I trust you are no longer shocked at me, Clarissa Avery?"

Clarissa had been living on three different levels while he spoke: sharply disappointed that he was against her work with the Underground Railroad, absolutely mesmerized by his ability to string thoughts and words and beliefs together with clarity and eloquence, and eternally grateful he detested slavery enough that he would rail against it from the pulpit. Perhaps there was hope for the two of them. But she had chosen to play the role of the woman opposed to flouting the decisions of the courts, especially the Supreme Court, so she could not express her truest feelings. In a bold move, she reached up with her leather-gloved hand and patted his cheek.

"There, there. Calm yourself, sir." She gave him her best smile. "I breathe a sigh of relief, Mr. Forrester, for I had it in my heart to like you. Now it's much easier to do."

"Is it?"

"Oh yes. You are against slavery—a practice I personally abhor—but you choose to confront it inside the law. That pleases me more than I can say."

"I'm glad to hear it."

"I'm glad to say it."

"I've taken you far off the beaten path, Clarissa Avery. We should make our way to your home directly or we'll be late for lunch."

Clarissa decided to stay bold for a while. "And that wouldn't do, would it, if you are trying to impress my parents, especially my mother."

He smiled. "It would not do, no."

Her boldness continued. "May I take your arm, sir?"

Inwardly, she shrugged. She risked her life on the Underground Railroad. Why did a burgeoning relationship with a man have to be so tame? Why couldn't she take some risks there too?

Kyle did not hesitate.

Which, to her, was a welcome sign.

He bent his right arm and offered it to her. "Shall we?"

She grinned the imp-and-devil grin and placed her hand in the crook of his elbow. "We shall. Lead on, Macduff."

"You do know that's a misquote, Miss Ross?"

"I do, Mr. Forrester. It actually is 'Lay on, Macduff,' where Macbeth is egging his foe on and inviting him to attack. However, common usage has rendered it as an invitation to follow, and I am quite happy with the common usage this Sunday afternoon."

"How are your boots holding up in this slush?"

"My boots? Father made them to last me until I'm in my coffin. It will take a lot more than snow and ice and a drop in the temperature to have them come apart at the seams."

"Hmm. I imagine that applies to you as well."

"Mr. Forrester, I can assure you it does." A thought popped into her head, and she chose to be impulsive. It had been an impulsive kind of night, and now it had become an impulsive kind of day. "But you don't have a pulpit to rail against slavery from, sir."

"What? Trying to keep up with your thoughts, Miss Ross, is like trying to catch hummingbirds with my bare hands and my two feet far too firmly on the ground."

"I'm simply referring back to our discussion of slavery in the great Republic. You said you would preach against it in the churches. But you are only a seminary student, sir. You have nowhere to plant those two feet of yours and give us a sermon against that despicable trade."

"*Only?*"

"I'm sure you are a brilliant student, Mr. Forrester. It's not my intention to belittle your efforts in hermeneutics and exegesis and homiletics. But, the fact remains, how will you fight slavery within the law if you have no law degree that gets you into the courts and, before God, no pulpit where you can boldly make your stand before a congregation?"

"It's odd you should bring that up."

"Why odd?"

"I have to give a public sermon as part of my studies. It gets evaluated, of course."

"Public?"

"Yes, anyone may attend. There are three of us preaching that evening, so I'm sure it would soon get tiresome for a young woman like you."

"Where is this taking place? And when?"

"In two weeks. At our church. At eight o'clock at night. Honestly, I can't see it being of any interest to you, Miss Ross."

"I suppose I can decide for myself what I find interesting or uninteresting, Mr. Forrester. I may very well be there. Despite your attempts to steer me away."

"I just think. . ."

"Hush. I've already made up my mind. There's my home. Let's go in and cheerfully enjoy our lunch."

And two weeks later she was at Christ's Church at seven thirty in the evening, mother and father in tow, to ensure she got into the family pew early.

Front row. In the middle.

She laughed to herself. *A few more feet and I'll be in Kyle's lap.*

"My dear," her mother complained, "is it necessary to be in such a rush? We'll be on display as much as the students what with all our hustle and bustle."

"We aren't Baptists, are we, Mother?" Clarissa retorted, settling herself and unwrapping her long woolen scarf. "Lutherans can sit as far forward as they like and come as early as they want."

More people were showing up than she had expected. It turned out one of the students was the son of a prominent banker in Gettysburg, and friends and relatives were joining his family to show their support. *So be it,* thought Clarissa. No one was there for Kyle Forrester except her and her parents. He had come to Gettysburg from New York City, and she knew that his own mother and father had passed away and that, like her, he was an only child. *An only, lonely child like me,* she mused as she waited for the service to begin, her eyes roving over the Christmas decorations in the sanctuary. Several of the wreaths, rich with burgundy, forest green, and large pine cones, she and her mother had fashioned and then placed. She wondered how unique being an only child made her or Kyle. Certainly, a child raised among siblings must have a different experience and perception of life than one raised without brothers and sisters. Was she used to getting her own way, since there was no competition with a sister who wanted her desires met over Clarissa's? Had constantly getting what she wanted made her more selfish or more demanding? Was she spoiled? Self-centered? A brat?

She pouted as she sat there in the pew, her wagon wheels turning over and over in her mind, and her mother saw the fat lip and frowned. *I am not a brat,* Clarissa said to no one in particular, though she never voiced the words. *I AM NOT A BRAT,* she repeated to herself with more vehemence. She could tell by her mother's disapproving stare that the mood of her unspoken words was scribbled all over her face, but she didn't care. It wasn't her fault she was an only child. She'd made the best of it, and she felt she had come out pretty well in the end. Kyle Forrester certainly had: seminary student at the top of his class (her father had made what he called *discreet inquiries*), a top competitor when it came to athletic contests, an excellent marksman (that she'd found out about on her own), a fine rider and horseman. . . . Even after they'd stood to sing a hymn and the service had begun with the banker's son giving them the first sermon with his mousy nose buried in his notes—*I am sorry for the adjective mousy, Lord, but it is accurate*—her thoughts continued to wander around her experience of Kyle Forrester from the past two weeks.

The lunch at her home after church had been a success. And although she had thought she'd have no interest in Kyle's parlor conversation with her father after the meal, she found herself drawn in by their talk of the possible secession of the Southern states from the

American Republic. Now, with South Carolina seceding from the Union the Thursday before, on the twentieth of December, she realized how prescient Kyle and her father had been, for both had laid down convincing arguments that several Southern states would indeed leave and break up the country.

"They will say it is all about states' rights," her father insisted as he sipped a third cup of black coffee. "And on one level, it is. But what they will not trumpet is the fact that the states' right which matters the most to them, above all others, is that of slavery. They will fight to retain their right to buy and own and work human beings on their cotton and sugarcane plantations. I would say some see it as a sovereign right. They shall hold on tightly to that right and never open their hands to release their slaves, unless compelled by force."

Kyle agreed and added, "What they call their right is the right to take away another's right to be free."

"Right to be free? What right, young man? The Fugitive Slave Law is already ten years old. You know very well that slave catchers can go any-where in the country they like and chain up runaway slaves and even free blacks." Her father shrugged. "And they will point to the Dred Scott deci-sion and say no slave can have rights or citizenship or protection under the constitution."

"I do not accept the Dred Scott decision, sir. It must be appealed. It must be overturned."

Her father shook his head. "The Supreme Court will not hear an appeal against their own seven-to-two ruling. Would you resort to force to overturn the court's decision?"

"No, sir. No I would not. But I would take it to the people. Let there be public referendum."

"No, no, that will not do, Mr. Forrester. Remember the war in Kan-sas? That was what an attempt to have the people vote for or against slavery brought about. A civil war among its citizens. Bleeding Kansas. No, a refer-endum will not do."

"What then, Father?" Clarissa intervened. "You say no to this and no to

that. So how shall slavery be brought to an end? How can America be a free country once again?"

"It never was a free country, my dear girl. Slavery was with us from the beginning. Jefferson wanted to end it with the Declaration of Independence, but South Carolina and Georgia would not have it. Thus, the passage pertaining to the matter was stricken from the document. You can blame Ben Franklin and John Adams for that. No, they left the question to another generation and turned their backs on it. You should be asking, when will America be free? For the first time in its history, when shall America be free?"

"And when shall it be free, Father? When? And how?"

But her father had only shook his head and poured himself a fourth cup of coffee.

They stood to sing another hymn, and Clarissa was determined to focus on the sermon presented by the second student, who was not Kyle Forrester, but a pleasant-looking young man with a handsome beard. Unfortunately, try as she might, she could not stay with him as he droned through the first two chapters of Genesis verse by verse, as if he were plodding through a muddy field after a hard winter's rain. *Where is the inspiration I need, sir?* Her imagination roamed back to her and Kyle. There had not just been the political talks. They had enjoyed three, no, four more walks together since the beginning of December, one of them with the most amazing sugar-crystal snowflakes falling lightly on their heads and shoulders. She had caught them on her tongue. And once, just once, he had impetuously leaned down and kissed one that had landed on a loose strand of her crimson hair. After which he had immediately apologized. This had annoyed her to no end.

"Oh, I wish you hadn't done that, sir."

His face was red. "I apologize, Miss Ross. I. . .I don't know what came over me."

"Oh, for heaven's sake, Kyle." She rarely used his Christian name. "I'm not talking about kissing a snowflake that got caught in my hair. I liked that. But you spoiled it by apologizing for it."

"I. . .apologize for apologizing then."

"You take back the apology, sir?"

"I do, Miss Ross."

"Then make up for it."

"Make up for it?"

"Yes. Do something else that is impulsive. Something that will surprise and please me."

"What?" he asked.

"Well, my goodness, sir," she responded with a good measure of exasperation, "if I tell you what to do, then it isn't impulsive anymore, is it?"

"I suppose not."

And then he was very impetuous, even impertinent, and absolutely surprised and shocked her. Lucky for him, she loved it.

He tilted her chin up toward his face, bent down, and gently, briefly, touched his lips to the brow of her eye.

Then he straightened and waited for her reaction.

"Well, Mr. Forrester. . .well, Mr. Forrester." She was tongue-tied. "Well, Mr. Forrester. . ."

"Yes, Miss Ross?"

She finally smiled. "Do it again, oh, do it again." And she placed a gloved hand on his arm. "Linger, sir. Please, linger." Then she laughed like the tinkling of silver Christmas chimes. "I don't have to teach you everything about wooing a young lady, do I?"

"I trust not."

"In any case, the rules for wooing other young women do not apply to me." She laced her arms about his neck. "I'm a redhead. You may take risks with me. You may be bold. I shall be bold in return. Do I frighten you, sir?"

"A little," Kyle confessed.

"Good. A redheaded woman should be a little frightening to a man." She turned her face up to his and the shower of falling snow. "But not so frightening he won't kiss her eyes when it's only a week until Christmas Day."

And his kiss was amazing. Two kisses. One on each eye and eyebrow. They made her giggle. Such childish kisses. Yet she refused to relinquish her embrace of his neck. And she knew she was strong. She knew he couldn't break away without using a lot more force than a gentleman would be prepared to use on a woman. Especially one he liked.

"You do like me, don't you, Mr. Forrester?" She smiled up at him. "I do have a bit of a hold on you, don't I?"

Kyle smiled a bigger smile than hers. "I'm very fond of you, Miss Ross. I admit I don't know all the reasons why."

"Good. A woman should be something of a mystery to a man."

"I do know some of the reasons, however."

They were standing in the backyard of her house. Only two lamps had been lit inside, and both were at the front. The only things that were bright in the back by the picket fence were the ice crystals of swirling snow. She snuggled into his chest.

"Enlighten me, young scholar," she murmured into the thick woolen cloth of his coat and cloak. "Please enlighten me."

" 'If the Son therefore shall make you free, ye shall be free indeed.'" Kyle's voice broke into her daydream. "You may be sure our Lord was not simply speaking about a spiritual freedom, as important as that is, for this was a man who fed the hungry with real food and who made the sick happy by giving them real healing, returning to them the capacity to truly walk and truly run and—may I not say it, when we shall gather here again tomorrow night for Christmas Eve and enjoy a ball afterward— dance and celebrate the freedom His touch had given them. No, Christ's freedom extends to every part of a man's life—his appetite, his health and his strength, his soul and his prayers, as well as his ability to move about freely, speak freely, choose freely, think freely, live freely. 'Ye shall be free indeed.'"

Clarissa blinked. What had happened to the boring Genesis sermon? Hadn't there been a hymn between that sermon and Kyle's? Hadn't she stood for it? How long had Kyle been speaking? Well, whatever she had missed, it was his fault she had missed it, for he was the one who had kissed her on her eyes the Tuesday before, and his kisses, just to her dark red brows, had been so potent they remained with her yet. As if they had never ended that snowy night, as if his strong, sweet lips were still sealed lovingly and oh so richly and tenderly upon her smooth white skin.

"One of my professors, who is here tonight," Kyle continued, looking, Clarissa thought, tall and strong and magnificent behind the pulpit in his robe of stark clerical black, "encouraged us to prepare sermons with the Bible open in one hand and the newspaper open in the other. In that spirit, I do not say anything shocking to you when I emphasize that our great nation is at a crossroads. One state has left us. Others shall follow in the new year, once the holidays have concluded and governments are back in session. What does the future hold? I tell you, we must be true to God. We must be true to scripture. We must be a free nation before God. We must be a Christian nation. And to be such a nation all men must be free in their souls and in their intellects and in their will to choose freely. And their bodies must be free. Without chains. Without bars on their windows. Without manacles on their wrists and ankles. We cannot be a nation honoring to God as long as one man or one woman or one child is enslaved. I say again, Christ did not just set souls free. He set lives free. He set bodies free. He set women and men free. 'Stand fast therefore in the liberty wherewith Christ hath made us free, and be not entangled again with the yoke of bondage.'"

A hush fell over the congregation. It was not a hush of boredom or disinterest or sleepiness or impatience; no, Clarissa recognized the sort of hush it was. Everyone was waiting with the sort of anticipation people had for the next strike during a lightning storm, the next peal of thunder—what Kyle would say next and how he would end.

"I preach from Galatians. Yes, Martin Luther's favorite book, Galatians. And why was it his favorite book? Because in it Paul argued that the grace of God set the captives free. Not unjust laws like we see coming from our Supreme Court. Faith in the supreme grace of a supreme God. And Paul made his argument under the inspiration of God Himself. So, what do I say to you with Christmas less than forty-eight hours away, a time when we celebrate the Son who came to set us at liberty from our sins? I say to our Lutheran churches: freedom now, freedom tomorrow, and freedom forever. I say America ought to be a Christian nation and therefore ought to be a nation of independence for all people, not just a privileged few. I say we stand fast in the liberty God has bequeathed upon us with the birth of our Lord Jesus and we do not go back to bondage of any sort—spiritual, intellectual, physical, or political. 'The Lord is that Spirit: and where the Spirit of the Lord is, there is liberty.' There is freedom! Amen!"

Kyle left the huge Bible open on the pulpit and sat down on the chairs behind it reserved for the seminary students.

His face was flushed.

It was as if, Clarissa thought, a storm had swept through the sanctuary and they were left to pick up the pieces, but the landscape had been altered by the winds and floods, and now everything had to be rearranged, and it was all different, almost new.

Slowly, awkwardly, the man who had led the proceedings for the evening came to the pulpit and asked the congregation to stand for a final hymn and a closing prayer.

"Kyle must walk me home," Clarissa whispered swiftly and fiercely to her mother.

Her mother nodded. "Of course, my dear."

"Alone."

"Yes, my dear. I'm sure you'll have a lot to discuss after a sermon like that."

"We will."

"Please be in by eleven. He may join us for some hot cocoa once he accompanies you home."

"I'm sure he'll find that agreeable, Mother."

Her mother smiled. "I'm sure he will. Any young man privileged enough to enjoy your company and good graces would find another ten minutes in your presence agreeable."

Clarissa did not know what privileges Kyle thought he did or didn't enjoy when he was in her company. But she knew what privileges she enjoyed. Indeed, demanded. A block from the church, they still had not said a word to one another. But she felt like a steam kettle inside, already on the boil for at least twenty minutes and ready to burst. When he finally turned to her and said, "I'm sorry, Miss Ross, have I disappointed you in some way? Was my sermon not to your liking? I realize I was a bit heated," she did not let him get any further. The street was deserted, but she pulled him into a nearby alley anyway and grasped the lapels of his winter coat.

"I adored everything you said, sir." She bit out her words in a fierce voice, tugging on his coat with so much force he almost lost his footing. "I adored it. And I adore you. Yes, I've said it, and I'm being forward, but it's nothing but God's truth. You're my lightning storm, sir; you're my thunder. And I'm the one who is heated, sir. Oh, you may be sure, I am heated beyond my capacity to keep it in, and you shall bear the brunt of it. And it's your fault, sir. It's entirely your fault."

She seized him in both her black-gloved hands and yanked herself into his chest. His arms came around her with an immense force that robbed her of her breath. It didn't matter.

"You yourself are my oxygen, sir," she managed to get out, "and you are my light. I cannot make do without either of those things, and I cannot make do without you, sir."

"But only God is our light and breath," Kyle protested.

"All right then. First God, then you. Is that theology acceptable to my seminary student and preacher cum laude?"

"It is."

"Do you wish to discuss it?"

"Here and now?" His face, she was happy to see, was incredulous.

She teased him. "If that is your desire, sir."

"I. . .I would rather. . ."

She grinned. "I feel the same way, sir."

Clarissa folded herself back against his chest and nestled into his strong arms and squeezed him as tightly as she could, closing her eyes in delight when he squeezed her back and took away her breath again, as well as any measure of resistance her red head might still be harboring against surrendering to his charms. She let him carry her utterly and completely away in her dreams and had no qualms whatsoever about letting him do it.

Chapter Four

Christmas Eve
Harrisburg, Dauphin County

*D*on't *you think you are taking things a bit too quickly with young Mr. Forrester?"*

"Too quickly? Mother, aren't I your impulsive daughter?"

"You're my only daughter. My only, lonely, impulsive daughter."

"So then you understand I live my life at twice the rate of forward propulsion of anyone else. At twice the power of steam and locomotion."

"I do understand that."

"And as you just said. . ."

"You're lonely."

"Yes I am. Or yes I was. Mr. Forrester has a way of cheering me up."

"I'm sure he does, my dear. Your father had that way about him at twenty-four too."

"I just wish he approved of the Railroad."

"He abhors slavery."

"But not acting outside the law to abolish it. I wish he thought highly of the Freedom Train. I wish he was proud of what they did. Then I could tell him I was one of their conductors."

Clarissa stopped her flow of memories and stamped her feet as the cold bit through her coat and boots. She was waiting for a signal from a somewhat dilapidated house on the other side of the railway tracks from where she stood. When she had first located the two-story affair, she had been certain they'd given her the wrong address. But after watching for ten minutes, she had seen the curtains move several times. People were inside. They too were waiting. And when the passengers arrived, they would let Clarissa know.

But how would she get them north from Harrisburg and farther along toward the Lake Erie crossing into Canada? She had been asked to go by locomotive from Gettysburg to Harrisburg because all the regular conductors were afraid of being compromised, there were so many slave catchers out and about. Everyone knew something big was up, so there were Southern spies throughout Harrisburg, believing they might have a chance to nab Moses, Harriet Tubman. Clarissa was such an unknown in Harrisburg that no one was looking for her when she got off the train and no one followed her. For that she was grateful.

What she was not grateful for was missing her Christmas Eve with Kyle Forrester. They had planned to sit together at the church service with her parents, have another one of their famous long, slow—and ultimately passionate and dramatic—walks back to her house for coffee and cocoa. Then they were going to open presents with her mother and father. It was going to be marvelous. Her mind and body tingled with anticipation Monday morning when she woke up and thought about how pleasant the evening was going to be. But then the summons had come. She'd just managed to make the Harrisburg train, and now here she was, hidden in the night's shadows next to an abandoned brick shack, dressed in men's pants and a man's long winter coat with a thick woolen toque from Canada pulled down over her head and ears, beginning to shiver, and imagining the stars as sharp, cold knifepoints pricking the skin of her face. This was not how Christmas Eve was supposed to be.

But she was helping men and women and children gain their God-given freedom. She was helping them get to Heaven. Could she honestly be doing anything better on the night Christians celebrated the birth of their Savior? No, no, but. . .if only Kyle could be standing beside her right now.

"What will you tell him?" she asked her father.

"That you have gone to help out a member of the family who is ill. And so you are."

"Hardly a member of the family," she grumbled.

"Not so. We are all part of the family of man, and the slaves are our brothers and sisters, our cousins, our next of kin."

"Well. What are the three of you going to do without me?"

"Why, have some Christmas cheer and open presents of course." Her father grinned. *"Don't worry. We'll save your presents for your return."*

Clarissa made a sour face. *"How very kind of you all."*

The curtain moved in one of the windows of the house she was staring at. But the signal was supposed to be the curtains fully opened for half a minute and then pulled tightly together again. So she thrust her mittened hands more deeply into the pockets of her long coat and blew out a lungful of air that turned into a small white cloud. There were other problems that had to be sorted out before the signal came anyway, so there was no point in her being impatient.

She had to move the passengers from Harrisburg to Lewiston, sixty miles farther north, and she had to do it alone. In the dead of winter. And find a barn she had never seen before, in a county she had scarcely been in more than twice. She closed her eyes and prayed. It was supposed to be a large group. How would she get them through the woods and across the farm fields on such a bitter night, and over such a distance?

"A wagon, Joshua. Or two wagons. Military wagons. Even slave catchers who have a bone in their teeth won't dare stop and search those."

Clarissa whipped her head around.

A tall man in a black hood was at her elbow.

Inwardly, she groaned. *Liberty.*

Outwardly, she snapped. "What do you mean by sneaking up on me like that? If I'd had a pistol, I'd have shot you. Next time, believe me, I will have a pistol and I will shoot you."

"Merry Christmas to you, Joshua, and may God be with you in the new year."

Clarissa had more to say but ended her retort immediately. She looked down at the toes of her boots, toes covered in snow. "Merry Christmas, sir," she replied.

"It's my understanding our Christmas present here is similar to the Twelve Days of Christmas, Joshua, similar in that we have twelve pipers piping."

Clarissa's dark eyebrows came together. "What?"

"I'm used to being cryptic so often I can't cease from being cryptic, it seems. There are eleven passengers and one conductor."

"Twelve. And with you and I that makes fourteen. It's too big a group to move safely, sir. Especially with so many slave catchers skulking around Harrisburg with their blood up."

"Hence the wagons."

"We'd need uniforms to make that trick work."

"I have them."

"I'm a woman, sir."

"But you don't look like a woman. So I think we shall be all right."

Blood and heat rose up in Clarissa. "I don't look like a woman? Is that what you think, sir?"

Liberty shrugged. "I've only ever seen you dress like a very old man."

She knew her eyes were on fire for they felt as if they were burning holes through her skull. "I can't stand you."

"But you will have to put up with me, Clarissa Avery Ross, for I am the only person you can rely on tonight."

"Don't you dare use my real name." She felt like flames were leaping out from under her toque. "Don't you dare."

"There is the signal."

The curtains had been opened.

"We must move swiftly," hissed Liberty, as he began to dart across the railway tracks in a crouch.

"Don't tell me what to do." Clarissa ran after him. "Even if you were Harriet Tubman, I wouldn't let you tell me what to do."

"As a matter of fact."

"As a matter of fact? What is a matter of fact? Am I to imagine you are Moses disguised as a vulgar lout named Liberty?"

They came in through the back door of the house.

A small black woman in clothes equally as manlike as Clarissa's pointed a Navy Six revolver at them.

"Tell me!" she demanded in a harsh whisper. "Hurry up and tell me!"

Clarissa's mind went blank.

But Liberty responded swiftly and smoothly: "'I looked at my hands to see if I was the same person. There was such a glory over everything. The sun came up like gold through the trees and I felt like I was in heaven.'" He grinned. "Your own words coming back to you, Moses. Your own words about how it felt to be finally free of the curse of slavery."

"Liberty." The small black woman could not suppress her smile. "Liberty." She lowered her pistol. "Come here."

She hardly reached up to his chest, but she gave him a fierce hug. "It's been too long."

He hugged her back. "It has been. But this is a wonderful way to spend Christmas."

"It is. And who is this man with you?"

"Uh. . .this is Joshua."

"Joshua. A good name for a liberator."

"It's. . .well. . .it is. . .for me. . .it is an honor to meet you, Moses," stumbled Clarissa.

Moses laughed. "Good Lord Almighty. Another woman just like me looking like an old man dressed up in a potato sack. How old be you, girl?"

"I'm. . .I'm nineteen, Moses, ma'am."

"Well, well, and I weren't a whole lot older than you when I started working on the Railroad. I'm glad you're here, Joshua."

"Thank you, Moses, ma'am. There's no other place I'd rather be tonight."

"Is that a fact? Well, I can think of a hundred places I'd rather be than cold as an ice floe in Pennsylvania, Joshua. But since we are helping these children find a freedom God granted them, but which others have stolen away, I would agree with you that there ain't a better place than right here and right now for us all to be. Come and meet the passengers I have guided north from Philadelphia."

They were huddled at the front of the house. All eleven of them. A smiling woman was passing out chunks of bread and cheese to them, and a small bent man followed pouring milk into wooden cups.

"But they are all children." Clarissa was almost speechless. "Moses, you brought them here from Philadelphia?"

"I did."

"Where. . .where are their parents?"

"Dead. Caught. Chained. Whipped." Moses looked grimly at the eleven faces as they gazed up at her while they wolfed down their food and drink. "We been here only fifteen minutes. And we need to give them another fifteen to rest up and warm up."

The woman passing out the bread and cheese glanced toward Moses with an unhappy darkness in her eyes. "We dare not risk a fire."

Moses nodded. "I know that."

"The wrong people might see the smoke from the chimney and grow suspicious-like. It is midnight."

Moses nodded again. "Cold milk an' cheese an' bread are delicacies for them. We much appreciate your help and shelter." Moses turned to Liberty and Clarissa. "What is your plan?"

"I have two commissary wagons," answered Liberty. "They're covered. I'll handle one and Joshua the other. We'll split the group into two."

"Hmm. I'd best ride in the back with your group, Liberty, as most men strike fear in these children's hearts, especially hooded ones. Joshua, I'd be obliged if you'd remove your hat and scarf so the children can see your face."

Clarissa hesitated. "So the children can see my. . ."

"They need to know you're a woman."

Reluctantly, Clarissa tugged off her toque. Her long scarlet hair tumbled over the shoulders of her dark blue coat. Just as reluctantly, she unwound her scarf, and her young freckled face popped out for all to see. Two of the children laughed and clapped their hands.

"My, my, Liberty," said Moses, "don't you have a redheaded beauty on your hands?"

"It appears so."

"What are you going to do with her?"

"Give her the reins to a team of four horses."

"You think she can handle them?"

"I have high hopes."

"I can handle sixteen horses if that's what you have in mind, sir," Clarissa practically growled. "I can handle anything."

Moses arched her eyebrows and laughed. "My, my. We have a hot fire in the stove."

"I expect you do, ma'am." Clarissa had decided to mind her manners once she realized she was in the company of Harriet Tubman, but Liberty always managed to find some way to gall her, and she found she could not bite her tongue. Her eyes spat fire and sparks at him. "I'm not yours to manage or mismanage, sir, so unless you have direct orders for me, which I will most certainly obey for the sake of the children, I'll thank you to keep any thoughts or opinions about me, and what you think I can or can't handle, to yourself."

Clarissa saw him shrug.

"I didn't say you were beautiful, did I?" he replied.

"Ohhhh." Moses placed her hands on her hips. "Maybe you gone all blind under that black hood of yours, Liberty."

"She's an operator on the Railroad. A conductor. That's all I require her to be. Her looks make no difference to me one way or the other."

"Believe me, sir, I'm most heartily glad to hear that." Clarissa snipped out the words. "In fact, I thank God."

"The wagons are in a large shed five minutes from here," Liberty told Moses. "When the passengers are rested, we'll make our way to them and get rolling. It will take the night to travel the distance."

Moses nodded. "Let's be moving."

They had no trouble getting to the shed. Clarissa would not speak to Liberty, just helped six of the children into the back of the second wagon. It had woolen blankets and heaps of straw. Then she climbed into the driver's seat.

Liberty opened the shed doors wide, looking about to be sure they remained alone. He came to Clarissa's wagon. She continued to stare straight ahead.

"Follow me," he told her. "We're heading to a farm where they will put us up during the day and feed us."

She nodded.

He handed her a flour sack that bulged with a blue uniform. "Put the pants and coat on over what you're wearing. And cover your face up again."

She took the sack.

"If we get stopped, I'll do the talking," Liberty went on. "You're Corporal Hackett."

Clarissa nodded a second time.

"Good luck," he said.

"I don't need luck," she responded in a voice colder than the night.

"Well, whatever you need, Joshua, I hope you get it."

"Sir, I already have it."

Liberty, clothed in army blue, nudged his team out of the shed and urged it along the road. Clarissa, also dressed in soldier blue, flicked the reins of her four horses and followed closely behind. For a brief moment, she poked her head through the opening of the cover as the wagon rolled forward, smiling at the children and telling them everything was going to be fine—"Wrap yourselves in those blankets and snuggle down in that straw." Then she closed the front opening as tightly as the back and kept her commissary wagon moving about fifty feet from the rear of Liberty's.

For the first quarter hour, she was tense, expecting trouble at any minute. Then she looked at the stars more often, reminded herself it was Christmas morning, thought about the children she was setting free, wondered how Kyle was doing—surely, he was fast asleep by now, or might he still be up, worrying about her, missing her, praying for her? What if he stayed awake all night on account of her?

"I hope so," she murmured with a smile. "That would be so romantic."

Two men suddenly slipped onto the roadway with muskets and forced her to stop her wagon.

Reining back, she saw that another pair had halted Liberty.

"Merry Christmas, Corporal," rumbled one of the men to her. "Mind if we take a look at what's so all-fired important that you have to carry it north from Harrisburg in the dead of night?"

Liberty had stepped down from his wagon and brought the two that had stopped him back to Clarissa's wagon. "It's army business, sir, and no concern of citizens like yourselves. Rest assured that it's stores and equipment urgently required in Lewiston over the holiday season, or the corporal and I would be at home with our families and opening our presents. Or fast asleep with visions of sugarplums dancing in our heads."

He laughed, but the four men with guns did not laugh, and neither did Clarissa, for she did not want any of the strangers to hear her less-than-masculine voice.

"Why are you wearing the hood?" one man demanded.

"An ugly wound. My musket misfired."

"Since you mention presents," another of the men growled, "I'd take kindly to you opening up them wagons as a kind of Christmas gift to all of us. We're a long ways from home, the weather's bitter, and our families are missing us at the table. Seeing what you got will make up for some of that and put our minds at ease."

Liberty shook his head. "I repeat, it's army business and strictly army business, sir. I do wish you a Merry Christmas, however, and I hope your own affairs hereabouts are quickly settled so you can return to your loved ones. Now we'll need to be on our way."

The man he had been speaking with, bundled in a heavy coat and wearing a scarf wrapped around his head and ears, shook his head and stepped to the back of Liberty's wagon. "Once I see what you're carrying you'll be free to pass. But not until then." He yanked open the cover and poked his head inside. "Well, well, well, now who have we here?" He laughed and turned his head to his companions. "Lookee here, boys, this really *is* our Christmas present after freezing ourselves half to death the last couple of nights."

The other men gathered around him at the back of the wagon, dropping their guard, lowering their muskets, peering inside, and while doing so, ignoring Liberty and Clarissa for the briefest of moments. She wished she had a pistol—why on earth hadn't she brought hers? Though whether she'd have the nerve to use it, to actually aim the revolver and pull the trigger four times, she had no idea. But not having it, all she could think of to do was to hurl herself on the men like a wildcat and slash at them with the bayonet in her boot. She knew it was a crazy idea, but how else could she possibly save Moses and the children?

She didn't give a thought to what Liberty might do. He didn't even cross her mind in her split second of indecision. Her long knife was suddenly in her fist, and she got ready to spring. *Lord!* she cried out a prayer in her mind. *Lord, Lord, Lord!*

"Gentlemen." It was Liberty's voice.

The men turned around quickly and lifted their muskets.

Crack. Crack. Crack. Crack.

The shots, so close at hand, startled Clarissa and made her grip her bayonet so tightly her knuckles went white.

Liberty's hand was extended before him, straight and rigid, and sparks and smoke spewed from the cap and ball revolver he was firing.

The four men collapsed in a heap.

On the coat of one, as he fell backward, Clarissa saw a stain spreading like water.

"If not you, I would have had to handle it, Liberty." Moses's head appeared at the back of the wagon. "I best get the children to Joshua's wagon. Then you can place the bodies in here."

"Yes." Liberty nodded inside his black hood.

He stood in front of the bodies in the dark, obscuring them from the children as Moses began to herd them to the back of Clarissa's wagon. Clarissa jumped down to help, returning the knife to its sheath in her boot. When all eleven were in and under the cover, Moses turned to Clarissa and placed a small but firm hand on her shoulder.

"You're pale, Joshua," she said. "I take no more delight in the death of the wicked than the Lord does. But those men would have strung you and me and Liberty up in two shakes and dragged all our young'uns back to slavery in the South. I could not countenance that. I could not. For slavery is the next thing to hell." She patted a pocket in her heavy coat. "If Liberty hadn't pulled the trigger, I would have. Now you make peace with him and help him with those men. Make sure you cover them with blankets. We'll bury them proper in Lewiston. Go now."

Clarissa hesitated. "I. . .I wonder if he felt anything at all when he fired at them. He stood there like. . .a statue. Cold. Unmoving."

Moses stared at her. "You don't know anything 'bout Liberty. He felt that shooting right down into his guts. But you never wound a snake, Joshua. You kill it."

Clarissa walked slowly to Liberty's wagon. She was not anxious to see him or the bodies. Before the shooting, he had simply been irritating. Now she realized she was frightened of him, and his black hood had taken on an ominous aspect in her mind. As if he were some kind of executioner.

He was struggling with the last man he was loading into his wagon. The man was probably twice the size of the others. Clarissa hung back a moment, then did her *Lord, Lord, Lord* prayer and came up to grasp the booted feet of the corpse.

"I can handle it," grunted Liberty.

"I'm sure you can," Clarissa responded. "But I need to do more than just watch."

"You are managing a four-horse team. That's a difficult task and more than enough for you."

"I've managed horses since I was nine, sir, and handling this team is not difficult. I can put my hands to a great deal more than that on this trip."

Together they lifted the body into the back of the wagon and made sure all four of the men were covered up. One was still staring upward, and Clarissa closed his eyes before drawing a ragged blanket over his face. A prayer for all of them began to form in her mind.

"It troubles you," Liberty said.

"A little."

"If I had not been here, what would you have done?"

"I had my bayonet out." She looked at his eyes that gleamed like dark wet stones from the slits in his hood. "You remember my bayonet."

"I remember it."

"I would have used it."

"You're sure?"

"I'm sure. And if I'd had my Navy Six with me, I would have fired before you did, sir."

She could almost feel a smile under his hood. "Would you have? Truly?"

"Long before. Others hesitate in such a situation. You hesitated. I would not have."

Of course, she *had* hesitated, and she knew it, and she knew Liberty knew it, but she saw no reason to make an admission that would give him an edge over her.

"Are you a praying woman?" Liberty asked her.

"I am."

"Then I'd be grateful if you'd pray for their souls and pray for our safety on the next leg of our journey."

"Why. . .I'd be. . .honored to give them that much. That would be the Christian thing to do."

"I take no delight in the death of the wicked, Clarissa."

"I've asked you not to use my name." Whenever he used her real name, it startled and bothered her. As if he knew all about her when she knew absolutely nothing about him. It was too intimate. And it broke the rules of secrecy of the Railroad. "Moses takes no delight in the death of the wicked either. Nor do I. Nor does God Almighty."

They both spoke the scripture reference at the same time: "Ezekiel chapter thirty-three, verse eleven."

Liberty nodded his head within his dark hood and jumped down from the wagon. He held out a hand to help her. Normally she would have ignored his offer of assistance. It annoyed her that, acting on an impulse, she did not. She took his hand and let him take her weight as she sprang from the wagon.

For heaven's sake, Clarissa Avery Ross, where did that come from? The dark side of the moon?

What was doubly annoying was that she let him help her up into the driver's seat of her commissary wagon as well. She even thanked him and gave him a smile that was bigger than her smallest smile. He snapped her a playful salute. She smiled even more and snapped one back.

"Thank you, Liberty," she said.

"I'm glad I was here, Miss Ross."

"Surprisingly, I am too, sir."

"I am just as surprised to hear you say that."

"Often enough, I surprise myself."

Such as in this instance. Which made her think her polite behavior toward Liberty must have come from the four moons of Jupiter, never mind the one moon of Earth that was close at hand.

He insulted you only an hour ago.

I know that.

He belittled your attractiveness.

Yes he did.

Yet now you treat him as if he's a prince.

Oh, I do not. Honestly, I do not.

It looks that way to me.

Well, and what do you know about it, miss?

The reins were tight in her hands as her team trotted behind Liberty's wagon. Again, she felt tense as they started out. Again, she gradually relaxed more and more as the miles rolled by under her wheels. The night swept by overhead, and now and then a few bits of snow swirled down. Images of the shooting kept appearing in her mind like daguerreotypes, and these brought her anxiety back for several minutes at a time. But then the darkness and the cold and the sound of the horses' hooves and the creaking of the wagon all combined to bury the bodies for a while. And she remembered that the children were alive—alive and free. And that it was Christmas Day.

Chapter Five

New Year's Eve
Gettysburg

hink of all the things the Lord has done for you this year past. Think of His many blessings. Think of how His chastisements have benefited you and made you a stronger man or a stronger woman, just as an apple tree that is pruned properly yields much more fruit. Spend the next few minutes meditating on all the good the Lord has done in your life. And thank Him."

It felt odd to be thinking about Liberty with Kyle seated beside her in the pew, but it was impossible for Clarissa to follow the minister's directions and exclude the black-hooded mystery man from her thoughts and prayers. Especially after Christmas Day.

They had made their way to the barn an hour before sunrise. Then the children had been spirited into the house to eat and sleep. Moses and Liberty and herself had said goodbye to them there and placed them in the hands of other conductors who would guide them farther north. They had prayed with them and returned to the barn to care for the horses, bury the men several hundred feet behind the barn in the soft earth under a dung heap, and curl up in the straw with thick woolen blankets. Liberty, out of respect for her and Moses, had taken himself up into the hayloft. Somehow, Clarissa had sensed he was watching her while she fell asleep, and it made her feel more peaceful and secure. That night, when she awoke to an operator gently shaking her shoulder, a mug of coffee in his hand, both Moses and Liberty were gone.

She kicked herself for looking about the barn for a note from him, but she looked just the same. He had not left a note or a word for her with any of the operators. However, Moses had asked the farmer who owned the barn to show Clarissa a verse from the family Bible: *"But he knoweth the way that I take: when he hath tried me, I shall come forth as gold. My foot hath held his steps, his way I have kept, and not declined."* Treasuring the words in her mind, she had taken the train back to Gettysburg alone in a prim and proper, but lush, burgundy and forest-green dress the woman at the farm had given her. Saved from when her daughter had been twenty-one and slender, it fit surprisingly well.

So, with all that, it had truly been the most wonderful Christmas of her life. And while her feelings about Liberty had not changed completely—she still found him scary and more than a little rude and arrogant—they had shifted enough for her to thank God she had met him and was working alongside him on the Railroad.

All of which did nothing to diminish her feelings for Kyle Forrester, who had burst into her life in 1860 like the hot blast from a cannon's mouth. She went to bed thinking about him and woke up in the same frame of mind. After which, he darted in and out of her thoughts each and every waking moment of each and every day. It was easy to thank God for him. And pleasant. Just as it was easy and pleasant to thank God for all those who had been rescued from a lifetime of bondage and set free—her freedmen. Which brought her mind around to Liberty once more.

It was as if the two men were sitting beside her on the pew, Kyle to her left and Liberty to her right. She supposed that sort of imagining ought to have made her uncomfortable, but it didn't. She flirted with the idea of Liberty being as handsome as Kyle and of both men vying for her attention—well, why not, that's the way courting was done—and it made her feel happy and warm to her leather-booted toes. In another hour, Kyle would be waltzing with her at the New Year's ball, and in another two or three weeks, she would be slipping through a cold January night and ferrying runaway slaves into the next county alongside Liberty. Despite the sense that other states might soon be following South Carolina out of the Republic, and the anxiety and stress the country felt because of it, Clarissa could not suppress her joy and excitement at having two men in her life she liked, and who she knew liked her—*oh yes you do, Liberty*—and she knew there was a happy smirk on her face as she sat with head bowed at her pew. And the excitement wasn't just about the two men. She was doing something that made a difference in the nation and the world—she was setting God's children free.

Then she was at the ball, and Kyle had one arm about her waist, and he was whirling her with speed and grace and precision over a polished wooden floor in the burgundy and green dress she had worn on her return from Lewiston. As soon as the music slowed, she sank her head upon the white shirt and black coat of his chest and decided the night was as perfect, in its own way, as the rescue of the children on Christmas Eve.

"Penny for your thoughts, Miss Ross," Kyle whispered as they moved in circles across the dance floor along with other couples, candles and oil lamps gleaming all around them.

"Oh, you'd need at least a twenty-dollar bill, Mr. Forrester," she replied, eyes closed, lips curving into a smile.

"Would I?"

"You would."

"Well, I hope there's room in there for some thoughts of me."

"I don't know if there is any more room, sir."

"No more room?"

"Hush. Don't pout." She laughed softly. "There's no room because you've already taken up most of it."

"I have?"

"Most certainly you have. So set your mind at ease, my young gallant."

Even while she was saying these words to him, and saying them most sincerely, the thought darted into her head: *I wonder if Liberty can dance as well as Mr. Forrester.*

But she shook it off.

Stay with Kyle Forrester, if you please, Clarissa Avery. You don't know anything about Liberty. You don't know what he looks like or how he presents himself in public without that ridiculous black hood of his. Steer clear for the present until you gain more information about the real man.

But I do know things about the real man.

No you don't. You know the man who acts as a conductor on the Railroad. You know absolutely nothing about the man under the hood.

Surely they are not two entirely different personalities.

They could well be. It is a trick of human nature. Remain with Kyle Forrester. With him there is no hood and no secrets.

Oh, everyone has secrets.

"It's just about midnight, my little dreamer."

Clarissa blinked several times and then smiled up at Kyle. "I know."

"I trust I may be able to collect my year's end bounty."

She laughed her silver chimes laugh. "I'm sure you shall, sir. There's no one else I'd rather surrender it to."

Someone shouted, "Happy New Year!" and Clarissa watched people throw the doors open to 1861. Church bells began to toll, and a group of men with deep baritone voices began to sing "Auld Lang Syne." Kyle touched her cheek gently, and she closed her eyes and tilted her chin up toward him.

Crack. Crack. Crack. Crack.

Clarissa jerked her face away from Kyle and stared wildly around her.

Crack. Crack. Crack. Crack.

"Shooting!" she exclaimed. "Someone's shooting a pistol!"

She saw Liberty aiming his pistol with his arm as straight and rigid as an iron bar.

It snapped and smoked and tossed off sparks.

Four men fell dead.

Forty men fell dead.

Forty thousand men fell dead.

She gasped and fell back into Kyle's arms.

"What is the matter?" he asked her, alarm scribbled all over his face. "Those are firecrackers, nothing more."

"It's gunfire. So much gunfire. Men dropping everywhere. . . everywhere. . ."

She saw a stain spreading over a hundred men's chests as rapidly as water spilled from a bucket into the dirt.

"Clarissa. It's fireworks. Only fireworks."

Crack. Crack. Crack. Crack.

"They are harbingers." Her heart was thudding in her chest. "I do not want the new year to be one I dread, but I cannot stop it, I cannot."

Kyle hugged her. "You don't have to. You don't need to. Regardless of what occurs, no year is all bad. No year ever is. There will be sunlight, trust me, Clarissa, sunlight and sunrise and stars in the night. No matter what else transpires. God will not leave us bereft of hope."

"Take me away from here, Kyle. Take me away from the gunfire. Walk me through the quietest parts of town you can find. Please."

He moved swiftly, snatching up their coats at the door and escorting her away from firecrackers snapping and banging on the roadway near the dance hall. In minutes they were walking past houses unlit by lamps or candles, past roofs and gables and chimneys and picket fences. The pop and crack of the fireworks was gone. When they came to St. Xavier Catholic Church, all darkened, Clarissa asked if they might linger.

"It has a picket fence like my house," she said. "And the cupola looks like the one at Christ's Church."

"It's a lovely church, and Father McGinnis is a fine priest and a good man. From County Armagh in Ireland."

"He is a good man. I've met him at our boot shop once or twice." She raised her eyes above the cupola and stared at the scattering of bright white stars. "The constellations are immaculate. Always immaculate.

Even when nations and the human race are in tatters."

" 'As the heavens are higher than the earth.' "

" 'So are my ways higher than your ways, and my thoughts than your thoughts.' " Clarissa completed the verse from Isaiah. "Thank God His ways are higher than ours. Most of our ways hardly rise ankle high above the mud and slop of winter."

"Take heart, Miss Ross. Many people in America have good intentions this New Year's Day, people in both the North and the South."

"I don't know what came over me. The fireworks made me think of gunfire, and the gunfire made me think of warfare, and I seemed to see men falling and falling, in long rows, like stalks of autumn corn being cut down."

"Have you been exposed to gunfire, Miss Ross? Have your senses been assaulted by excessive violence?"

"No, no. . .no. . .I don't know what came over me. . . ."

Of course, she knew very well what had come over her. The killing on Christmas morning. The dead bodies she had helped bury under the dung heap. The threat of other states leaving the Republic now that the holiday season was coming to an end. The long, black clouds of impending conflict. She had always prided herself on not being overly sensitive or excited about death and war and muskets and politics. But something had reached out to her in the icy winter darkness and found her, and she felt a frightening hand clutch her heart more and more fiercely.

"At least I have my town," she said. "And all its beautiful houses and peace. Its places of worship and faith. Its trim fences and shrubs. Even in winter, our trees have a stark beauty with or without the snow on their naked branches. And the people are fine. Not perfect—who is perfect, Kyle Forrester? But they are fine, and some are exceptionally fine."

"I believe that."

"I suppose I've always been high-strung. But it was worse when I was eleven or twelve. Mother had to take me on long walks to settle me down. Nothing else seemed to help except that. Summer, autumn, winter. I've walked all these streets countless times. I know every nook and cranny, every home and who lives where. I know the pets that have come and gone, and I've watched toddlers grow into young women and men. I have my favorite shade trees and my exceptionally favorite sunny spots. I know where the best crab apple trees are, and I've raided them too." She laughed to herself. "I'm talking too much. Like a woman leaning over a picket fence to chat with her neighbor. On and on. I apologize."

"Clarissa. There is nothing to apologize for. If it helps, I shall walk the streets of Gettysburg with you until dawn. Provided we stop by your house to obtain your parents' consent."

"Ha-ha. Which you will never get. But I appreciate the gallantry you have just extended to me." She put her arm through his. "Come. Escort me home. They'll be wondering what's happened."

"They said we had until one."

"Because that's when the ball ends and the hall shuts its doors. They assumed we'd be there the whole time. Now, I'm sure they've realized we are no longer in attendance. So let us head to my white picket fence and my seven gables and set their minds at ease. Oh, they trust you, don't be afraid of that. However, a prompt arrival at the front door will make all the difference. Are you in agreement, Kyle Forrester?"

"I am."

"Then let us away, sir."

They had hardly gone a block, past several handsome homes of gables and shutters and the town's ever-present picket fences, before Clarissa squeezed his arm.

"Perhaps you can promise me something," she said.

"Anything," he replied.

"Anything? My, my. You haven't even heard what I'm about to ask."

"Well. . ."

"Do I truly have you wrapped about my finger to such an extent, sir?" she teased. "A tall, strong man like you?"

"I do feel somewhat tethered, Miss Ross. But happily so."

"Really? I'm glad to hear it. I know I'm being rather bold to speak along these lines, but it was my understanding all men wanted their independence at any cost."

"Sometimes. . .intimacy is what brings a man the liberty he seeks. Not a lack of it."

She smiled and squeezed his arm again. "What a perfect explanation. So, having snared you, I've been your liberator and not your captor?"

"You might put it that way."

"Well, I like the idea of being the woman who sets you free rather than being the woman who places you in some sort of prison. So, if I'm an aspect of your freedom, can you return the favor and bless me by promising there won't be a conflict within our republic?"

"Oh Clarissa, you know that's not a promise within my power."

"But convince me anyways, sir. Lead me to believe it shall not happen."

"It need not happen. If more states join South Carolina and secede, they can form their own nation with their own laws. Their laws will not impinge on ours, and their judges will not sit on our Supreme Court. So no more Fugitive Slave Law in the North. No more Dred Scott. Do you see? America shall have more freedom than it's had for decades."

"That does make me feel better," Clarissa admitted.

"If all parties realize this, the South can go their way; we can go ours."

"And there doesn't need to be armed conflict."

"Not at all."

She groaned. "There would still be slavery."

"But not up here. And no law permitting slave catchers in our towns and counties. Nor would we return any runaways to the states that seceded."

"You would assist all efforts to keep them safe and secure on our side of the border?"

"Of course I would. It would be the Christian thing to do. And the right thing to do so far as our laws were concerned. . .as well as God's laws."

"Hurrah!" Clarissa threw her head back and laughed. Ringlets of scarlet hair escaped her bonnet and curled to the shoulders of her cape and her coat. "I feel wonderful again."

"Thanks be to God."

"Yes, God. And the walk. And my quaint little town. And you."

"I'm honored."

She skipped a few moments, still grasping his arm. "War will not come."

"Well," he cautioned, "it need not come."

"War will not come. I say, it will not come."

Her childlike enthusiasm and optimism were infectious. He could not help but join her in her declaration: "It will not come."

"It will not come to New York. It will not come to New Hampshire."

"It will not come to Massachusetts," added Kyle. "It will not come to Boston."

"It will not come to Connecticut. It will not come to Rhode Island. It will not come to Providence."

"It will not come."

"It will not come to New Jersey," she called out. "It will not come to Indiana. It will not come to Pennsylvania. It will not come to Philadelphia."

"It will not come," Kyle called back.

"It will not come to Pittsburgh. It will not come to Harrisburg. It will not come to Gettysburg."

"It will not come. It will not come."

Chapter Six

April 1861
Lancaster County

*C*larissa was crouched behind a tree, watching a farmhouse, with twelve runaways huddled around her, waiting for the sun to hurry up and set, chewing rapidly on a long stalk of spring timothy. Her eyes were on the farm, but her mind had wandered back to her skipping along a Gettysburg sidewalk on New Year's Eve.

She had been full of whimsy and, she admitted later, a large helping of silliness that she pulled Kyle Forrester into during the early hours of New Year's Day. She hadn't seen much harm in being foolish in the face of so much uncertainty about the fate of her country. Her Grandmother Avery—God rest her sweet soul—had often remarked that a long face changed nothing at all, except to make a woman look as bad as she felt inside, and thus to present to a troubled world an unpleasant profile that made everyone who saw it feel worse. *"Shine, Clarissa Avery,"* Grandmother had admonished her. *"Shine like a diamond if you are going to carry my name about with you for the rest of your life. Promise me."*

So Clarissa didn't regret her craziness at the end of one year and the beginning of another. Kyle had gallantly tried to make a promise to her that there would be no war, and she had just as gallantly tried to keep her promise to her Grandmother Avery, in heaven, that her one and only granddaughter wouldn't show a long face to the world even if there was a war. Which Clarissa fervently prayed there wouldn't be, well aware there were others praying just as fervently that there would be.

Mississippi, Florida, Alabama, Georgia, and Louisiana had seceded in January. Texas in February. Nothing had happened since, and she was holding her breath, waiting for another Southern boot to drop. But maybe one wouldn't drop. Maybe the seven states that had left the Republic were content now. They had formed what they called the Confederate States of America in Montgomery, Alabama, right after Texas joined what Kyle called the "illegitimate rebellion," and now they were going about their business and ignoring President Abraham Lincoln and Washington. Except they had begun to create their own army. And had taken over all the United States forts and arsenals in their territories. So that was worrisome.

She chewed the long green stalk of timothy more vigorously. Glanced at the sinking sun, glanced at the farmhouse, glanced at her twelve freedmen, as she always liked to call her passengers on the Railroad, glanced again at the farm where several men were leading large workhorses—Percheron, she thought—into a massive red barn. She put her eyes on the sun once more. It was taking too long. Spring sunsets were too slow. Winter ones were ideal.

"But *so* cold," she murmured.

Yet liberty was liberty, whether obtained during the April planting season or under a white January moon that was rigid with frost.

"And speaking of liberty," she murmured again, plucking a fresh piece of grass to place in her mouth, "where are you, sir?"

And that was one of the truly uncanny moments, she mused later, of her very short life.

For Liberty was at her elbow instantly.

All in black and—with his hood—reminding her of an executioner, a bandit, a roguish clergyman who hid his face from God and his congregation. Or Ichabod Crane's nemesis in *The Legend of Sleepy Hollow*.

"Liberty." She refused to admit he had startled her once again. "All you need is a pumpkin for your head to be Washington Irving's protagonist."

Perhaps he smiled under his perpetual hood. She was certain his dark and distant eyes did on the other side of their slits.

"Some people consider that a horror story, Miss Ross."

"Yes, well, you do fit into that Halloween festival the Scots and Irish brought with them from the old country."

"I've not had the opportunity to celebrate that odd holiday."

"You yourself are odd enough, sir, so you ought to try it."

"When is it?" he asked, his voice muffled and distorted, as always, by the thick cloth of his black hood.

"The last day of October."

He snorted. "A lifetime away."

"The world will still be here this autumn, sir."

"But not, perhaps, our nation as we know it now."

"Why do you say that?" Clarissa frowned. "Do you know something?"

"No."

"Has another Southern state seceded?"

"Not to my knowledge."

"How was our Gettysburg when you left it?"

"Quaint and quiet."

It was almost night, and she decided to risk a question she had been meaning to ask for months: "Where do you live in Gettysburg, sir?"

He did not reply for a moment. Then he said, "I know where you live, and that is sufficient."

Instantly, her temper flared. "It's not right you should know so much about me and I know absolutely nothing about you."

"I'm a conductor. It's important I know who I work with."

"I'm a conductor too."

"I'm a more important one."

"Are you indeed?" She knew her eyes were blazing. "And you base that odious misconception on exactly what facts?"

"I'm older, wiser, have been on the Railroad longer, and I don't have a lady friend to make a mush of my brain the way you have a beau to make a complete mess of yours."

She exploded. "What?"

"*Shh.* Slave catchers from Virginia and Arkansas are thick as ticks on a Maryland hog tonight."

"I don't care where they are from, and I don't care about your hogs either. How dare you pry into my private life?"

"Our work is hazardous. There mustn't be any weak links in the chain, or people die and slaves are recaptured."

"So?"

"So it's my job to be sure you are safe and that we are safe with you."

"I can't believe it. Do you prowl about my house like a common thief? Or an unkempt alley cat?"

"I don't. But the seminarian Kyle Forrester moons about your house enough for six or seven alley cats."

She wanted to strangle him. "You and I were getting along much better until now."

"He is all right as far as most seminarians go. But he has a lot to learn about women and about life."

She was one split moment of indecision from slapping him across his hooded face. Or tearing the hood from his head and pummeling him properly. "When I was fourteen, I beat up a schoolyard bully named Billy Thomas for stealing my lunch and constantly harassing me and my friends. I gave him two black eyes and a bloody nose, and it was one of the proudest moments of my life. I even made the big lout cry. Oh my, how I enjoyed that. How I loved cutting him down to size. Served the blackguard right. I was suspended for a month, and I didn't care. It was well worth it." She glared at Liberty. "I feel like giving you a licking right now. Don't think I can't do it, sir. I'm stronger and faster and meaner than you think."

"Like a badger," he responded, looking at a lantern swaying back and forth in the farmyard.

"Exactly like a badger," she retorted.

"Or a wolverine."

"Exactly like a wolverine."

"There is the signal, Joshua; we must be off."

"Don't you dare turn away from me when I am speaking to you." She grasped his arm and squeezed until she was certain it hurt, although he did not flinch or make a sound. "You yourself have a great deal to learn about women and life, sir. To press the matter further, Mr. Forrester is a gentleman, which you are not, and enjoys my good graces, which you no longer do. I wish he were by my side right now instead of you."

Liberty shook off her grasp and stood up in the dark grove of trees thick with spring leaves. "That would not help you much, Miss Ross, since he disapproves of what you are doing and would not lend you a hand in breaking the law, no matter how often you bestowed your good graces on him. Including your frequent hugs."

She swung as hard as she could with her closed fist but only hit empty air. He was moving quickly across the field to the farm and gestured for the runaways to follow him. They did. She was the last person to leave hiding. And so angry she could barely see the glimmer of the lantern in the blackness.

I'll murder him. I'll murder him as soon as we have these passengers safely on their way to New York, and I'll tell everyone slave catchers did it. With their bare hands. Because I intend to kill him with my bare hands. Just the way I dealt with that bully in eighth grade. Only this time I'll send him all the way to God. Or the devil. Yes, most likely I shall be sending him straight to the devil.

How much she meant it, whether she intended to pounce on him the moment she had him alone in the woods or the barn, like the tomboy and wildcat she knew she could be, and teach him a lesson he would never forget, she was destined never to find out. For as fate would have it—or Providence, which was what she believed saved Liberty from her fury—the Amish operators on the farm had news that startled the wrath right out of her. It was as if life itself punched her in the stomach and robbed her of all her air. And she had not seen it coming.

"Hello, Amos," she said to a tall, lean, bearded man dressed in Amish black, along with a broad-brimmed black hat, as he ushered them into the barn where the Percherons were in their stalls. "It's very good to see you again."

"*Ja.*" He nodded. "And you, sister. Rebecca will be bringing food and drink from the house directly. Brother Ezekiel is making up a pack for your journey to Lebanon. That will be in a day or two."

"How far is it, Amos?" She had no idea if they were indeed Amos and Ezekiel and Rebecca, for the Amish regularly used names from the Bible, or whether those were simply their operator names. It didn't matter. "And thank you for taking us in."

"God is not a slave driver. Neither should His children be."

"Amen."

"Were you having to run quite a lot, sister?" he asked, searching her face.

"Why?"

"You are flushed."

"Oh." She looked away from Amos to where two of the women passengers were making a seat for themselves on a stack of hay. "It's nothing."

"All right." Amos gestured to Liberty. "A word with the two of you, *bitte.*"

Liberty came over. "What is it?"

Clarissa stepped away from him.

"News came today," announced Amos.

"What news?" responded Liberty.

"You know the president was sending ships to resupply Fort Sumter, ja? Off the Carolina coast?"

"Yes." Clarissa spoke up. "I knew that."

"On Friday and Saturday, the Confederacy fired their cannons at Sumter from the shore."

"I am not surprised." Liberty barely reacted. "It is unfortunate, but you could see that firing upon Sumter was a possibility."

"That was days ago." Clarissa's mind was turning over quickly. "We've been sleeping in the woods for most of the week, heading this way after dark. There was no opportunity to get any information like that."

"We only found out this morning." Amos ran his hand through his beard several times as if deciding whether he should say more. "The fort surrendered."

"No." Clarissa felt a coldness through her entire body, and all her anger at Liberty dissipated instantly. "No."

"The president has called for seventy-five thousand troops to quell what he calls the Rebellion. Well, and many people are calling it that. Lancaster is full of such talk among the *Englisch*. It is war, my friends. So sad. So very sad, ja? The country torn apart."

"And the nation is responding to the president's request?" asked Liberty.

Clarissa thought Liberty looked far too calm. Not that she cared. Or perhaps she did care—she wanted him to look as agitated as she felt.

"It is early yet," replied Amos. "But, judging from the mood in town, and what others have told me is in the newspapers from Philadelphia and New York and Boston. . .ja, he will get his seventy-five thousand and more."

"And the President of the Confederacy is already raising an army of one hundred thousand," added Liberty.

Amos nodded. "It is upsetting. We must pray. Perhaps even now this madness can be halted before it goes too far."

"Have any other states seceded?"

"*Nein*. But. . ."

Clarissa had no patience left, not for Liberty, not for Amos, not for her country hurtling toward a brutal conflict. "For heaven's sake, Amos, what is it?"

"Virginia has been grumbling about the seventy-five thousand troops the president wants. They have threatened not to help furnish them. So. . .who knows what they will do next?"

A woman taller than Amos slipped into the open barn carrying a tray of bread and sliced ham, while a round and heavyset man behind her held pewter pitchers of what looked like milk. "No more politics, Amos," she warned. "Food and drink and prayer are more important for these people than rumors of war and ill feeling." She smiled at Clarissa and Liberty. "*Welkommen*. It is so good to see you both again. I'm glad you are working together."

Clarissa managed a crooked smile.

"And you must be starved." The woman knelt by the runaway slaves and set down the tray of food. "We are so blessed to have you here. Thank God you are safe. And on this farm, we shall keep you safe. Ja, the Lord and our people shall keep you safe. My name is Rebecca, and this is my husband, Ezekiel, with the fresh milk, and our politician is Brother Amos." She chuckled. "Such a good president he would be."

Amos grinned through his thick black beard. "Ja, and so if I were president, there would be no war, Rebecca."

"Indeed not, and thank you for that." Rebecca turned back to the cluster of runaways. "I know you wish to eat."

"If we could, ma'am." A young woman spoke up. "All we had the last two days was wild apples and creek water."

Liberty coughed.

"Oh, and Mr. Liberty, he had his t'ick black coffee and his t'ick brown sugah for us." She and several of the other runaways laughed. "It was like to drinkin' boiled tar. Only Mizz Clarry cottoned to it."

Clarissa snorted. "I did not, Sara. I tolerated it. Mornings and evenings are cold, and I was willing to put up with boiled tar."

"Well, I'm afraid we don't do boiled tar in Lancaster." Rebecca smiled and folded her hands in prayer. "But let me give thanks and you can see how you like our bread and milk and ham, ja?"

Everyone in the barn bowed their heads, including Liberty, and all the runaways folded their hands like Rebecca, even the men. She prayed in German, but everyone understood the *amen*. After the prayer, Rebecca handed out tin plates and then dished up food for all the runaways. They went at it as if they hadn't eaten in days or weeks. Which wasn't far from the truth, Clarissa thought as she watched them, unless apples and stale bread and creek water and boiled tar counted as real food.

She always marveled at how quickly the runaways could adapt. At first, there was the understandable fear and silence that smothered them because they were afraid of being captured and unsure of who conductors like Clarissa and Liberty were—especially Liberty in his ridiculous hood. And telling them his face was badly deformed hardly helped matters. After a day or a night of them all being thrown together, however, the runaways would speak more often, even smile. If they had to spend several days with their conductors, as they did on this passage through Pennsylvania, their words came more freely and so did their laughter. Teasing Liberty about his coffee would have been unthinkable for them only three days before. But now they were trusting Clarissa and Liberty far more and loosening up considerably. Clarissa loved the unity and was glad they still had several days together until they reached Lebanon.

She watched them eat without a thought of food for herself. Rebecca brought her a tin plate with ham and bread and offered her a tin cup of milk as well. They sat and chatted with her while Clarissa devoured every crumb. Did she want more? Well. . .yes. They both laughed.

"Racing through the woods and fields," Rebecca remarked as she came back with another plateful for Clarissa, "climbing all those hills, constantly looking over your shoulder, no wonder you are famished. You spend so much time on the Freedom Train it's a wonder you aren't skin and bones."

"Ha." Clarissa was shoveling ham into her mouth. "I'll never get that thin. I like food too much. This ham is smoked perfectly, Rebecca."

"*Danke*. Ezekiel prides himself on his work with the hogs and the smokehouse—not a pride in himself and his abilities, no, but in what God can accomplish through his willingness to work hard and do everything as perfectly as he can."

"Well, it's much appreciated. I like running the Train through Lancaster because I love bringing my passengers to your station. It's so safe and comfortable here."

Rebecca smiled. "Ah, then praise God. It is little enough what we do, but I'm grateful it makes a small difference in the face of such wickedness."

"Those who work on the Train think highly of the Amish and Quakers. Very highly. One of our chief conductors says she can trust the Quakers' promises, and that they are right to call themselves a Society of Friends."

"Amen. The Quakers are good neighbors to us."

"We feel the same way about the Amish and Mennonites. You have earned our trust. We do not fear anyone or anything once we are under one of your roofs."

Rebecca placed her hand firmly on Clarissa's shoulder. "Your words make my heart glad."

"*Gut.*" Clarissa put her hand on Rebecca's. "*Gut.*"

"Let me add my thanks." Liberty stood in front of them. "Our passengers are exhausted. They have come all the way from Alabama over the past month. A night and a day here to rest will give them fresh strength."

Clarissa looked down.

"It is an honor to serve God and the men and women you bring to us." Rebecca got to her feet. "Now I know you two will have much to discuss before you sleep. We shall be watching the barn all night. First Ezekiel and then Amos, and after him, another man, Eli. So, you will be safe. Should a problem arise, someone will come to you and inform you. The sheriff here always assists the slave catchers, but I think he is caught up with the news about Fort Sumter this week, and about Lancaster helping the state meet the quota of troops President Lincoln has asked for. Even if a group of slavers approach him, I doubt he will have the time for them. I have heard he has been offered a commission in the army as a captain. No, he will not have time to help slave catchers beat the bushes for runaways. Yet it is so sad that it must be war that stays his hand and not his Christian conscience."

Liberty did not sit beside Clarissa. "I will stay up a few more hours. Just in case there is trouble," he told her.

She nodded, not looking up. "All right."

"Once the men are ready, I'll get them up to the loft."

She nodded again.

"Is there anything you need?"

She kicked at the straw with the toe of her boot. "Yes. But nothing that is in you to give."

"You mean an apology? No, I won't be offering you an apology."

"I suppose I didn't think you would."

"All our conductors are examined from time to time."

"You mean spied on."

"I know of three who turned their passengers in to the local authorities and collected the reward money."

She snapped her head up and glared at him. "And you honestly think I am capable of that?"

"I don't, no. I was more concerned with what you might inadvertently divulge to young Mr. Forrester."

"Divulge? How would you know what I said or didn't say to him in private conversation, sir? Do you reside in one of his coat pockets?"

"I know his professors. I know his classmates. I would have heard something eventually."

"What?" Clarissa's eyes narrowed to slits of fire. "Who are you? Where do you live in Gettysburg? Are you working at the seminary? You have to tell me something."

"I don't."

"Yes you do, sir. I have placed my life in your hands. And the lives of countless others many times over. How do I know I can trust you? You obviously don't trust me. So tell me why I should trust black-hooded Liberty the conductor? Give me something to erase the doubt and disappointment that is rising in my heart against you. Please. You must. Or we won't work together again after Lebanon."

"Miss Ross. . ."

"We won't. I swear to God, we won't." She felt like getting to her feet and pacing, the way her father paced when he was upset, but she decided to stay seated. "Moses knows all about you. The people that run the Railroad know all about you."

"They don't know *all*."

"I don't care. They know more than I do. Which isn't hard, because I know absolutely nothing. Nothing, sir. Yet I am the one who risks her life with yours every time we ride the rails and ferry new runaways to a safe station."

"We keep our secrets for a reason."

"Apparently I don't have any secrets where you are concerned. Even when it comes to my romance with Kyle Forrester."

"I told you. I've done what I've done simply to be sure you can be trusted."

"And can I be trusted?" demanded Clarissa.

"Yes. Very much so."

"Thank you. So now prove it."

"*Prove?*" echoed Liberty.

"Tell me something about yourself. I don't care what."

"Miss Ross. . ."

"Quit answering my queries with *Miss Ross, Miss Ross*. I find it irritating. Besides, it is against the code of the Railroad."

"Joshua. . ."

"Using that name is equally annoying. I don't want you to use any of my names. I want you to give me some information about yourself."

"I don't know what I can say."

"Tell me about your hood."

"My hood?" Liberty responded.

"Does my question require further elaboration? You only have the one hood, am I right? No one else I've met on the Railroad wears one. You'd think Moses would if it was so all-fired important. Yet there you are with that absurd bag over your head. What purpose does it serve except to hide your identity from the people you work with and who you entrust your life to? Surely it does not matter if they see your face, since they would have turned you over to the slave catchers or one of the sheriffs by now, hood or no hood, if they were falsehearted. Moses knows such a device isn't necessary. Why do you? Unless you wear it to spite me?"

"I can assure you. . .Joshua. . .that I was wearing this hood long before you arrived on the scene."

"Were you? Because your features strike fear and loathing into the hearts of the runaways?"

"No."

"Don't try and convince me you have some sort of wound or suppuration. I wasn't born yesterday. Nor did my mother pluck me from the turnip patch the day before yesterday. There is no scent of blood or infection on you. No hint of rotting flesh. You are as clean of offensive odors as my parents or my beau. So, now tell me. Trust me. Why the hood, Mr. Liberty? Why the black executioner's hood, sir?"

Liberty did not move or speak for at least a minute. Clarissa refused to be intimidated and would not break the long silence with her own voice, and she had no intention of looking away either. She forced herself to be patient, no mean feat, she soon realized. But finally, Liberty spoke, in a masculine voice muffled by the thick fabric of the hood, the only voice she had ever heard come from his hidden mouth.

"It is not to spite you, Miss Ross. Still less to hide myself away from you or any of the conductors or operators. Or any of the slaves, for that matter. And, no, there is no wound to speak of."

He paused.

This time she did speak up. "So then, why, sir?"

His hands became fists. Then opened again. Then became fists. "There are. . .there are slave hunters who might come up from Mississippi one day. They would never come into Gettysburg. Or, if they did, never cross any of the paths I take on a daily basis. But on the Railroad, out in the fields or streams or hillsides, we might well meet face-to-face. And I would be recognized." Through the slits in the hood, she felt his eyes fix like daggers on hers. "I am of the South, Miss Ross. My family is a well-known plantation family, and I, being one of its sons, am well-known too. Many folks from Jackson would know my face, for my family has done business there since I was a child. In Vicksburg they would know me. In Biloxi, for we have another home there since my father loves the sea. In Natchez they would know me, and know me well, for our plantation is there. It is a vast estate with a vast mansion. We grow cotton and sugarcane. Natchez is the chief port on the Mississippi for shipping our crops north to the rest of America or shipping them south to New Orleans and thence overseas to Europe. Slaves work our plantation, Miss Ross, and they have for more than a hundred years."

Clarissa felt as rigid as ice.

Rebecca and Ezekiel and Amos were talking with the runaways. Sometimes there were bursts of laughter or bursts of thanks to God. But she did not move a muscle, not so much as a finger, and she doubted she blinked or batted an eye.

"Mississippi is a close-knit state. Natchez is an even closer-knit community of wealthy plantation owners. Their fathers and sons will fight for what they see as their right to work their plantations as they see fit. Their fathers and sons will die for the Mississippi way of life. I, having opposed that way of life since I was a boy, though I kept it locked up in my heart, would be seen as a traitor if it was discovered I was a conductor in the Underground Railroad."

"They would flay you alive," whispered Clarissa, half to herself and half to him.

"What they might do to me is of no concern. I have seen them lynch Mississippians who were caught aiding the Underground Railroad. And seen their family and their relatives, who knew nothing of what had been going on, hounded from Mississippi and disgraced. Some were tarred and feathered. All had their property seized and their assets confiscated by the government. Many never lived down the shame. A number took their own lives. Others starved, for they had no income and no savings and no hope for any sort of employment worthy of a gentleman. Even if they grew desperate enough to stoop to a job common to the average man, no one in the South would hire them. The lady folk were denied the role of nanny or forbidden to bring in money as seamstresses. So they moved to the North or they found some way to scratch out a living with a shack and a vegetable garden and a goat that gave them milk and cheese. Yet often enough those gardens were trampled, and the goats slaughtered or stolen, and the shacks burned to the ground."

He paused again.

Clarissa could feel her eyes tearing. Now she did blink. Again and again. "You would not wish any of that on your kith and kin. You would not."

"No man would. No son. Neither would you, Miss Ross."

"No, sir. No I would not."

"Understand the Mississippians are not monsters. Not devils. It is the way of life they know and believe in. It has been that way from the beginning. They see it as God blessed. My parents are good people."

"All right."

"I traveled to England with one large shipment of cotton bales and sugarcane. It was a coming-of-age trip. Twenty-one and all on my own. I handled the financial end of everything. Upon our return, the captain had cause to put into Boston. Fortunately—or providentially—a squall came up while we were still several miles offshore. Waves raked the deck fore and aft. I let myself be washed overboard. And I made sure I was seen being washed overboard. The sea was a foaming madness, but I have been a strong swimmer since I was twelve. I propelled myself away from our ship, under the water, while the sailors were shouting and throwing lines into the waves. The squall was over in a few minutes, but by then the vessel had been blown at least a half mile from where I was swimming. They could not see me in the chop, and I watched them prepare to put a boat over the side and stroked even harder. The ship's crew did not spot me, and I eventually came ashore near Winthrop and made my way to Chelsea. I never went into Boston, of course, for the ship made harbor there. I had enough gold for new clothes and the train to New York City. There I saw my sad story in the papers. Drowned off Boston Harbor. Of course, it was not sad for me. Now I could reinvent my life and live it the way I wished. But it was horribly sad for my poor mother and father. They loved me and had given me the best sort of life they knew how, the same sort of life that had been passed down to them by their parents and grandparents, and back many generations to my ancestors who made the voyage from England in 1676. Believe me, before God Almighty, Miss Ross, when I say I did not wish for my mother and father the hellish pain of losing a beloved young son, as they thought they had. But I needed to be free of the scourge of slavery, and free of inflicting it on the men and women whose only crimes were to be forced to Mississippi from another continent and to wear a darker skin, both of which were no crimes at all. Yes, I had to be free of that. And the price I paid was the loss of my name and my lineage and my inheritance and livelihood. And the price my family paid was to mourn the loss of a son and brother and heir."

Another pause. And all Clarissa could think of to say was, "I'm sorry, Liberty, I am. . .I am so very sorry."

He pushed on, and she wished now she had never asked, for she knew that the telling of his story was like cutting himself with a knife.

"My family must not grieve and mourn a second time. They must not be disgraced or lose their home or income—even though it be off the sweat of slaves. At least my father is not a tyrant or unjust or fond of the lash. No, Miss Ross, at least he is not the Simon Legree of *Uncle Tom's Cabin*. I must not be discovered. They must not bear any more pain on account of me. What I have chosen to do is on my head. Not my mother's. Not my father's. Not my sisters' or brothers' or aunts' and uncles'. Not my neighbors'. I alone am responsible for my actions. And I alone will pay the price for them. I am happy to do so. Better I am lynched than my father and my brothers and my father's brothers in Natchez. But even if I am strung up, my murderers will never see my face. Not in a thousand years."

Then she swore he chuckled under the hood.

"At first, I thought a beard might be sufficient," he went on. "But I had a very good beard when I sailed to England. Clean shaven, bearded, it makes no difference. I've been seen with my family a hundred thousand times in either configuration, if I've been seen once. So the hood it is, and whenever I'm moving passengers, I have it on. Awake, sleeping, out in the woods, hiding in a barn or farmhouse, it covers my head. If I am captured, I put my revolver to my face and pull the trigger. No one from the South must see what I look like. No one from Mississippi. No one from Natchez. No one who knows my family name. As far as anyone is concerned, Iain Kilgarlin, heir to the estate, was lost at sea. I am not him. I am someone else. He can never resurrect."

Now she felt eyes like knifepoints on her again. "Is that trust enough for you, Miss Ross? Before God, no one else knows."

He turned away and began to climb the ladder to the loft.

Clarissa sat and did not move or shift her weight. She felt as if she had been struck by a stone. A large one. Many large ones. There was nowhere she wanted to go. Nothing she wanted to say. No one she wished to chat with. She looked at the hands—her hands—that were folded in her lap, and the spots of water from her eyes that spotted them.

"You are the most impossible man I have ever met," she said under her breath. "One moment you can infuriate me like no man alive and drive me into a towering rage. The next you are capable of filling me with pity. And the next. . .the next, sir. . .all I can feel for you is love."

Chapter Seven

July
Gettysburg

*C*larissa had spent several hours plying the needle as a seamstress with her mother and a group of ladies, including her young friend Ginnie Wade, and was walking away from the Wade house on Breckenridge Street, parasol held high against an already hot sun at eleven thirty in the morning. She loved the seamstress work, for she earned a few dollars from it, could chat with Ginnie—who was only a year younger—could laugh and listen and forget about the things that she felt were pulling her far underground. However, strolling on her own, with no walking companion, she found it difficult to keep her mind from straying to her troubles. *Look at the roses in people's gardens,* she told herself. *Look at the peonies. There—someone still has a patch of irises opening in the most perfect purple hue. That puppy is darling, the way he's leaping and bouncing. And there goes Professor Saxon in his elegant carriage. Occupy yourself, Clarissa. Fill your mind with color and images and cheerful faces. And wave, for heaven's sake. Your beau is a student of the professor's and, this summer, a tutor working under him.*

But she could not keep the thoughts out that she didn't want in.

Such as the ones that swirled around the battle that had occurred a few days before on Monday the twenty-first—the North utterly routed and defeated. Smashed like a bowl of eggs. She had not wanted war to come. How foolish of her to cry out on New Year's Eve, "It will not come. It will not come." But once Virginia had joined the Rebellion, along with Arkansas, North Carolina, and Tennessee, she had accepted the inevitable and hoped for a quick, easy victory, a Confederate surrender, and the world returning to sanity and normalcy by autumn. Now everyone was opining that it would be a long and bloody war, and that the North had better pull itself up by the bootstraps or it would lose it.

Lose it!

Before the battle—they were calling it Bull Run in the New York, Boston, and Philadelphia papers, but papers out of Richmond used the name Manassas—she was confident the clash would sound the death knell of slavery in the Republic. Now, with the Union defeat, she had to wrestle with the fear of slavery extending from coast to coast and north to south, with no end in sight.

Oh God, that can't happen, can it? Will You permit the travesty to exist forever and blight our country perpetually? What will we do? Run slaves across the border into Canada for another hundred years? With slave catchers growing bolder and bolder, and enlisting the aid of Northern sheriffs who would act on behalf of the slave owners in an increasingly ruthless fashion?

"I hate war, but we must win this one," she muttered. "If we don't, this republic will be hell. We need better generals. Better officers. More infantry. More cavalry. More cannons. More of everything, including courage—they say our boys outran jackrabbits! No more of that. Never again. Please, Lord God, never again. Fix our minds and hands to finish this task and win this war and snap the chains off every man and woman and child working cotton and cattle and sugarcane on the plantations. Yes, in Alabama and the Carolinas and Florida, but in Maryland and Kansas and Missouri too. And Mississippi—even in Natchez, even on the Kilgarlin estate. *No, especially there.* It must end there most of all. Loss of income and inheritance? Let them grow corn. Or tobacco leaves.

Let there be miles of wheat waving in the sun. But no more slavery, Iain Kilgarlin, not a drop more of blood from the veins of those God has declared free—'He hath made of one blood all nations of men for to dwell on all the face of the earth.' There is no difference. We are all the same."

Several women walked past going the other way. They gave her odd looks as she spoke to herself, but she didn't even notice them. Thinking of the Kilgarlin plantation made her think of Liberty, which made her think of Kyle Forrester, which made her feel confused: *I cannot sort out the country or this war or the prolongation of slavery, and much less can I sort out the affairs of the heart.* Liberty was in Gettysburg right now. She had no idea who he was, yet he had been fighting against the slave trade for two years. He had most certainly been waging his own war, which showed her that, for all his faults, he did not lack principle or moral fiber or the kind of bravery that did not flinch from the hounds or guns or hate of the wretched Southern slave drivers. Had he not proven how far he was willing to go at Christmas when he shot those four men? He would see to it that the Republic did not become a slave nation. They would have to kill him before he let America perpetuate human bondage ad infinitum.

But what about Kyle? What was he doing? Yes, he'd built a fine sermon around slavery and freedom last December, but what was he doing now when President Lincoln had called for five hundred thousand additional men, while their enemy was calling for four hundred thousand? Was Kyle willing to fight? Would he enlist? Her father had said they would make him an officer in a snap of the fingers. Why, even her father had tried to enlist, but the army had told him they needed the manufacture of boots and tack more than they needed him to fire a musket and march twenty miles a day. That was an enormous relief to her mother and her but did not stop the question from spinning about in Clarissa's brain: *What about Kyle Forrester? What would he do?*

"Excuse me, miss. Excuse me, if you please."

Several men rushed past her at a run, all carrying luggage of various sizes, almost knocking her off her feet.

"I suppose I do excuse you!" she called after them, the heat rising inside her. "What on earth puts you in such an all-fired hurry, young sirs?"

One of them glanced back and grinned. "I apologize, miss." He was a redhead like her. "We're afraid we'll miss our train. My friends and I are on our way to Washington to join the army."

"Oh." She calmed immediately, like a kettle taken off the boil. "That's tremendous then. Good luck to you and God bless."

"There's thousands of Pennsylvanians heading there now. We all plan to show up in one great mob."

"Why do you find that necessary?"

"We were refused before Bull Run. For ridiculous reasons. Hundreds and hundreds of us were. They won't refuse us now."

Clarissa instantly decided to change course and follow them to the train station. A large black locomotive was hissing and steaming there, and she quickly discovered that the men who had almost bowled her over weren't alone in their mad rush to get to Washington and enlist. The platform at the depot was teeming with at least two dozen like them, and they were accompanied by family and beautiful young sweethearts who were hanging off their beaus' arms. *Imagine saying goodbye to someone you had fallen in love with, knowing they could take a musket ball to the chest and die a few weeks after you gave them a final kiss.* She shook her head. That she would not be prepared to do today, and she doubted any of the other young women were prepared to do it either. Yet here they were— making a huge sacrifice for God and country and for the chance to strike a death blow to American slavery.

But they are not all enlisting to end slavery, Clarissa Avery Ross. You know that from the papers and the talk about town. They are joining the army to save the United States of America, to keep it intact as one nation. Not to shut down the plantations.

Perhaps not. Perhaps not yet. But in time they will see that is a big part of the fight. In time it shall sink in.

Do you think so?

I do.

She continued to watch as several more men joined the throng, juggling bags that bulged with who knew what sort of items—shirts, trousers, suspenders, socks, loaves of bread, jars of jelly. From what little she knew of army ways, she doubted any of the shirts or pants would be worn. The men would all be in uniform in a few weeks' time and the many items of civilian life discarded. Fathers shook their sons' hands. Mothers hugged their boys who had grown up too fast—some looked hardly older than sixteen or seventeen to her. The scene both excited and depressed her. She was grateful to see so many Adams County boys rallying to the cause—it made her proud of Gettysburg and the people from the farms that surrounded it—but it also put a grim November in her soul when she thought of battlefields scattered with broken limbs and sightless eyes. She shuddered. Why must it be so? Why must this be the way the world resolved its most difficult issues—war and maiming and death?

Then she saw him.

Towering over most of those around him.

Kyle Forrester.

Her heart roared in her chest. What, was he leaving for Washington too, and not a single goodbye to her, not a kiss on the cheek? He was her beau—at least sometimes she thought he was—but certainly no less than a friend to her and a friend to her mother and father, now up and gone to war without a word, without a note? A fiery mix of emotions boiled up in her. She was proud that he had decided to enlist and fight slavery in a tangible way. But she was upset that he had not talked about it with her. And she was even more upset that he felt it was all right to leave her without saying goodbye, even though he might never see her again. Perhaps she did not matter as much to him as she thought she did. Perhaps she did not matter at all.

You yourself have been unsure about whether you have feelings for him or for Liberty.

I have feelings for both. That is what makes me unsure about whether I ought to commit to one or the other.

Well, then, it may be that he senses that indecisiveness on your part. So it makes him unsure of how to act toward you or who you are to each other.

But we are friends. We are at least that. A friend says goodbye to another friend. Especially if a long journey is involved.

Are you friends?

Of course we are.

But not more than friends?

Yes. No. I don't know.

If you don't know, I'm sure he's picked up on that, and I doubt he knows who you are to him or who he is to you.

Well. . .

You are both one big mess.

Clarissa made a sour face, which she knew would look awful to anyone watching her.

Then made up her mind. Thrust out her lower lip in a pout. Folded her parasol shut. And marched toward the crowd of women and men on the train platform.

Kyle was shaking hands with several young men who had just joined the group surrounding him. She arrived on the scene and stood defiantly behind them, face and eyes set like stone. *I am not so short at five-six that you will not notice me, Mr. Kyle Forrester, nor so far back in this press of bodies that you will not recognize my face. I shall remain rooted to this spot, regardless of how I am jostled by the multitude, until you address me. And if you refuse to address me, well then, sir, I intend to board the train and travel to Washington too. And I will glare until my eyes drill holes in your head. Perhaps I'll join the army. As a nurse. Or disguise myself as a boy with a fair complexion and enlist. What will you do then, if you find me marching into Virginia at your side, my dear young seminarian? Hmm? Will you still pretend I don't exist and shy away from speaking with me? I am a Yankee woman, sir, and I will have my way. It is not just Southern women who are strong, oh no. I am twice the lady any of them are, and I say I shall have my way with you. You cannot ignore me or resist me forever, and this Yankee woman shall have her way and she shall have her say. As God is my witness.*

"Miss Ross."

An older man was at her side, lean and wiry. The president of the Lutheran seminary, Professor Samuel Saxon, whom she knew very well.

"Professor Saxon." He had startled her. "Sir."

"What brings you here at his portentous moment in Gettysburg's history, my dear?"

"Why, I. . ."

"Have you come to see our seminary students off? Has Mr. Forrester introduced you to any of them?"

"No, yes, no. . . . I mean, I have not been formally introduced to any of Mr. Forrester's fellow students. . .but I am here to show my support of their sacrifice for our nation. . .and of their desire to fight to end the American notion that slavery is any sort of particular or peculiar state's right. . .sir."

Saxon grasped her by the elbow and tugged her gently aside. "Have you told Mr. Forrester what you do?" he whispered.

"I. . .I. . ."

"Have you confided to him your work with the Underground Railroad? Have you mentioned my name or how I have assisted your efforts?"

"No, no, sir."

He nodded. "Very well." He smiled. "It does not matter to me if you have, Miss Ross. The South is now a belligerent. It cannot send their men across our borders to secure escaped slaves and African freedmen for their plantations anymore."

"Yes, sir. Is our work done then?"

"By no means. There are still slaves escaping bondage in Missouri and Maryland and Kansas. Not to mention the entire Confederacy. We must help the ones in Missouri and Maryland obtain their freedom, just as we shall continue to assist those from the secession states make their way to our borders and liberty."

"I understand."

"Now then, allow me to introduce you to the four students who are traveling to Washington to enlist in the grand cause."

"All right."

She managed to compose herself as Professor Saxon brought her into the cluster of friends and her eyes met Kyle's. His widened in surprise. She kept hers flat and a very dull green and noncommittal.

"Seminarians, allow me to introduce to you one of the fairest flowers of faith in Gettysburg," Saxon began. "She is a member of Christ's Church and was confirmed there. Her name is Clarissa Avery Ross. . .*Miss* Clarissa Avery Ross."

All the young men except Kyle Forrester murmured, "How do you do, Miss Ross?"

She inclined her head in its white summer bonnet. "How do you do, young sirs?"

"This is Theodore, our brightest theologian. And this is Thomas, truly our Greek scholar par excellence. Now, this strapping fellow from Ohio, our James, is a preacher of preachers, a master of the homiletical enterprise. And, finally, here we have Bartholomew, our wizard with Latin and Hebrew and Aramaic."

"Uh." Clarissa shook each of their hands in turn, caught off guard that Kyle's name had not been mentioned. "It. . .it. . .is an honor to meet you all. Thank you for your service to our nation and to the godly cause of setting the enslaved at liberty. Thank you, sirs, thank you. I shall most certainly keep you in my prayers." Then, gritting her teeth, she deliberately turned to Kyle and extended her white-gloved hand. "And good luck to you too, sir. God bless you as you put on the blue uniform of the Union and take your faith and beliefs to the battlefield. May you soon return home to us. May you all soon return to Gettysburg and to your friends. And I hope I may now count myself as one of your friends, young sirs."

The students all grinned.

"Certainly you may, Miss Ross," responded Bartholomew, his spectacles perched, she thought, rather precariously on his nose.

"Yes indeed," replied Theodore, with his trim but still bushy, black-as-tar beard. "And may we have permission to write now and then, Miss Ross?"

Clarissa smiled. "Certainly you may, young sirs. I'll jot my address down if any of you have a pencil and paper."

Immediately a scramble began as the four students bent and hastily rummaged through their bags. Clarissa stared at Kyle—she hoped he identified correctly that her demeanor was icy—as he remained immobile. "I suppose letters from a young lady whom you've became rather well acquainted with do not interest you in the least, Mr. Forrester?"

He looked puzzled. "What do you mean?"

Now she could not hide her peppery annoyance. "You do not want me to write you while you are away at war, sir. That is plain to me."

"What need would I have of such letters, Miss Ross?"

"What, indeed, sir, since our friendship of many months duration is apparently inconsequential to you?"

"Inconsequential?"

"That is my word of choice, sir."

"But I. . ."

"I have paper and pencil, Miss Ross," interrupted James eagerly.

"As do I," added Thomas and Theodore at the same time.

Clarissa turned away from Kyle with a bitter smile on her lips. "One will suffice, young sirs. Thank you, James." She scribbled quickly on the notepad he handed her. "There. That should do it. You may share my address around the four of you. I do look forward to hearing from you, gentlemen. Do not disappoint me."

"Oh, we won't," replied Thomas. "At least I won't."

"Nor will I," said James.

"Nor I," echoed Bartholomew.

"None of us will." Theodore tipped his hat. "Rest assured."

"Good. Then I may expect letters from Washington informing me of your enlistments?"

They all said yes in unison as if they were a trained chorus.

Clarissa laughed happily. *Well, at least I get a dash of enthusiasm and an ounce of satisfaction from some men in my life today.*

The whistle on the train blew several times.

White steam billowed over the platform.

The cars were opened, and the men—Clarissa supposed anywhere from twenty-five to thirty of them—began to board, offering their loved ones and friends final handshakes and hugs and kisses on the cheek. She waved her gloved hand to the students as she stood beside Professor Saxon. Kyle did not budge, and she cast a glance at him out of the corner of her eye.

"You will be late, sir," she finally said, not wanting to but exasperated at his tardiness as the last men climbed aboard the train.

"What, Miss Ross?" he responded.

"Do you intend to attain Washington by foot? They are closing and sealing the cars."

"So they must."

She rolled her eyes. "Why aren't you joining your friends and colleagues?" Then she had a wild and hopeful thought. "Did you wish to say something to me in private, Mr. Forrester? Is that why you are lingering?"

He stared at her. "You are mistaken."

Immediately her temper flared, like sparks shooting up a chimney. "Indeed, I must be. I must be mistaken about everything when it comes to you. For I thought you were a friend and a gentleman, perhaps even a beau, or almost a beau, when clearly you are none of those things to me, sir. None of them."

"Clarissa. . ."

"Do not address me by my Christian name, sir. Don't you dare."

"I don't think you understand. . ."

"I understand, sir. Oh yes, I understand perfectly. Don't think I shall lack male companionship while you are gone, sir. I shall be surrounded by well-wishers. Oh, most certainly, and I shall welcome round to my parents' hearth and home young gentlemen who think it a blessing to be honored with my friendship and my presence. You shall not be missed,

Mr. Kyle Forrester. In fact, I doubt I shall even notice you are absent. I will understandably be quite occupied. Now, if you will excuse me."

"Miss Ross," Professor Saxon said.

"Good day, Professor." Clarissa began to step away from the train. "I apologize for my sharpness. I am still very young and not well versed in the ways of women and men and social etiquette. I have, however, learned an invaluable lesson today."

"Miss Ross. I insist."

She stopped. "What is it, Professor?"

"There has been a grievous error on your part."

"Truly? And what is that, sir?"

"It has just become clear to me—forgive me for my slowness here—that you are under some sort of misapprehension concerning young Mr. Forrester's plans and position."

"Am I, sir?"

"He is not boarding the train to Washington."

"Apparently not this one, sir, as it is presently pulling clear of the station. He will have to catch another."

"He will not catch any other. His work here, under my supervision, is much too important to terminate on a war that may well be over by Christmas. No, he is not enlisting in the army of the United States, Miss Ross. I am grooming him to be a leader in the Lutheran Church in America, both in the Pennsylvania Ministerium and the General Synod. I intend that he one day take my place at the seminary here in Gettysburg. I do not wish that all my plans and pains—and God's plans too, I trust—should come to naught due to an ill-conceived shot from a Mississippi musket three weeks hence. No, Miss Ross, he has not boarded this train, nor is he boarding any other train, for the purpose of enlistment. He is in the Lord's army, miss, and there, I pray, he may remain. I trust that now you understand his position and that no insult or slight was intended toward yourself. Indeed, I can personally vouch for how well he speaks of you. Very highly, Miss Ross, very highly."

"Oh." Clarissa stood frozen to the platform at Professor Saxon's words. The four students she had befriended were waving to her from one of the windows of the slowly moving train, and she finally took notice and lifted a slender arm with its long white glove that reached to her elbow. "Oh, I see."

The train was gone, sliding down the iron tracks, the locomotive expelling large gouts of dark gray smoke.

Clarissa turned to Kyle, her face scarlet. "I owe you an apology, sir. I fear my youth and my temper and my inexperience in the ways of the world and polite society often get the better of me."

Kyle grinned and inclined his head. "I continue to find your youth and temper and inexperience in polite society infinitely surprising and charming."

"Do you, sir?"

"It is my confession."

She was not in the mood to smile, but a small one slipped over her lips just the same. It seemed to her that there were a lot of things she could not control about herself. "In that case, may I ask you to see me to my home? I should like to chat on the way and make what amends to you I can for my unladylike behavior."

"I'd like that very much. Just as I like your unladylike behavior very much."

"Do you?" Her smile broadened, a smile liberally sprinkled with summer freckles. "Then, sir, we may have a future in store for us."

He offered his arm, and she slid her gloved arm through it.

"That's my hope, Clarissa Avery Ross. That's truly my hope and my prayer."

Chapter Eight

September
Gettysburg

Clarissa finished signing her name to the short note of encouragement she'd penned to Theodore. His two-page letter, smeared with dirt and rain spots, lay open beside her on the writing desk. She folded her note into an envelope and set it aside for the morning's mail. Then she leaned back and thought about everything that reading his letter had stirred in her. Finally, she got up, left her garret, and went downstairs. She found her father in his den with the door open and a book in his lap. An open door meant he didn't mind if she or her mother looked in on him.

"Father?"

"*Oliver Twist.*" He looked up and smiled. "How are you this evening, my dear girl?"

"I am well. No, no I'm not."

"I see. Please take a chair and tell me all about what is not well."

She dropped into a well-worn leather chair she knew had been purchased new just prior to the War of 1812 by Papa Ross, her father's father. "I received a letter today from one of the seminary students I saw off to Washington in July."

"Ah. Good. And how was that?"

"It was fine at first. He told me how they were all attached to the same regiment and the same platoon in the Army of the Potomac."

"Wonderful."

"Then he confessed he had taken a ball to the leg during some inconsequential skirmish on the Virginia border. He called it inconsequential—I don't."

"I'm very sorry to hear it."

"He made light of it, but at the end of his letter, he confessed gangrene had set in and they had. . .the surgeons had removed his left leg above the knee."

"Dear Lord. Poor boy, poor boy."

"He is laid up in a military hospital in Washington. Of course he is being very brave about it all."

"I am sure young Theodore will recover handsomely."

"I am not at all sure that he will, Father. I wish it would be so. Indeed, I pray it would be so. But. . .I have an unpleasant feeling about all this."

"Mother and I will pray with you. Our minister will direct the church to pray."

"There is. . .there is something else."

"What is that, my dear?"

"I read about Theodore's sacrifice, and I cannot help but compare it to Kyle Forrester's lack of sacrifice."

"I see."

"These boys are students like him. Why, they are all the same age—twenty-one, twenty-two, twenty-three—and they are in danger every day from Confederate pickets. They eat their food out of tin pans, the meat and potatoes indifferently cooked. As autumn and winter come on, they will be chilled to the bone. . .all in the service of our country. . .all in the cause of ending slavery in the Republic. . .and there sits Kyle in his ivory tower on Seminary Ridge, wanting for nothing, feted by the Lutheran notables that come to town, a soft bed every night, three hot meals a day, no skirmish lines to face, no minié balls to dodge, no privations to endure, nothing more taxing to put his hand to than the conjugation of Greek verbs or the writing of doctrinal treatises for Professor Saxon and his cause célèbre of minimizing the importance and infallibility of the original Lutheran Confessions. . .while Kyle's peers stare through musket sights at secessionists they are trained to kill and who are trained to kill them. . ."

"Now, now, my dear girl, slow down. . ."

"I can't slow down. I've never known how to slow down."

"You paint your young man in the most dreadful of colors. Your mother and I were under the impression you had feelings for him."

"I do. Of course I do."

"He is not so bad a fellow as you make out. Remember, it is Professor Saxon who insists he remain in Gettysburg to assist him at the seminary."

"I know."

"And he is helping provide important spiritual leadership and counsel to the other students at the seminary and to the Lutheran community here as a whole, both the English-speaking and the German congregations."

"I'm aware of that, Father. I admire him very much. God has granted him wonderful gifts and talents. We get along splendidly. But."

"But. He is not fighting the Confederacy directly and he is not fighting the progenitors of slavery directly, so you find fault with him."

"I. . .I suppose I do."

"You think him weak? Unpatriotic? Lacking in courage?"

"I don't know—something is not right."

"If Professor Saxon released young Kyle from his service, and if he enlisted immediately after he obtained this release, would this please you? Would this settle your heart?"

"I expect it would."

"Even though he would be absent from Gettysburg? And absent from your side?"

"I would be willing to make that sacrifice."

Her father arched his eyebrows. "Be careful what you wish for."

Clarissa wound and unwound her hands in her lap. "I can't help it. I'm being honest about how I feel. Of course I'd rather have him here. But not. . .but not when all the other men are out there fighting to save the Union and. . ."

"Fighting to set men free," her father interjected. "Have you told young Kyle all this personally?"

"No, sir. I suppose it was all bottled up inside. I had no idea my feelings were so strong and so decided. Reading the letter from Theodore stirred them up till they caught fresh fire."

"Perhaps I might offer a word of advice."

"Of course, sir. That is why I sought you out this evening."

"Now that these feelings have come to your attention, and come full-blown, you are thinking of confronting your young Mr. Forrester with them, are you not?"

"Well, sir, I am bound to do so. He must know how I feel. We've grown quite close, and it would not be right of me to pretend I did not harbor these misgivings about his present position in life and all the blessings he has at his fingertips while others his age are. . ."

"Quite right," her father interjected. "But it would not do to subject him to your cannon fire until you discussed all this with the man who has put young Kyle where he is right now, and who has placed all the blessings you so strenuously object to at his fingertips."

"You mean. . ."

He nodded and closed *Oliver Twist*. "Yes, my dear, I do mean that and I do mean him. I would suggest you make an appointment to meet him at his home, however, for if you sat down with Professor Saxon at the seminary. . ."

"Kyle would know and Kyle would wonder what it was all about."

"Exactly."

"I will try and see him tomorrow. I must." Clarissa stood up. "Thank you, Father. I think I'd have tossed and turned all night if I hadn't gotten this off my chest."

"I'm glad to have been able to help, my girl. And I'm sure a good night's sleep will put things in their proper perspective. Resting the brain always does."

"Especially a fevered one like mine, you mean?" She laughed.

"Always a good and appropriate ferment, it seems to me."

"Sometimes. May I take this spare candle with me?"

"Yes of course, that's fine. Good night, my girl, and may God bless you."

"God bless you too, Father."

But it was not a good night. She thought about Theodore and worried. She thought about Kyle and worried some more. She thought about Liberty—Iain Kilgarlin—and worried until her brain felt like scrambled eggs. Theodore was not a love interest; she was concerned about his amputation and his recovery from his wound. But Kyle and Iain, that was a different matter. Whom did she love? Or did she love either of them? Did she love anybody? She flipped her pillow to one side and then to the other, but it never felt comfortable. Somehow she got up at dawn and made her way downstairs to a ham and cheese omelet, then dashed off a note to Professor Saxon that their hired hand, William—a freedman who also worked with her father at his boot and shoe shop—took up the hill to the seminary on horseback. She received a favorable response, which William handed to her upon his return. She asked him to dress appropriately and fetch the carriage and matched sorrels, wore her six-hoop green dress, a green bonnet, and carried a green parasol when she climbed into it, and was at the professor's house for ten o'clock coffee and tea.

"I do not have a class again until eleven," he informed her, pouring Clarissa a cup of Irish breakfast tea. "Pray, tell me what is on your mind, my dear. I've received no notice of a cargo that needs to be brought safely across the border."

"No, sir, it isn't that." She sipped at the tea. Even though the July day was already almost too warm, she was grateful for the tea's heat both in her throat and on her hands. "It's about. . .it's about. . ."

"It's about young Mr. Forrester. Am I correct?"

Her face reddened. "Why is it so obvious to you?"

"My goodness, my dear, I'm well aware of how much time you spend in one another's company."

"I don't wish to dance around the subject. I just didn't think anyone had noticed our. . .prolonged involvement with each other."

"Hmm. Well, Miss Ross, all of Gettysburg has taken note. Many have you married off by Christmas."

Her face reddened even more. "*By Christmas?* Oh no, no, no. There are no wedding bells in my immediate future. In point of fact, Professor, I am not entirely sure of my feelings toward him."

"No?"

"There is another young man who works on the Railroad. Risks his neck on the Railroad more so than many of us, may I say? And that is so because he is a scion of a famous and well-to-do Southern family. They have a plantation on the Mississippi."

"Indeed." The professor stopped in the midst of adding sugar to his cup. "Then that makes him a very principled and courageous man."

"Yes it does."

"For if Southerners captured him. . ."

"He is aware of the danger. Yet he will not relent from rescuing men and women from slavery."

"Bravo."

"And that, sir, is my dilemma. He is fighting the greatest scourge to America's honor, literally with his two bare hands, and when I compare Kyle Forrester to him. . ." She stopped.

The professor waited a moment for her to finish, then nodded and stirred his tea several times so that his spoon chimed against the cup's bone china sides. "Mr. Forrester pales in comparison. Is that it?"

"Yes, sir."

"Would it help if I told you he is more valuable to our country here than on a picket line aiming a musket at another young man like him who is clad in gray?"

"I was hoping you could help soften my disposition toward Kyle Forrester, sir. The thing is, I have just received a letter from Theodore—"

"Ah," the professor interrupted. "And how is he?"

"He has been grievously wounded, sir, and they have taken his left leg due to the gangrene."

"Oh no. I'm sorry to hear this."

"When I compare the sacrifice that Theodore has made for the cause, along with that young Southern man I've just mentioned, who works on the Railroad. . ."

"I understand." The tinkle of the spoon. "But you must appreciate that Kyle Forrester is a man of exceptional gifts and abilities. Any number of brave youth can serve their country and our cause by bearing arms against the Confederacy. They cannot, however, do what Mr. Forrester is doing—foster our spiritual roots. If America is to be a great nation, it must have a great faith. What if we win the war but lose our own soul? Kyle is helping America rediscover its soul. We do not just fight with muskets and cannons, my dear. We fight with pen and speech, exactly as we did in 1776. We fight with scripture and with prayer and with pulpit. We must not take Kyle away from that important work. We dare not. You see how essential your young man is to our cause, Miss Ross? He is a patriot."

Clarissa hesitated and looked down into her teacup, then looked directly into the professor's eyes. "Your words are very fine, sir. You are eloquent. But there is Theodore on a hospital bed fighting off gangrene. And there are the slaves in Virginia—whipped and chained and broken for another day, another week, another month. They say many of our officers are incompetent, sir. . ."

"They merely lack experience," the professor broke in.

"But even without military experience, Kyle Forrester would never be incompetent, sir. You know that."

Professor Saxon nodded grudgingly. "I do."

"Imagine—as I often do—Kyle, in the role of an officer, leading his men into Virginia and rescuing hundreds of slaves. Or bringing about the surrender of hundreds of secessionists, in action after action, and thus blunting the Confederacy's force along with its will to fight. Imagine him as a regimental commander, a divisional commander, a corps commander. Why, sir, he has the ability to rise to a three- or four-star general and command the Army of the Potomac. In such a position, with so many soldiers under his colors, he could bring Richmond to its knees and bring this war and the curse of slavery to a swift end."

"You speak of eloquence?" The professor smiled. "Such an argument you bring to the bar. You make it sound so logical and straightforward, I wonder if Jeff Davis himself would not submit." He shrugged. "But wars are not so easily won. And a general's command decisions, although brilliant before the map table, often fall to pieces due to climate or topography or the surprise movements of the enemy, or the cowardice and timidity and ineptitude of the officers beneath him. Taken all in all, while I know you wish young Kyle would rise to become another liberator like Washington, I see him in a better light, as another Martin Luther who would bring a greater reformation to this republic than we have seen in a hundred years. I fear I cannot advise you otherwise, my dear. I remain firm in my stance that he remain with me here at the seminary and strengthen American democracy at its very core. He cannot do that prancing about on a pony and waving a saber. Build a stronger country out of the ashes of this conflict? Set the captive free? He cannot do better than make his fight here in Gettysburg—in Gettysburg alone can young Mr. Forrester forge the fate of our nation. I'm sorry, my dear. I will not ask him to leave his post. And, without my backing, I daresay he will never walk away from it. Gettysburg, Miss Ross, Gettysburg. That is his destiny and the Lutheran faith's destiny and America's destiny. He must not abandon this dot on the map."

Clarissa felt as if ocean waves had swept over her. The professor's logic seemed more irrefutable than her own. Yet he did not convince her. Sitting in a backwater town like little Gettysburg—there, she had said it, if only to herself—regardless of there being a reputable seminary here, regardless of how charming the town and its townspeople were, Kyle Forrester would make no great difference to the future of America. But a general rallying troops against the Confederate states, defeating its armies, laying low its proud plantations, and marching on Richmond to obtain the Confederacy's final and irrevocable surrender—yes, oh yes, that would be something that would change the nation's destiny. That would make Kyle Forrester unforgettable. That would set America free and make her whole. That, and only that.

"Perhaps I may be able to convince him otherwise." Clarissa set down her cup. The tea was cold, and she had hardly drunk any of it. "Thank you for your bold words, Professor. But I would see him as a colonel or general in the Union army and bringing the Confederacy as swiftly and suddenly to its knees as possible."

"Colonel or general? My dear girl, how long do you think this war is going to last?"

"Some say years after our defeat at Bull Run."

"Bull Run was a debacle to be sure but hardly a commentary on the Northern effort as a whole. We've had victories in Virginia since that dark day."

"Yes. And will have many more decisive ones if I have my way with Mr. Forrester. With all due respect, sir."

"I admire your stand."

Clarissa rose to her feet, and the professor rose to his along with her.

"I doubt he will hear you, Miss Ross. Nevertheless, I wish you well. I know you mean his best and the nation's best."

"Thank you, sir. I do, I truly do. I'm confident he will hear me."

But he did not.

She asked him to walk with her through Gettysburg that Sunday evening. Many other couples were out strolling, but few were as young as they were. So many Pennsylvanians had enlisted, it seemed as if the men of Gettysburg consisted solely of those who were in their sixties and seventies. Clarissa was acutely aware of what an anomaly it was to have a young man at her side while they roamed the September evening streets. She pointed this out to Kyle. Along with a number of other things—the need for good officers in the Union army in order to bring the war to a speedy and victorious end, his gifts and skills as a leader of men, how insignificant Gettysburg was and how much more important it would be to situate himself in Washington at the helm of a regiment in the Army of the Potomac. But he countered all her arguments with arguments of his own: he could not do the cause of abolition any good with a minié ball lodged in his brain; the Lutheran seminary was in a unique position to influence the future course of the faith of hundreds of thousands of Americans; his gifts were better utilized in education and preaching than in prancing ponies and saber waving—which convinced her that Professor Saxon had gotten to Kyle since her discussion with the professor at his home. No matter what she said to convince him, she came up empty.

"Oh Kyle!" she finally blurted in exasperation. "How can I respect you when you act like such a coward?"

He bristled. "What? So I'm a coward if I don't go along with your way of thinking?"

"It's not just my way of thinking. It's everyone's way of thinking. How many young men do you see out tonight with their sweethearts? They are gone and fighting in the war. . .our war."

"I am fighting in my own way."

"How? By teaching Greek to the few students you have left at the seminary? By preaching practice sermons at Christ's Church to people who already know what you're going to say and who already agree with you before you even say it?"

"I am writing important treatises for Professor Saxon."

"Oh, for heaven's sake, he isn't illiterate or inarticulate. He can write them for himself. He doesn't need you. Your country needs you."

"This is how I've chosen to serve my country."

"You aren't serving your country. You're just serving Samuel Jefferson Saxon."

"Who is serving America."

"Who is serving the Lutheran Church. No matter how much good he wishes to do for this nation, he is doing it as a Lutheran and a Reformed theologian, and America is a lot more than Lutheran doctrine or Reformed theology. I want you to be bigger than this little pinprick on the map of Pennsylvania."

"Why are you so ambitious, Clarissa Avery Ross?"

"Why are you so intimidated by my ambition, Kyle Thomas Forrester?"

"I am not intimidated."

"You are a hundred miles from Washington, but you might as well be on the moon. You aren't making any difference at all to the defeat of the Confederacy or the abolition of slavery. But if you would enlist as an officer, you could lead the sort of men who would make all the difference in the world."

"I could not. I would not. I have my own way of making a difference, and even if you don't see it, I am fighting the Confederacy and I am fighting slavery."

"You are not."

"What about you? What do you do? Wander about town and sew pillowcases in your spare time? What are you doing to end slavery? What are you doing to set the captives free, Miss Ross? What? What?"

Clarissa lost all control. "I'm a conductor on the Underground Railroad. I've been setting men and women free for years while you. . .*you* sit up there in that high and holy Lutheran tower of yours, wondering how many angels can dance on the head of a pin."

"The Underground Railroad?"

"Yes, it's true. That is what happens when I disappear to visit sick relatives for days or weeks at a time. I am getting slaves to freedom in Canada."

"You are not."

"I am. Ask your beloved Professor Saxon. He knows the whole of it. While you've been shuffling papers for him, I've been setting slaves free for him. Which do you think is more important?"

"More important in whose eyes?"

"In the professor's eyes. In anyone's eyes. In God's eyes." She stopped. "In my eyes. Though I don't suppose that matters anymore. If it ever did."

Kyle seemed to sag in front of her, as if he were going to melt into the ground. "So, you've been lying to me."

"I don't call that lying. Our work is secret and it's done in secret. We are forbidden to talk about it lest we compromise lives."

"All along. Week after week. Month after month. Lies."

"Stop it, Kyle."

"All you are is a pack of lies."

She slapped him across the face. Tears shot down her cheeks.

"Take me home!" she demanded. "Not another word. Take me home immediately."

She had withdrawn her arm from his. They walked side by side like two soldiers marching. When they reached her house, she climbed the steps to her front door. He did not join her.

"This is the end of us," she told him.

He nodded. "I expect it is."

"I do not spend time with a man who insults his woman and his friend. You are doubly the coward I thought you were."

"And you, my dear, doubly the falsehood. I bid you good night."

"You brute." Her tears came again. "I could never love a man like you. You're not even a man, in my eyes. Goodbye, Mr. Kyle Thomas Forrester."

"Goodbye, Miss Clarissa Avery Ross."

She took the staircase straight to her room in the garret and slammed the door shut. Sinking down on the bed, she wept until she could hardly breathe. There was a rap at the door.

"No!" she barked. "Go away! I can't talk to anyone now. I can't."

She fought with the tears that burned her face another half hour. Then she began to sink into a troubled sleep. Only partly awake, her fingers fumbled with an envelope on the pillow. The note inside was short, but she could barely read it in her state. Theodore was dead. He was dead from gangrene. Tears slashed down her face in a fresh torrent of pain. It felt as if her insides had been cut open with a sword. *Lord, Lord, Lord,* she prayed. *I can't bear it, I can't. No more, please. I feel like a dead woman myself, and it's as if men are shoveling dirt over my grave.*

Chapter Nine

September
Gettysburg

Someone was shaking her shoulder. So gently she scarcely felt it. She murmured, "No."

"Clarissa."

"No."

"Clarissa."

"What? What is it?"

"You must get up. It's ten in the morning, and Professor Saxon is here to see you. It's urgent."

She recognized her mother's voice and opened her eyes. She was under her Amish quilt and in a cotton nightgown. Her hair was up in a bun. She thought about it for a few moments and the last thing she remembered was lying on her bed crying, with the note about Theodore's death in her hand.

"Did you put me to bed, Mother?" she asked.

"Yes. Someone had to."

"Theodore died."

"I know."

"Kyle and I had a terrible fight. We aren't going to see each other anymore. The courtship, if there ever was a courtship, is over."

"I know, my dear."

"How do you know?"

"Because I read the note you had in your fingers. And Professor Saxon told me what happened with you and Mr. Forrester."

"How does he know?"

"Kyle told him."

Clarissa suddenly sat up. "I suppose all of Gettysburg knows."

"That's very likely."

"What does Professor Saxon want? To say how sorry he is that Kyle will be remaining in this backwater town to write his theology for him?"

"Hush, Clarissa Avery. You love Gettysburg."

"Not this morning."

"In any case, the professor is not here about any of that or about you and Kyle. This is Underground Railroad business. And he appears quite agitated."

"The Railroad? Agitated?" Clarissa jumped out of bed and began to get dressed. "Why didn't you say so?"

In five minutes, she was downstairs and speaking with Professor Saxon in the parlor. Her father was seated and listening carefully. Her mother was serving all of them coffee and biscuits. The professor was pacing as Mrs. Ross settled into her favorite chair, sipping from her cup.

"It is all this muddle about what laws are still binding," the professor grumbled. "Some think the Fugitive Slave Act remains in force and the Dred Scott decision as well. No one disputes that the states which are in armed rebellion have lost the right to cross our borders and capture runaway slaves or abduct freemen. But what about Maryland or Missouri or Kansas? Lincoln is playing politics with them. He does not want those three to join the rebellion so he looks the other way regarding their citizens who openly practice slavery. His concern right now is the Union, not abolition. So long as those three states remain loyal, he will not say a thing about their slave catchers crossing the borders into the North. Not everyone agrees with this policy, but enough do, and they permit the slave hunters to enter into Pennsylvania or Delaware or New York, or anywhere in the Union, with impunity. Indeed, many officers of the law in the North feel they are bound by duty to continue to assist slave catchers from states that are not belligerents. It is a hopeless tangle. Three days ago, a pair of our conductors were shot and killed next door in York County and all ten of their passengers scooped up and dragged back to bondage in Maryland."

"Oh no." Clarissa put her fist to her mouth. "How wicked."

"Now we have another party of runaways being brought across into Chester County at midnight from northeastern Maryland. Their goal is the Amish station at Lancaster. You know the region better than anyone alive, except for the conductor named Liberty. I'm asking you to help. I say this in front of your parents because I know how dangerous this assignment may be. The slaves are from the households of Mr. McGinty and Mr. Le Claire. They are two of the worst slave drivers on the planet. You may wish to refuse this work, and I'll understand."

Clarissa shook her head, and her red curls swayed defiantly. "I shall not refuse it. How many passengers are there?"

"Three women and four children and one man."

"I can handle that."

"Clarissa." Her mother spoke up. "You are only nineteen. Please."

"I'm twenty on the thirty-first of October, Mother."

"It is too dangerous."

"Oh my goodness, I've met with danger on the Railroad before."

"Surely you don't expect our daughter to work alone, Professor." Her father set down his coffee. "That is a great deal to ask."

"I do not ask it. No one does. Liberty will be there."

Iain, thought Clarissa, with a jump of joy that she found surprising, disturbing, and delightful. *Iain Kilgarlin.*

"Very good," responded her father. "Very good."

Clarissa stood up. "You see, Mother? I'll be perfectly fine. He is one of the ablest conductors on the Railroad and a personal favorite of Moses."

Her mother was pale. "I am not at ease with this."

"It is about thirty miles to York, another twenty-five to Lancaster." Professor Saxon consulted his pocket watch. "You can just catch the train to both if you move with alacrity. My carriage is outside, and I shall get you to the station. Travel as befits a lady. Carry your disguise and any weapons in a portmanteau."

"I know how to travel, sir, thank you."

"You will be met at Lancaster by our Amish confidants. They will get you into Chester County and down to the border with Maryland. Liberty will be waiting there. Can you be ready in five or six minutes, my dear?"

"My portmanteau is always packed. I shall be ready in two." She crossed the room and leaned down to hug her mother in her chair. "I'll be more than all right. The Amish will take good care of me."

Mrs. Ross hugged her daughter back with an unusual ferocity. "But they will not fight for you."

"Liberty will. Believe me, Mother, Liberty will."

Her father climbed to his feet, and she embraced him.

"Pray for me," she asked him.

"We have never stopped, my girl."

"It's fortuitous." Clarissa hugged her mother a second time. "I must get away from Gettysburg for a few days. I must get free of Kyle Forrester. I must."

Mrs. Ross patted her daughter's back. "Yes, dear, I understand that. I didn't think you needed a plateful of danger too."

"I'm very sorry for what transpired between you and young Mr. Forrester," Professor Saxon said. "I hope I am not in any way to blame."

"No, sir." Clarissa ran up the stairs to her room. "Kyle is old enough to make his own decisions and bear the consequences." She called back: "We were like cats and dogs anyways. Always squabbling about something. I'm sure he's as glad to be rid of me as I am to be rid of him."

That was not entirely true, and she knew it. Her heart felt hollow and her stomach hurt. The only thing that gave her any sense of lift that morning was the prospect of doing something brave and adventurous for the Railroad. And getting out of Gettysburg. And—she gnawed on her lower lip while she thought about it—seeing Iain Kilgarlin. As mysterious as he was, as scary as he could be in that hood of his, Clarissa still felt safe around him. And now, of the two men in her life, he had wound up surpassing Kyle Forrester in every conceivable way. Iain was a man of courage and principle that Kyle could not even touch. She had a strange impulse—one she did not entirely dislike and was not sure she would entirely restrain—of rushing into his arms when she saw him in Chester County. It was an impulsive thought, and she knew she was capable of impulsive actions. Yet she doubted she would follow through on it. She knew the boy who sold newspapers on the corner better than she knew Iain Kilgarlin. She had never hurled herself into any young man's arms and was not about to do it today.

The train ride was swift and uneventful. Two gentlemen sought to strike up polite conversations with her and she gently rebuffed them both. Amos and Ezekiel had a small wagon pulled by two matched bays waiting for her at the station in Lancaster, and when she alighted from the train, she was dressed like a stocky old man whose words were gruff and few. The three set out immediately for the roads south and east that led to Chester County and the Maryland border.

"We are not as fast as the steam locomotive," apologized Amos. "It will take us several hours to get to where we are going."

"We'll be fine." Clarissa smiled. "Tell me about your church. How is everything? How is everyone? I know the war is upsetting, but I'm sure good things are still happening in Lancaster."

"Oh ja, ja, God remains in His heaven. The poor choices men make will not force Him out of office."

The roadways were hard and dry, and they made good time. But it was almost completely dark as they drew near the location where they were supposed to meet Liberty. After going back and forth on back roads for an hour, Clarissa was sure they had missed him. The moon was slight, the stars plentiful, and the beauty of the night sky might have given her more peace if everything had been going according to plan. Her annoyance and irritation grew until she wanted to wrest the reins from Amos's hands and drive the two-horse team herself. Somehow she felt that if she had the reins, she would be able to sense in which direction they ought to go, more so than Amos or Ezekiel. She knew it didn't make sense, but experience had taught her that things didn't always need to make sense to be the right things to do.

Still, she did not take the reins. She knew that would have hurt and insulted Amos, and he was a dear man. But she did close her eyes and pray and try to get a feeling for what was out there around them, and when she opened them again and glanced about in the darkness, she pointed to the left.

"There," she said in a quiet voice. "Go there."

"Why?" argued Amos. "What good will that do?"

"Please. Go there."

"You have angels directing your steps?"

"Can't I?"

Amos shrugged and steered the team to the left. They passed through brush that was empty of leaves, the branches scraping the sides of the wagon. This went on for almost a minute. Suddenly they could make out a chimney, a caved-in roof, a door hanging off its hinges, and the rib cages and skulls of dead cattle. Then there was a pinprick of light. It vanished. Appeared again. Vanished again.

"Stop the wagon." Clarissa put her hand on Amos's arm. "That is the signal."

He reined in the team.

Clarissa sprang from the wagon and ran through the blackness toward the ruined farmhouse. She had not intended to rush into Liberty's arms—that had been a notion she had discarded hours before—but it happened just the same. He caught her up and held her and whispered in her ear: "Easy now, Miss Ross. The floor rotted away years ago. You'd tumble straight into the root cellar and break your neck. And we can't have that."

"Oh." She did not pull away from his grasp. "Thank you."

He released her.

For those few seconds, she realized she had enjoyed his proximity to her, and his strength.

"Are they. . .are. . ." She collected her thoughts. "Are the passengers here yet?"

"No. I don't expect them for another hour."

"When did you leave Gettysburg? I've been traveling by rail and road most of the day."

"I've been here since just after those conductors were shot. I hid in that busted-up cellar Friday night. No one's been around."

"That long? What did you have to eat?"

"An odd mix of items. Bread as hard as cobblestones, raisins like iron, and a few carrots that were as soft as taffy. I could bend them into Os."

"That doesn't sound very appetizing."

"Along with a few canteens of water, it was more than enough. Do you have food and drink for the passengers on the wagon?"

"Yes."

"It's not a very large wagon."

"I guess we'll have to squeeze together like lambs in a pen."

"Mm. Well, let's get to Amos and Ezekiel. I imagine they have oats in the back there for the team, and there's a stream about a hundred yards west of the house they can water them at."

"Liberty."

"What?"

"Iain." She risked it. "Iain."

He did not respond.

"If you've been gone from Gettysburg since Thursday or Friday, then. . ."

She stopped.

"Did something happen in town?" he prodded her. "Is there

something I ought to know?"

"Apparently, everyone in town knows. So I suppose you ought to know too."

"Know what?"

"It's not an earth-shattering development. I just thought. . . I wanted you to hear from me that. . .that. . .I've ended my relationship with Kyle Forrester. That's all."

He stared at her through the slits in his hood. "You have?"

"I have."

"Why did you do that?"

"We don't see eye to eye on a number of things. Including how important I think it is that this war be fought and won. And how critical I think abolition is."

"He disagrees with you?"

"He thinks he can win the war and end slavery by writing theological treatises for his professor at the seminary."

"He won't enlist?"

"No. And he doesn't think there should be an Underground Railroad."

"I knew that. Well, every man—every woman—must decide for themselves how to live out their days and hours during a crisis. I suppose he feels tutoring at the seminary and writing doctrine for his professor is one way to keep America on the tracks."

"America? America can be run off the rails by this conflict. He should be right here, right now, beside me, preparing to help the man, women, and children coming over to us from Maryland to a better life in the Commonwealth of Pennsylvania. After that, he should either help more slaves gain their independence or he should enlist and fix bayonets."

"Fix bayonets? You can be fierce, Miss Ross. It's no wonder you ran him off."

"I expect he's still running. And hiding in that ivory tower of his, Greek verbs jumping about in his head." Clarissa was certain her face must look like a tomahawk. "Well,. I haven't run you off."

"You won't."

"You've used my Christian name often enough. Would it trouble you if I used yours, instead of Liberty?"

"I thought you were a stickler for the rules."

"Sometimes." She tried a smile. "And sometimes I break them."

"Call me what you like. It's been a very long time since anyone has addressed me as Iain Kilgarlin. Especially in a Yankee accent."

"Thank you. I. . .I confess I looked forward to working with you tonight. . .Iain Kilgarlin."

"Considering how we started out, that's an enormous step forward. If it matters to you, I've always looked forward to the opportunity to rescue men and women at your side. Always."

"Oh." Clarissa's heart roared inside her chest. "Oh, I see." She clenched her hands into fists in the dark and summoned up a larger portion of boldness and courage. "I wanted to say something else."

"What is that?"

"I am. . ."

"Wait!" he hissed. "Listen!"

She stopped talking and heard splashing and muffled voices.

"People are crossing the creek," whispered Liberty. "There's a ford there. I found it Sunday. Whoever is crossing over to us, at least one of them knows this place."

"So it's our passengers and their conductors," replied Clarissa.

"Maybe. Maybe not. Did you bring a pistol?"

"Yes."

"Get it out. And come with me."

He ran at a crouch toward the creek. She was right behind him, her fingers wrapped around the butt of her Navy Six. Soon they could make out human shapes and the taller shapes of horses. Liberty dropped to one knee in the grass, and she did the same.

"Who is it?" demanded Liberty of the night. "I have a gun. My companion has a second gun. Quickly now."

A woman's voice, soft and musical, came clearly to them from the direction of the creek. " 'On Jordan's stormy banks I stand and cast a wishful eye, to Canaan's fair and happy land, where my possessions lie. I am bound for the Promised Land.'"

The professor had instructed Clarissa in the proper response, and she spoke it into the dark before Liberty even parted his lips: " 'No chilling winds or poisonous breath can reach that healthful shore. Sickness and sorrow, pain and death, are felt and feared no more. I am bound for the Promised Land.'"

"Hallelujah." The woman's voice was low but exuberant. "Hallelujah, Jesus."

A man rushed up to Clarissa and Liberty, water streaming from his face and hat and clothes. "Thank God you're here. We've had a hard time of it."

His face was jagged with fear.

"What is it?" Liberty tucked his revolver into his belt. "Are you being pursued?"

"Yes, sir. They can't be more than an hour behind. Probably much less now."

"Do you know who it is?"

"Men from McGinty and Le Claire. There are at least two groups. Some are mounted."

"How are your horses? How many do you have?"

"We had to walk 'em the last half hour. That's how I know the catchers are a whole lot closer. We got four horses. And five passengers. And me, Tad Whitehead."

"I'm Liberty."

"Yes, sir, I see by the hood."

"This is Joshua."

Tad touched his soggy hat brim. "Sir."

Clarissa just nodded.

"We were told there would be eight passengers," said Liberty. "And two conductors."

"A man and his wife and child. . .they drowned a ways back. And Henry, the other conductor. . .he were caught and lynched by Alexander

McGinty. Just after we lit out."

"You're sure it was Alexander McGinty? The head of the family?"

"Yes, sir. I had my spyglass on the hanging."

"Then he means business. Does he have hounds?"

"Yes, sir."

"Hounds and Alexander McGinty himself. Why is your group so all-fired important that he is out at night riding with his men?"

"One of the women. . . He was in love with her, I'm thinking. That's what she says."

"We need to get out of here. Take everyone to the wagon. It's just by the farmhouse there. But don't board till the team's been watered." Liberty, unconcerned about noise now, shouted, "Amos! Ezekiel! Get the team watered right away!"

"Ja!" came the cry in return. "We done that ten minutes ago! Went over to the creek right there! You and Joshua talk so much, you ought to find an altar!"

Tad stared at Joshua and Liberty.

"He's a she," Liberty explained.

Tad was perplexed, his face screwing into lines and wrinkles. "That's hard to believe."

"Isn't it? But take my word on it, the sunrise pales in comparison. It pales badly, Tad."

"Yes, sir."

Clarissa felt heat rise rapidly from her toes to her head. Liberty had never paid her a compliment that acknowledged her femininity or her beauty. Ever. She stood rooted to the spot, letting the happy sensation wash over her.

"Get them to the wagon, Tad. Now." Liberty caught Tad's arm as he turned to run back to the creek. "Leave two of your best horses for Joshua and me. Then you and one of the women ride the other two. Tell the drivers—their names are Amos and Ezekiel—that Liberty said to push it as if the devil were on their heels. Joshua and I will try and delay the slave catchers."

"Yes, sir."

"Do you understand what I've just told you?"

"Yes, sir."

"Ride."

Tad vanished into the dark.

Liberty looked at Clarissa through the two narrow slits in his hood. "Do you understand what I'm asking you to do?"

"I think so."

"If you want, you can ride with the wagon."

She went from bliss at his earlier compliment to inferno at his latest suggestion. "I am not riding with the wagon."

"They will likely need your protection, as the Amish are never armed."

"I. . .am. . .not. . .riding. . .with. . .the. . .wagon. Sir."

"For an overweight old man, I'd swear you had red hair."

"I'll be the one swearing if you don't permit me to remain behind. Anyways, it's not your decision to make. I'll stay behind if I want." She whipped the hat from her head, unwound the scarf she always used to cover most of her face, and shrugged off the oversize coat. Her long hair fell in curls over her shoulders, and her face gleamed in the blackness. "Unless you give me a direct order to go. Then I will. Otherwise, I'm not leaving you, Iain. So. . .are you giving me a direct order to join the wagon?"

Clarissa could see, even through the slits in the hood, that his eyes did not leave her face.

She tilted up her chin and thrust out her lower lip defiantly. "Well?"

"I'm giving you a direct order to stay, Clarissa Avery." He reached out and gently stroked the side of her face. "Is that all right?"

She put her hand over his. "More than all right."

"Is your pout. . .is your pout kissable?"

"You're a big, brave, heroic man. Why don't you take a chance and find out?" She placed a hand firmly on his broad chest. "But not with a hood on. Sorry, sir. I draw the line there. Fond as I've grown of you,

I don't fancy kissing a cotton pillowcase you've dyed black with boot polish."

In a flash, a knife was in his hand.

He made one swift cut with the blade and exposed his mouth.

His action frightened and excited her. "Liberty," she began, startled at how fast he'd moved.

Clarissa let go and allowed his strong arms to pin her to his chest— *oh my, Liberty, there is a fierceness in you Kyle Forrester never had the nerve to deliver.* She wound her arms about his neck as tightly as she could. She grew light-headed, as if she'd had too much sun or too much punch, and she felt as if she ought to swoon, like some Southern belle, within that powerful and manly embrace of his. His lips were on her hair, her forehead, her cheek.

I've never permitted myself to indulge in thoughts about you, Liberty, never. You are simply the scary and rough-talking head conductor on the Railroad who has infuriated me more than once. This is utterly beyond me. Maybe I ought to just faint and let it be.

"But I am a Yankee woman," she whispered, "and I can handle this, and I can most certainly handle you. Oh yes, sir, most certainly I can handle you."

There were no more feelings of fainting. His passion had stoked hers like a north wind made flames flare and sparks swirl, and she felt stronger than ever. Although his mouth never touched hers, his desire for her was obvious—he held her more tightly, and more tightly, until she hardly had any breath left in her.

"Oh, I like this, Liberty," she managed to say, continuing to return his strong hugs with her own in a redheaded ferocity, delighted through her entire body and soul. "I like this side of you very much."

Chapter Ten

October
Chester County and Lancaster County

*C*larissa crouched by a corner of the farmhouse. She wished there hadn't been so much waiting. It had been over half an hour now, and that gave her too much time to think. She didn't want to think. Now she had no choice.

"We'll hear the hounds first. Then the hoofbeats. Then the splashing when they enter the creek. I have a hunch there's at least one person with them who knows about the ford. Or they may swim it on their mounts. Either way, once I start shooting, you start shooting. It'll be hard enough to see something, let alone hit anything. But fire away anyways. When you've emptied your pistol, jump on your horse, get through the brush, and light out on the trail back to Lancaster. I won't be far behind."

Liberty had had plenty to say to get her prepared for the slave catchers. But not once had he spoken to her while they embraced. And she knew why. He did not want her to hear his voice. What did it matter? But once their explosive passion had died down, he had turned the hood back to front, ensuring his mouth was covered again, and cut new slits for his eyes. And when he finally did speak to her, his voice was as muffled and distorted as it had always been.

And where had that explosion come from? Yes, she was impulsive. Yes, she hurled herself into situations. But she'd had no idea she had that much desire for Liberty bottled up in her. After the fiery hug was over, it frightened her that it had happened at all. Well, perhaps *frightened* was too strong a word. But she certainly felt uneasy.

Yet even that was not the whole of it. Part of her was uneasy. Another part was thrilled. Jubilant. Ecstatic. So, as she crouched there in the early hours of the first day of October, one moment she was sure she had made a mistake by taking Liberty into her arms and holding him tightly like that, and another moment she was overjoyed at what had happened and at how good it had felt to have his arms around her. She relived the entire event over and over again, and it never ceased to both alarm her and excite her.

So, which was it? An impulsive redheaded mistake? Or a bold redheaded conquest? As far as she was concerned, the only way open to her that would make it clear whether Iain and Clarissa were right for each other was to have what had just happened happen all over again. And there needed to be a kiss. Then she'd know. But another opportunity like that might not present itself for a good while. So if it didn't take place over the next few days, it might never take place at all, because he'd go back to his Gettysburg, and she'd go back to hers, and they'd never see each other again until they were summoned to get slaves across the border into Pennsylvania once more. If they were ever summoned.

My brain is working like a windmill in a hurricane. The only business I can truthfully deal with is the business at hand. And the business at hand is to shoot into the dark. Maybe I'll hit a slave catcher, and maybe I won't. I'm not keen on hitting anyone really. But it would devastate me if I hit a horse or dog. So I hope I just scare everyone off. That seems doubtful with hard-edged men like that beastly Alexander McGinty. But I'm praying for it anyways. I want them to feel they are being attacked by ghosts.

"Hear that?"

She jumped.

Liberty was suddenly right beside her.

"I wish you wouldn't do that anymore," she complained.

"What?"

"Just pop up like some kind of wild jack-in-the-box. After all, we've embraced now."

"We've embraced?"

"Oh yes, didn't you notice? Or was your mind elsewhere?"

"You can hear the baying of hounds."

She stopped thinking of what words she was going to stab at him with next. The sound of the dogs was unmistakable, and it grew louder every second she listened. Her head and hands went to snow and ice.

"Some of them will be on this side of the creek when I open fire," Liberty told her. "Some will be crossing over and in the water. Others will still be on the far bank. The gunfire will throw them into panic and confusion. And they won't know how many of us there are. Two? Three? Four? They won't be able to tell. They'll be too busy trying to get out of the way of the bullets. Even after we've stopped firing, they'll be spooked and cautious. It will take them some time to feel safe enough to move about and get organized. Every minute they hang back gives our people time to reach Lancaster. Do you understand?"

Some inner heat flared up and thawed the frost in her hands and head. "Of course I understand. I'm not a child."

"How fast can you ride?"

"Faster than you, sir."

"Then we are ready, Miss Ross?"

"Yes. We are. Mr. Kilgarlin."

"Good luck."

"And God bless you, sir. May your hand be steady and your nerves on a cake of ice."

He was gone. She peered ahead into the darkness. Was certain she heard the splash of men and horses and hounds. Took her finger off the trigger guard and placed it on the trigger itself. Was grateful her mind grew sharp and calm, something that often happened to her under duress, even though she understood better than anyone that she was only known for her temper and her tantrums. But her mind had a way of settling in when she truly needed it to. And for that she did thank God, not out of habit or because her Lutheran and Christian faith required it, but because she honestly was thankful she could hold her concentration, almost indefinitely, until a crisis had passed or resolved itself. It was as if another Clarissa Avery Ross took over, that a doppelgänger lived in a corner of her body and soul—ready to assume command of her faculties when life became cold and dark and deadly, and to bridge the abyss of fear and doubt, bringing her safely to another side of the world she dwelled in along with millions of other Americans. It was a gift she never took for granted. She praised God it was with her now.

Crack. Crack. Crack. Crack.

Liberty's shots yanked her from her thoughts and prayers.

Huge gouts of yellow flame lashed out from his gun barrel.

She counted to three, four, five, and then squeezed the trigger of her Navy Six.

Sparks and fire burst in front of her eyes.

She heard men cursing and hounds yelping and horses shrieking.

Once her revolver was empty, she jumped onto the buckskin that Tad Whitehead, the conductor, had left for her. The saddle was flimsy and worn, but it was good enough. She kicked the mare's flanks with her heels.

"I'm going!" she shouted above the snap and bang of the second revolver Liberty had pulled from his boot.

"Go!"

She made her way through the tangle of brush at a trot, but once she reached the open road, she urged the mare into a lope. For three or four minutes, she was on her own, one eye on the North Star, the other on the path that led to Lancaster. Then Liberty was there, hood and all, his large white gelding pounding the hard-packed earth with its hooves.

"Faster!" cried Liberty. "Let's put some distance between us and them!"

"Are they coming?"

"Not yet. Still cowering. And shooting at phantoms. But in another five or ten minutes, with no return fire, they'll set the hounds on our trail. So let's make tracks."

"I'm fine with that, sir. I like giving a spirited horse its head."

"Is that because a spirited horse reminds you of yourself?"

"Perhaps, Mr. Kilgarlin." She laughed and tossed back her mane of curly red hair because she was certain he would like that. "Perhaps."

They flew side by side on the horses. After fifteen minutes, Liberty told Clarissa to rein in and dismount. Then he ordered her to reload. She had done it only once before—powder, patch, ball, crimp it down, move on to the next chamber. Her heart thudded in her chest.

"What are we doing, Liberty?" she demanded. "You know they're on our heels."

"When we see the first rider, we shoot," he said. "They won't be expecting an ambush."

"I don't want to shoot a dog," she told him, struggling to reload all six chambers in her revolver.

"Or a horse," he added. "Am I right?"

"Or a man."

"Then shoot over their heads. Once they see the gun flashes, they'll make for cover. That's what we want to do—slow them down and give the runaways more time to reach Lancaster." He tugged his horse into the bushes. "Hide in here."

In ten minutes, horses and riders and hounds came racing along the roadway. Clarissa began to shoot as soon as Liberty did. One of her chambers misfired, but the others were good. Two riders were thrown, and the others yelled in fear and anger and galloped off the road into the dark. The hounds kept coming.

"Ride!" snapped Liberty. "Ride, Clarissa!"

She swung up into the saddle and dug in her heels. Liberty kicked two dogs away and thundered after her. Once again they rode for fifteen minutes, dismounted and reloaded, waited for the slave catchers, then ambushed them a second time. Clarissa fired over their heads, as she had done the first time, but this time she saw a man hit the ground with a scream: "I'm hit, Mr. McGinty!" She may have been missing on purpose—Liberty wasn't.

In moments they were mounted and roaring north on the roadway once more.

"You ride well!" Liberty shouted over to her.

"I've been with horses all my life!"

"We'll pull one more ambush and then go like arrows for Lancaster, no more stopping. Can you handle that?"

"I can handle anything."

"I believe that."

"I'm glad I've made a believer out of you, Iain Kilgarlin."

This time they rode at a fast canter for half an hour before doing a third ambush. The catchers were moving more cautiously, and it took them twenty minutes to reach Liberty and Clarissa, which was a decent rest for the pair's mounts. The gunfire made the catchers holler and scatter. A man cried out and fell backward off his horse, and the catchers let loose with a fusillade of shots. Clarissa took off at a gallop, assuming Liberty was right behind her. When she glanced back, he was not there.

She wanted to rein in. She wanted to go back. But she knew Liberty would be furious with her if she did. She could almost hear him saying, "I can take care of myself." She was certain he'd say that because she was certain she'd say the same thing, and somehow she felt increasingly connected to him, as if a rope bound each one tightly to the other.

Clarissa went on without him for at least fifteen minutes. Then he was beside her, bent low over his horse's neck. Even in the dark, she saw the blood, blood that made it look as if his coat and shirt had been splashed with a tin cup of water.

"You've been shot." Her whole body went cold. "Liberty, Iain. . ."

"You did well to keep riding. If I fall back again, keep moving forward. You can just see the glimmer of Lancaster's lights."

"I'm not leaving you now that I know you've been hit."

"They're right on our backs. They've left the dogs behind and are coming full gallop. We don't both have to die. Just keep going."

"Nobody is going to die, Iain Kilgarlin. And you can't keep telling me what to do."

"I'm a chief conductor."

"And I'm the woman who held him in her arms. I'll do what I think I have to do to protect you."

"You are so stubborn."

"And you are so lucky I am. Any other woman would have stopped talking to you months ago, Underground Railroad or no Underground Railroad. It wasn't that long ago I considered you the rudest and most obnoxious man on earth."

"And now?"

"I intend to tame you and bring out the best in that ornery soul of yours. So don't try and order me around anymore."

If he replied to her retort, she did not hear it. She glanced to her front a moment, and when she glanced back, his saddle was empty. Crying out a cry she had never heard herself utter before, she wheeled her horse around, saw his body on the road, swung down, and ran to his side. He was on his stomach, and when she turned him over, her hands were slick with his blood.

"No," she groaned. "No, no, no."

"Leave me." She could barely hear him. "Get back on your horse and get into Lancaster where you'll be safe."

"I'm not going anywhere."

"You're helping runaways. They won't spare you."

"I don't care what they think they can do to me. I'm getting you up on my horse."

"How is an itty-bitty scrap of nothing like you going to do that?"

"An itty-bitty what? You said that last December! I'll show you how itty-bitty I am!"

"Sure. Show us all. And when you're finished with your show, we'll hang you."

The voice was rough.

And emerged from the darkness around her.

There were no dogs. Just four men on horses. All had their pistols pointed at Clarissa and Liberty.

"End of the line, slave lovers," said a huge man with a thick beard. "You owe Alexander McGinty a debt you can never repay. So I'll take your lives as partial payment on that debt. Then I'll go into Lancaster and find my property, and that will settle the debt for good."

"You aren't going into Lancaster, Mr. McGinty. You're turning around and heading back to Maryland."

Clarissa watched a dozen men walk their horses out of the night and form a circle around her and Liberty. They all wore badges. And carried muskets or shotguns.

"The law has always cooperated with me in Pennsylvania," rumbled McGinty fiercely. "What's going on, Sheriff?"

"A war, Mr. McGinty. And laws formed by Southern judges and Southern congressmen just don't hold water with us Pennsylvanians anymore. Now turn around."

"This ain't justice. Those slaves are my property by right. *By right!*"

"We don't recognize that right anymore, Mr. McGinty. Turn around."

"I'll go to Washington about this. I'm an American citizen from Maryland, not the Confederacy, and I own those slaves, body and soul."

"While you're at it, you can go to the Quakers and see what they have to say about it. Find out what they think about you owning men's and women's souls, souls that only God Himself can create. Ask the Amish too. Heck, you can even ask me." The sheriff poked his shotgun at McGinty. "Ever see what this can do to a human brain? Turn around, Mr. McGinty. This is your final opportunity to get home in one piece."

Clarissa listened and watched, but all the time she was ripping at her coat and making bandages for Liberty's wounds. A deputy holding a lantern climbed down to help her, about the same time as McGinty let loose with a string of the rawest curses she had ever heard and began to angrily lead his men back the way they had come.

"You'll hear from me again!" he shouted. "You'll for certain hear from me again, Sheriff!"

"He's bleeding out," the deputy said, putting the lantern close to Liberty's body. "It's no use."

"I'm not giving up on him!" snapped Clarissa. "I'm not!"

"Get his coat off. Pull off his shirt. We've gotta find those wounds and stop 'em up."

"Then help me."

The deputy began tugging at Liberty's coat with her. "Someone get his boots off."

Several other deputies joined them.

"He's a goner," said one.

Clarissa felt like slapping him. "I don't care."

"It's a waste of time."

"I told you, I don't care. And I didn't ask for your opinion. I'm going to save him. You can stand and watch if that's all you're good for."

"Tear off that shirt," said the first deputy. "Someone loosen his belt. And get that thing off his face."

"He doesn't want it removed," Clarissa told him.

"Get it off. Cut it off. For all we know he took a bullet to the brain. That hood is soaked in blood."

One man was yanking Liberty's boots from his feet; another was helping Clarissa rip off his shirt; the sheriff was removing the belt and tossing it to the side. Someone had a canteen of water and was kneeling and ready to put it to Liberty's mouth, and a frail man with a large black mustache was struggling with the hood. Clarissa wiped the back of her hand across her forehead and knew she'd left a bloody streak. A bearded man placed a hand on Liberty's chest and said he felt a heartbeat, the sheriff was tying a strip of cloth to a bullet hole in Liberty's arm, and the frail man continued to wrestle with the hood. She finally thrust him aside, used both hands, putting all her strength into it, ripping the black hood free. And gasped as she stared into Kyle Forrester's dying face.

Chapter Eleven

January 1862
Gettysburg

It was as if she wanted to etch every part of her hometown into her head and heart. Wanted to exchange bad memories for new and better ones, get rid of ghosts and replace them with flesh and blood, thrust murky and upsetting experiences far away and embrace experiences that were fresh and appealing and filled with hope.

Clarissa marched—not walked or strolled, marched—from her house just off York Street, along Baltimore until she turned right on Breckenridge, waved to her friend Ginnie who was shoveling snow by her front door, carried on until she decided to double back and take South Washington Street to Gettysburg College, crossing the railroad tracks. Then she chose not to carry on to Mummasburg Road, turned around, recrossed the tracks, and headed to her right when she reached Chambersburg Street, putting the Lutheran seminary with its distinctive cupola, a larger version of the one atop Christ's Church, squarely in her line of sight, along with Seminary Ridge, upon which the seminary had been built thirty years before. At this point, she made up her mind to stretch her legs far more than she'd planned when she set out, headed straight to the seminary, nodded to several students who tipped their caps, carried on past them, and took an icy path that wound its way down and across a flat field and then up to another prominence called Cemetery Ridge. On the way, she first crossed Fairfield Road, stepped gingerly over a frozen part of Winebrenner's Run, clambered over a five-foot fence, crossed the Emmitsburg Road after three carriages had rattled past, climbed another five-foot fence, then tramped up the short slope to the top of the ridge.

"Oh my. Thank You, my Lord; this makes the long hike all worthwhile."

Cemetery Ridge gave her a magnificent view of Gettysburg as she caught her breath, breath that wound about her face and dark blue winter bonnet in threads of white. Smoke from hundreds of chimneys rose straight into the gray sky like pencil lines. After a few minutes of taking the view in, she carried on into the cemetery itself, Evergreen, past its handsome brick gatehouse, which served as the caretaker's residence, and meandered among the gravesites with their black iron fences and their white and gray monuments, pausing to read several epitaphs of persons she had known growing up.

Eventually, she made her way from the cemetery and began to walk the length of the ridge, which she knew to be about two miles. Now the town and seminary were at her back, to the north, though she could clearly see the snowy slopes of Seminary Ridge off her right shoulder to the west, despite the low clouds. It did not take her long to reach the stone wall that marched its way across the crest of the ridge. She loved the rough and ready scrambled look of the field rocks and had played on them when she was a child. Some parts of the wall had tumbled down. Her mind on her memories, she picked up a few of the loose stones and put them back. When she'd been a little girl in her crimson ringlets and dresses, the wall had seemed enormous to her, and she'd skinned her knees more than once climbing it, often enough drawing blood, alarming her mother, but refusing to cry even though it stung. Now that she was a grown woman, the wall didn't quite reach those skinned knees of hers, one of which bore a scar of her misadventures on Cemetery Ridge. *If only all scars were so pleasantly earned.*

The grove of chestnut oaks had been her favorite haunt though, right where the hardscrabble stone wall zigged and zagged at what her father called "the fence built by the farmer with a degree in geometry." He referred to the two ninety-degree angles the wall took by the chestnut oaks. The oaks had grown over the past twenty years just as she had grown. Bare of leaves, they still looked splendid to her. She made up her mind to return in June or July when the grove was in the full flush of green and all the leaves thick. Winter had its stark beauty though. It made the landscape look more like an engraving, with the pastel details one saw in summer totally obscured.

By the time she reached Little Round Top, and the big Round Top, at the end of the ridge—she'd played in those woods as much as she'd played on the stone wall, her mother always shouting at her to be careful—she was so chilled she felt like she imagined a snowflake might feel as it tumbled cold and perfect from the heavens. She gazed down, shivering, at the naked limbs of a peach orchard—she had often enough eaten fruit from that orchard when her father had purchased baskets of it for Mother to make cobbler and preserves—and the barren black-and-white field that grew wheat in the spring and summer. Yes, her town and its surrounding farms were lovely. She'd spent so many harsh hours on the Underground Railroad she'd almost forgotten how lovely. But now she needed a hot tea and a hot fire and her favorite moccasins lined with rabbit fur.

Clarissa climbed down from Cemetery Ridge, walked along the Emmitsburg Road until it intersected with Baltimore Pike, waved off offers of rides from well-meaning young men driving buckboards, then followed the Pike into town until it became Baltimore Street, which took her to York and, finally, her own front door. She discarded her winter coat and cape and bonnet, her scarf and mittens and boots—it felt like she had been wearing pounds and pounds of clothing, and she was exhausted—and stepped into the parlor, where a blaze was bright in the fireplace, making the room as cozy as summer.

"Have you expunged all your ghosts?"

She looked at the man in the large leather chair. "Not all of them. Not you." She came over and took one of his hands to her lips and kissed it. "And I don't ever want to."

"Where did you go?"

"Cemetery Ridge. Did you ever walk over there from the seminary?"

"I did. I like the grove of chestnut oaks for naps, and I like climbing up Round Top to give the arms and legs something strenuous to do. And I've picnicked at Cemetery Ridge—all by myself."

"Well, you don't need to have picnics all by yourself anymore, my dear boy. Once you are back on your feet—"

"I'll be good as new by the end of the month. The doctor was adamant about that."

"Oh, he was *adamant*, was he?"

"Strict orders—get up and get going. 'Three months convalescence is more than enough for a strapping young man like yourself.'"

"He said all that?"

"Well, something like that."

"The sooner, the better. I have plans for you, sir."

"I'll bet you do."

"And what shall I call you? Have you made up your mind?"

"I have."

"So. . .is it Kyle? Is it Iain? Is it Kyle Iain Forrester Kilgarlin? Or something much more complicated than that?"

He laughed. "Something far simpler. Iain Kerry Kilgarlin. My name at my baptism. Kerry bestowed because that's where my father's side of the family is from, County Kerry in Ireland."

"Are you quite sure?"

"I am quite sure they're from County Kerry, and I'm quite sure that's the name I'd like to be addressed by in the future. I wore a hood long enough. That one deputy who hailed from Boston recognized me. He met my father and me in New Orleans a few years back. The word will have gotten around by now. I intend to write my parents a letter. No more hiding. It will hurt them, I know that. But it will also bring them some measure of joy to find out I am alive. Even if I am a Yankee."

"I can't imagine it will be easy to write such a letter."

"Perhaps not."

"How is it going to be delivered? The mail service is notoriously unreliable between North and South these days. In fact, sir, it does not exist."

"Captured Southern officers get paroled and return to their home states. I've already made inquiries by telegram. I can send my letter on to Washington, and they will see it gets into reliable hands that will carry it safely to Dixie."

"Will your parents be harmed as the word gets around among the plantation owners?"

"I used to think so. I told you that when I was still under the hood. But I've been gone and presumed dead for two or three years now. And my parents had absolutely no knowledge of my actions, nor will they be seen to have been complicit in them. I believe their neighbors will feel sorry for them. There will be a certain amount of shame attached to the family because of who I have become and what I have done—of course, there will be that. But I don't think they'll be punished or publicly humiliated. Their son will be vilified. Not them."

Clarissa sat down on an arm of the chair, facing him, and frowned so sharply her dark eyebrows came together. "I don't want you to be vilified. It's an ugly thing to think about. I have enough ugly things to think about."

"You know what one of the most pleasant things to think about is for me?" He reached up and took a long tendril of her scarlet hair in his fingers. "Being able to touch you."

"Thank you."

"I was hoping you weren't still having nightmares."

"I'm not having nightmares. I think about what happened while I'm wide-awake. I almost lost you."

"But you didn't, Clarissa."

"Holding you so closely as I rode. And I rode like a wild woman; I rode like I had escaped from an asylum. Hoping my body's warmth would be enough to keep you breathing. The deputies pounding on the doctor's door in Lancaster. Him not sure what to do. Fumbling around in his surgery like a drunk."

"I know."

"Me yelling at him. Someone going to get his assistant who had his house on the next block. The assistant getting the pistol balls out. Blood everywhere. As if we were in a slaughterhouse."

"I know. I'm sorry."

"You shaking like a tree in the wind, a tree that's losing all its leaves. Wrapping you in blankets. Lying beside you on a cot to give you as much of my heat as possible. All the time staring at your face—am I looking at Kyle Forrester or Iain Kilgarlin? Who are you? Why all the games?"

"We've been through all this. I couldn't let you get attached to Liberty, so Liberty was unkind to you."

"Unkind? He was a monster at the beginning. You, sir, were an absolute monster."

"And I had to make sure you broke off with Kyle," Iain added.

"So you were mean to me again. Terribly mean. Even cruel. Why?"

"Clarissa, we've gone over this a dozen times now."

"I still don't understand why."

"Because I had a price on my head. Because I didn't think I had a long life ahead of me. Because I was having my own nightmares and premonitions of death. No, I couldn't let you in on my secret. I didn't want us to become intimate or romantically involved. I didn't want you to grow too close to a man who was going to wear a bullet in his brain. And I was convinced that bullet was going to arrive very soon."

"But then you cut a hole in your hood just so you could kiss me. How do you think that made me feel?"

"How did it make you feel?"

"It made me feel wonderful, you idiot."

"And I felt wonderful too."

"So, why did you make us feel wonderful if you had no intention of letting us fall in love with each other?"

"Because I fell in love with you anyways," Iain admitted.

"When?" Clarissa asked.

"When you took the old man's hat from your head at that wreck of a farmhouse in Chester County. And shook out all your long red hair. And unwound your scarf so I could see your perfect face. And told me in no uncertain terms you were *not riding with the wagon*. That's when I realized I was a goner."

"A goner?"

"And that I'd been a goner for a long time. But at the farmhouse, alone with you, with danger coming at us from across the border, seeing your courage, seeing your defiance, just as I'd been seeing it month after month as either Liberty or Kyle Forrester, and finally letting myself get pulled in by your astonishing beauty, something I had fought against for years as the scholarly seminary student who attended Christ's Church and agonized over you each Sunday morning—well, I had no fight left in me. So I gave in, cut the opening in my hood with my knife, and kissed your hair and your face, even though I knew it was the kiss of death."

"Kissing me was the kiss of death? Do you think I find that flattering?"

"It was the end of one life and the beginning of another. A better one. You resurrected Iain Kilgarlin. You made a new man out of the old man. The bullets didn't change my destiny. You did."

"The bullets almost ended your destiny. What a fright you gave me. I was sure you weren't going to live, no matter how hard I prayed."

"But I did live."

"By the grace of God."

He nodded. "By the grace of God and the grace of your heart and spirit and face."

"Oh Iain Kilgarlin, you charmer." She laughed and messed his hair with her fingers. "You always get out of this argument the same way. Always."

"Luck of the Irish."

"The truth is, you *are* a different man. You're not Kyle. You're not Liberty. You're not even the Iain I knew before you were shot. You're someone completely different."

"And you like the difference."

"Kyle and Liberty and Iain all had their moments. But Mr. Iain Kerry Kilgarlin? He has it all. Yes, sir, he has everything this Yankee girl could want. He makes her swoon."

"Does he really make you swoon?"

She giggled and gave him a quick kiss on the cheek. "No, not really. But if he tries a little harder, he might."

"I'll work on it. I'll study hard."

"You do that. Meanwhile, I'll help Mother with dinner. Are you planning to assist Father at the shop this evening?"

"I am. Right after the peach cobbler."

"Who told you we were having peach cobbler?"

"My Irish nose. Other Irish smell potatoes a mile away. Or stew. Me? If I were in the garden of Eden, you could have tempted me a lot more with a peach than with an apple."

"I'll bear that in mind."

But what played in her mind—despite the happy banter with her new beau who was an impossible mixture of Liberty, Iain Kilgarlin, and Kyle Forrester, Underground Railroad conductor, Irishman, Southern aristocrat, seminary student, and Lutheran minister—was the night he almost died in her arms. It plagued her constantly. And she knew she never wanted to face an experience like that again. She dreaded the day he told her he was healthy enough to enlist in the Union army. For what could she say? She had pushed Kyle Forrester in that direction and demanded he put on Yankee blue, and she had insisted that if he did not, he was not a man. How much of that the Liberty side of him had taken to heart, she had no idea. But she was certain one of two things was going to happen once he was fully recovered from his wounds: either he would return to his dangerous work on the Underground Railroad, or he would join the Army of the Potomac. What she'd prefer was that he didn't heal completely. That he would stay in Gettysburg and make boots at her father's side until the war was over. That she could hide him here in her quaint little town until the minié balls stopped flying and the cannons stopped roaring in Virginia.

"It is safe here, my beautiful man," she would murmur to herself when she was alone. "So safe. So protected. I love this place. I love you. Stay here. Let's grow as old as America together. You do not have to win this war. You have won me, and that's enough. No matter what happens, we can face it together. We'll never be conquered. Please."

But she was certain God would not answer her prayers and that he would recover. Certain Iain would not listen to her pleas and that he would enlist. Certain he would take the train for Washington one morning. Certain that once he left she would never see him again—not alive, not in Gettysburg, not at her side. He and she would be *never again, never again.*

Chapter Twelve

May
Gettysburg

I have a commission, Clarissa. Can you believe it? The seminarian is a captain in the Army of the Potomac. What do you think of that, my fine, beautiful, feisty Pennsylvania girl? Your prayers are answered."

Clarissa was sewing in the front room when he burst through the door and into the house, waving a letter in his hand. The stone, a heavy stone, sank into the pond in her heart so completely there were no ripples, no ripples at all. She got to her feet and tried to smile for him. He swept her up in a tight hug and spun her in a circle before setting her down. Despite her misgivings about what had just transpired, she laughed at his boyish enthusiasm. And then she immediately remembered what a bullet wound looked like on his body, and her laughter stopped.

She felt dead inside. Absolutely dead.

Iain did not notice her shift in mood. "I'm assigned to the Second Brigade, Second Division, Second Corps. Do you know what's particularly significant about that, my love?"

"I don't."

"It's the Philadelphia Brigade. They're making a name for themselves. Despite all the Northern fiascos. They're fighters, Clarissa."

"That's good." Then she thanked God a question rose in her mind so that she was able to do more than just offer dull responses: "How could you be in that brigade when you're from Adams County and not Philadelphia?"

"My papers show me as a resident of Philadelphia who lives in Gettysburg for the purposes of furthering his education. I started out in Philadelphia after I jumped ship in Boston Harbor."

"I see." Back to her dull replies. It annoyed her, but she couldn't muster any true enthusiasm for his enlistment or officer's commission. She had sung a different tune a year ago, she knew. But that was before she fell in love with Liberty Iain Kerry Kilgarlin, as she sometimes called him. That was before she saw his blood on her hands and heard his dying breaths in her ears. "Is there anything else?"

He grinned. "There is. I'm assigned to the 69th regiment. There's the 71st, the 72nd, the 106th, and mine, the 69th. Do you know why they placed me in that specific regiment?"

"No."

"It's Irish volunteers. Born in Ireland or born Irish-American here. Isn't that grand? I'll be fighting alongside the lads."

Despite her gloomy mood, she could not keep one corner of her mouth from curving up and producing her crooked grin, a grin she knew he loved. "The more you become Iain Kilgarlin, the more you begin to sound like an Irishman and the more you use Irish expressions. Soon you'll be saying, "*sure and begorrah*," like some New York City Irish police officer."

"Ha-ha." He kissed her quickly. "I love that face you make."

"I know. Thank you. It comes and goes without my bidding, so I can't take any credit for its sudden appearances and departures."

"Once they saw my family hailed from County Kerry, my fate was sealed."

She hated that expression. "Your fate was sealed?"

"I mean, there was no other Pennsylvania regiment I could be in but that one. Iain Irish Kilgarlin. You couldn't put me with the Germans or Dutch, could you?"

"I suppose not."

"I must tell your father. Won't he be excited?"

"I'm sure. Men always are when it comes to war. Women? Not so much."

"What do you mean?"

She saw that her words had put a halt to his headlong rush of enthusiasm.

"I'm going to miss you, Liberty Iain Irish Kerry Kilgarlin. What do you think I mean? That I'm happy to send you off so that you can return in a pine coffin, if you return at all? Do you know how many widows Gettysburg has already?"

"I thought. . .I thought you wanted a war to set the slaves free."

"You know that's not why the North is fighting, Iain."

"Not yet."

"You know Lincoln simply wants the Union restored at any price. And the boys in blue are fighting for the same reason, to retain the Republic. To keep it in one piece. No one cares about slavery."

"Some do."

Clarissa folded her arms over her chest. "Most don't."

"I recall you telling Kyle Forrester last year that attitude would eventually change."

"Well, the 1862 Clarissa Avery believes otherwise. She's read too many newspapers now and heard too many political speeches and looked over too many published reports from the battlefield. No one cares about abolition or emancipation. They just care about winning and bringing the South to heel. And we don't appear to be doing very well at that."

"I'll not be fighting just to win, Clarissa Avery Ross. I'll be the officer you always wanted—the one leading his boys into battle to bring independence to every man and woman. Not just white Northerners or white Southerners."

"You'll be battling your own people."

"My own people are the people who need freedom and the ones who are helping them to get it."

"The South says it's fighting for freedom."

"White freedom. And white freedom to enslave others. You already know that's not who I am. That's why I became a conductor on the Underground Railroad."

"You used to say—when you first told me who the man under the hood really was—that if Southern troops captured you and realized who you were, they'd lynch you."

He shrugged. "They might. They'd see me as a traitor. Or they might not, if they knew the North would retaliate by hanging Rebel officers."

She sighed and reached out for his face. "I guess I can't talk you out of this, can I?"

"You're the one who talked me into it."

"I don't think Liberty needed much convincing. Kyle Forrester, yes. Not Liberty or Iain Kilgarlin."

"Am I still so many personalities to you?"

"In a way, you are. I'm still trying to stuff all the parts of you into my one man and into my one head."

"If it helps. . .I'll miss you terribly. Terribly."

He took her in his arms, the strong embrace filling her with a bright joy in the midst of a gloom that issued from her dark and dying heart. She grasped him as tightly as she could, as if she might be able to keep him in one place, keep him in Gettysburg, keep him in her house, the house she'd been raised in and where she'd dreamed a young woman's dreams of falling in love. *Don't go, don't go anywhere. You've done enough. You risked your life as a conductor on the Railroad—let others risk theirs now. Stay here, stay with me. Let prayer and preaching be your weapons, like the Kyle Forrester who told me that so many months ago.*

She broke off the embrace. "You. . .you didn't say when you had to report for duty."

"It's not so bad."

"Tell me."

"August."

"But. . .it's the end of May now. That only leaves us two months: June and July."

"I'm aware of that. Clarissa, you know it could be worse. Far worse. I could be reporting to my unit in two weeks."

"So then why aren't they making such a demand?"

He shrugged. "I feel fit as a fiddle. But the army docs want to give it a little more time to make sure."

"I won't argue with them." She rubbed her hand over her face, bent her head, and closed her eyes. "I wish I could bring the 1861 Clarissa Avery back. I do want abolition and emancipation. And even though hardly anyone is fighting for that in 1862, maybe they will in 1863 or 1864, if this war goes blundering on. Something more than a union has to be worth the sacrifice of so many lives. The idea of liberty has to be more than a political statement. It has to be in the cities and towns and farms. It has to be in the neighborhood. It has to be next door."

"You're talking a long way ahead when you say things like that. Many Northerners won't accept that degree of freedom for slaves. The Union doesn't consist solely of Quakers or Amish or operators on the Underground Railroad."

"I have to look ahead. If you're going to go off to war and never come back, your life has to be worth it; what you die for has to be worth it. It has to be bigger than this conflict and this rebellion; it has to be something that matters to the whole world and the whole universe."

"Hey. Hey now. Calm down. You already have me six feet under. What's gotten into you?"

"Seeing you get shot, that's what's gotten into me. Most women don't see those things. Only the nurses do. The others don't even think of the blood and the broken bones and the gangrene. It's flags and marching bands and handsome uniforms, so far as they're concerned. I can't help but think of what gunfire does to skin and bone, can I? The images never go away. No matter how much we talk it over or I pray about it, the daguerreotypes are always there, the photographic plates always in my head."

He gently folded her into his chest. "I'm sorry, Clarissa. I guess I'll always be sorry for the pain the shooting has inflicted on both of us. Maybe I didn't need to ambush the slave catchers that final time. Maybe I didn't need to lag behind and fire two or three more shots. Maybe I was headstrong and careless and foolhardy. But I'm alive. You saved me. The doctor's assistant saved me. God saved me. And either I get back to fighting my fight on the Railroad or I fight it in uniform, like my beautiful Clarissa Avery wanted me to do a long time ago. Whatever I do, I'm doing it for God and country and for those in chains. But most of all, I swear I can't be strong if I'm not doing it for you. I can't be happy and I can't be strong."

"Oh Iain. . ."

"I'm not saying that to please you or to make you say things to me you don't want to say. It's just true, that's all. You mesmerize me. You enthrall me. You make me more than I have any right to be. You make me great. If I can't fight for you, I can't fight. That's who I am. I'm not only the man you resurrected but the man you made all over again. I'm the sixth day of creation."

She had no idea why the tears began to cut down her face. "I know that. I know you're different now. Some things are the same, but you're a different man. It's not my doing. God is the one who makes things new. . .not humans. . .not women. . .not even headstrong me."

"Not even headstrong you?"

"Well, do you think you're the only one with Gaelic inclinations in this courtship? The Ross family, we're Scots."

"That explains a great deal, doesn't it?"

"It does explain a great deal. My fighting spirit, for one thing."

"And you love oatmeal."

"I do." She did not want to lift her head from his chest. The sound of his heartbeat made her feel a special kind of strength she didn't always have. *Stay here, Iain, stay with me.* But they were both fighters. "If you must go and strike a blow for freedom, who is this Scots girl to say no? This woman who is a conductor on the Underground Railroad? This redhead who would sooner have a good argument than a good dress or a good meal? This Yankee who wants abolition and emancipation more than she wants to draw another breath into her body? So I give you to the cause, sir. I give you up to God and my republic, and I pray you will give me a free country in return, free for all, not just a privileged few."

"I'll do that. Before God and His Son, Jesus Christ, I swear I'll do that."

"And I would like you to give me all the time you can spare while we're still together, Liberty Iain Irish Kerry Kilgarlin. I feel like I'm just getting to know you and how all your many parts fit together. I need a few more weeks. I need what's left of May, all of June, and whatever you can set apart for us in the months of July and August. I'll make sure your uniform fits properly. I'll take it in, bring it out. Sew on brass buttons. Iron your pants. Polish the boots Father crafts for you and make sure they are kind on your feet. Help you choose your horse, for a captain must have a horse. I'll do anything to be with you another second or another minute. Do you understand that, sir?"

"The *sir* does understand that. And does the *miss* know the *sir* feels exactly the same way about her as she does about him?"

"The *miss* does. He made that plain long before today. Long before we rang in 1862. He made it plain at a rotted-out farmhouse in Chester County, Pennsylvania, when he took a knife to his hood just so he could kiss Clarissa Avery Ross's crimson hair. She'll never forget that moment. That's when she understood she had brought the mighty Liberty to his knees and that love was in the air."

"A Yankee girl stole my heart."

"Yes she did, sir. Oh yes she did. And she intends to keep it."

Chapter Thirteen

July
Round Top
Gettysburg

*A*nd she kept it by keeping Iain by her side as much as possible during the hot and humid summer days of southern Pennsylvania. They walked together, had picnics, enjoyed carriage rides, and she even watched him swim, fully clothed, in the waters of Rock Creek and Plum Run, though she did not join him, for such a thing could not be done without causing a scandal.

"Oh, never mind the gossips," Iain teased her at Plum Run. "Jump in, dress and bonnet and all. The water is wonderful."

"No thank you, sir." She remained on the bank. "We already have one war going on. We don't need another in Gettysburg."

"No one will notice."

"Ha. Every person in town will know an hour after I take the plunge."

"We could have a water fight."

"Quit tempting me, Iain Kerry Kilgarlin. I would like nothing better. And I'd beat you too."

"So, dive in and prove it."

"Will you leave off with your wickedness? I'm not coming in. However, I will take you up on horseback riding, and I'll whip you at that."

He grinned and tossed water at her with a splash of his hand. Holding her parasol over her head as the July sun beat down, she made a face and stepped farther back.

"I thought we already did the horseback riding," he said.

"That was while we were being shot at. I'd like to have a contest without half a dozen cutthroats on our tails."

"My new horse will leave you in the dust, Miss Ross."

"Don't count on it, Mr. Kilgarlin."

They had selected a horse for Iain's war service from one of the local farmers and breeders, a steed that was big and strong and a vivid black—like a glimmering midnight, she thought, and not like coal or tar or boot black—a fine seventeen-hands gelding they finally named Plum Run, after Iain's favorite swimming hole. He had wanted to name the horse after her—Avery or Ross or Temper—the last suggestion had almost made her lose hers when he playfully insisted—but she finally drove the point home that she was not having a horse, any horse, ever, named after her.

"Next, I suppose," she had complained, "you will want to have a regimental mascot named after me—Clarissa or Avery or Missy—and it will be a dog or a mule."

"That's a good idea," he'd replied. "Thank you for suggesting it."

Her eyes had narrowed. "Honestly, dear boy, my only suggestion is you *don't* name a dog or donkey or pony or cat, or anything in the animal kingdom, after me. If you do, believe me, you would be safer facing Stonewall Jackson and his brigade in battle than me."

"I'll keep that in mind, Miss Ross."

"You do that, Mr. Kilgarlin."

They did have their horse race; they had several of them—usually doing a mile run along Taneytown Road, or on Emmitsburg, between the Codori farmhouse and the peach orchard a few hundred yards farther along—but Iain and Plum Run always got the better of her and her mare, North Star, though one Sunday afternoon she made sure Iain realized he had only beaten her by a neck.

"And it's just because your horse has a longer neck, that's all," she grumbled, her bound-up hair unraveling on both sides of her perspiring face. "You aren't faster than us, just longer than us."

"I see." Iain was leaning forward and patting Plum Run's glistening neck. "Would you like to picnic?"

"Well, that's a grand idea, my love, but I wish you'd mentioned it back at the house. I don't have any desire to go back and pack up a basket. I'd rather be out here in this glorious July weather with you. . .you and your long-necked gelding. Mind you, it is rather hot and humid, isn't it?"

"Follow me to some shade trees."

"Huh. You can follow me, sir. Or I can ride at your side."

"Let's take the road past the wheat field and find us some shelter at the Round Tops."

"All right. There are a dozen trails up to the woods."

"Choose the one you like."

She did, riding past the ripening crop of wheat on their left and leading the way up the slope to Little Round Top and then, at the crest, picking her way down and up onto the higher hill, the big Round Top, her mare stepping over rocks and branches and scree. Iain and Clarissa reined in where there was a thick cluster of trees and flatter rocks to sit on. After dismounting, both horses having had a good drink below on the banks of Plum Run, Iain surprised her by tugging items out of his saddlebags, bags she supposed he had placed on his horse to get it used to military ones. He produced a large flask of lemonade, still cold since he had packed it in ice, a half dozen slices of smoked ham, a loaf of black bread, a small jar of pickles, a cup of butter—also cold—two slices of peach pie, and some fresh cucumbers, which he handed over to her along with a shaker of salt.

"What do you think?" he asked. "Am I a wizard or not?"

"Well, with my mother at your side, you certainly are." They prayed, and she began to bite into one of the dark green cucumbers. "When did you find time to put all this together without my catching you at it?"

"That wasn't hard, Avery." He often liked to use just her middle name. "You were bathing for over an hour before church."

"Oh, I was not."

"You were. So your mother and I assembled everything in a corner of the icebox, and just after lunch, when you'd disappeared for a second bath—"

"I did not have a second bath, and you know it."

"—I got all of it into the saddlebags here, you none the wiser, and now, *panem et circenses!*"

She laughed. "You and your Latin. And what does that mean?"

"It means 'bread and circuses.' You know. We need food, and the things that make us happy, in order to stay happy."

"I see. And besides ham and butter and bread—and peach pie—and your horse—what makes you happy?"

"You already know the answer to that," Iain replied.

"Do I?" She lifted one of her shoulders in a shrug. "Tell me anyways."

"I adore you. I cherish you." He took the flask of lemonade from her hand. "Let's tease less and compete less. At least today. At least right now."

She smiled. "All right."

"There wasn't a Sunday when I was a seminarian that I didn't run to church to be sure I could sit where I could see you without you noticing it."

"Oh." She could feel some heat in her face. "I'll be twenty-one this fall. You'd think I'd have gotten past blushing by now."

"When I began working with you on the Railroad, Avery, I thanked God. It was like He'd given me a dream. I enjoyed your strength, your bravery, your sharp wits, your faith. You became so much more than the pretty face at Christ's Church. You were a woman of immense stature to me. Heroic. Beautiful. Unstoppable once you put your mind to something. You refused to let discouragement or cowardice in the door."

"Thank you." She put a hand to her cheek. "But you really must stop this, my love. You are putting heat into me that is adding to the heat of this summer day and making the day quite impossible."

"I am so deeply in love with you, nothing else is important—food, sleep, the prospect of combat, picking up my seminary studies after the war—nothing."

She glanced and realized he had scarcely touched any of the picnic items from his saddlebags. "Iain, I love you too, but I don't want to hold a scarecrow in my arms when we hug. Please eat something. I like picnicking with you, but not if I'm eating alone."

"The picnic will have to wait, sweet Avery."

"Oh, and for what?"

"I have. . ." He stopped, then tried again. "I have a ring."

Clarissa's mind emptied immediately. "What?"

"I have a ring. A ring for you. If. . .if you want it."

She was sure her entire face had gone scarlet. "A ring?"

"I'm not asking for your hand. Well, yes, I am, but not for today or tomorrow. I spoke with your father. I advised him that I was not seeking a swift marriage and then an even swifter gallop off to war, a war from which I might not return, which would leave you a widow far too soon for your young age. I told him I only wished to say, with the ring, that I would come back, God willing, and make you my bride, if you wanted to be my bride, and he understood and said he felt that would be best."

Clarissa had a hard time finding her tongue. "You. . .you apparently had. . .a great deal to say. . .to say to my father. . .but what. . .what do you have to say to me?"

"I don't want to be forgotten."

"Oh Iain, I am never going to forget you."

"And I'm not asking you to pine away. You're so young and brave and pretty. If I don't return to Gettysburg, you move on and marry and raise a family here, far from the guns in Virginia."

"Please don't talk like this."

"But, so long as I remain alive and intact and have my arms and legs and hands. . ."

"You could lose all your limbs and I'd still want you, Iain Kilgarlin."

". . .I want to give you a ring that's a promise between us. That if I return. . .when I return. . .we'll marry. . .marry and live together forever in some big old Gettysburg house, have a passel of kids, take care of your parents as they get older, take care of each other when we get wrinkled and gray. . ."

"Iain." Clarissa began to laugh, holding her hand to her mouth. "First you had me all nervous and blushing, and now you have me laughing. Wrinkled and gray? Honestly?"

"Well, I do want to stay with you that long, Avery."

"I want to stay with you that long too, but you needn't be so dramatic about what happens to us when we age. Can't you make this moment a bit more romantic?"

"All right. You're blue sky. You're sunrise. You're stars and galaxies. You make every breath I take good. Every morning, every day, is better because you're in it, because you're in it and you love me, and it makes me feel like I'm sixteen or seventeen and so young and so excited and so wanting to ride away with you."

"Thank you." She smiled. "I wish you would."

"I never could get you out of my mind, whether I was Kyle Forrester or Liberty or a seminary student or a conductor on the Underground Railroad. And I can't get you out of my mind as a Mississippi boy or an Irish American. If I could put you on the train to Washington and get permission to have you share my saddle and ride with me into combat on Plum Run, I'd be the happiest man alive."

"That sounds like a grand adventure."

"But I'd never want to expose you to musket fire or cannonades or some Reb cavalryman's slashing saber."

"I've braved the risks on the Underground Railroad, my dear Iain. War is ugly, but I would never be afraid to face it with my beautiful, brave, and heroic man at my side."

"Thank you, but unless Bobby Lee comes knocking at your door, you'll just have to wait upon my return. Which, with the way this war is dragging on, is likely to take years. In lieu of me, I offer up this ring, something you can wear and gaze at and hopefully remember me as you admire its sparkle. You're the most amazing woman in the world, Clarissa Avery Ross. I love you, I want you to be my bride, I'd fight through a thicket of bayonets just to be at your side, and I'm not going to let this war get between you and me and keep us apart. God willing, I'll be back to sweep you off your feet and see you all decked out in white with a bouquet of summer roses in your hands. But will you say yes? Will you wait for me? Will you take this ring? Will you be my bride in 1864 or 1865 or 1866?"

He dropped to both knees in the dirt, holding up the slim band of gold that glittered with its diamond.

"Are you serious, sir?" Storms of emotion gusted through Clarissa, and she wanted to cry and sing and scream at the same time. "Wait until 1865 or 1866? I can't do that."

"But I. . ."

"I love you far too much to wait that long."

"Avery. . ."

"Hush. You've had your say. A lot of say. Now, hear me out, my lovely man. I adore you. It took some time getting used to all your personalities, but I'm fairly well settled in, and you're the man I want to live and die with. Oh sweetheart—" She went to her knees in front of him and curled her arms around his neck. "Yes, I'll be your bride. Yes, I'll accept your wonderful ring. Yes, I'll wait for you. . .but not until 1866!"

She began to kiss him, placing her lips rapidly all over his face.

"How long will you wait?" he gasped out between the kisses she rained on him.

"Not long, my love. You know how impulsive and impatient I am."

"How long?"

"I'm not going to haul you to the altar at Christ's Church before you and Plum Run board the train for Washington, my handsome Irishman. But if they ever give you any leave. . ."

"They won't give me leave, Avery."

"Or you come limping back here to convalesce from a bullet wound, or Plum Run bucks you off, and you wind up on crutches with a busted leg, and they send you home to get it all better under my tender ministrations. . ."

"You're dreaming, my redheaded beauty. . ."

"I don't care what happens or how it happens, so long as it's not a pine box—the next time you set foot in Gettysburg, you have to marry me. Right there and then. And God help you if it takes longer than a year, because if it does, I will fetch North Star here and ride to the battlefield where you're waging your war to set the captives free, find your regiment and find you, gallop around by your side, dodging minié balls and repeating your commands at the top of my lungs so troops a mile away will know what to do. And as soon as there's a lull in the fighting, I'll get a chaplain to marry us as we sit in our saddles—you think I'm joking, but I assure you, the redhead is not joking, sir—and I don't care which shows up first, a Union chaplain or a Rebel one. Heavens, if neither shows up, I'll call for a flag of truce and demand Stonewall Jackson marry us—I understand he's a devout Presbyterian, which ties in well with my Scots heritage—but marry you I shall, though the artillery of both armies should be booming overhead. Are you taking me seriously?"

"Do I have a choice?"

"You don't. So better you snap a bone and come home to me to recuperate if you don't want a wild Gaelic woman, with crimson hair blowing about her face as if her head's on fire, racing down upon you on her horse and waving a sword and singing 'The Battle Hymn of the Republic.'"

She suddenly felt so happy, so free, so strong, so full of thanks to God, so in love, she burst out with a couple verses of the song.

"Mine eyes have seen the glory of the coming of the Lord;
He is trampling out the vintage where the grapes of wrath are stored.
He hath loosed the fateful lightning of His terrible, swift sword.
His truth is marching on.

"Glory! glory! Hallelujah!
Glory! glory! Hallelujah!
Glory! glory! Hallelujah!
His truth is marching on.

"In the beauty of the lilies Christ was born across the sea,
With a glory in His bosom that transfigures you and me.
As He died to make men holy, let us live to make men free,
While God is marching on.

"Glory! glory! Hallelujah!
Glory! glory! Hallelujah!
Glory! glory! Hallelujah!
His truth is marching on."

Clarissa laughed, unpinning her hair and tossing it back in a wave of scarlet. "I'm not much of a singer, but I hope you get the idea. I love being in love with you, I love the fact you're going to set men and women free, I love being hidden away in the woods with you, and I love the ring—when on earth were you planning to put it on my finger?"

He laughed too. "I didn't want to interrupt your kisses. I like them."

"Oh, I'm glad you do. We'd be in a bit of a ditch if you didn't. Well, I'll be sure to give you a bushel more, kind sir, and one day there will be a kiss on the lips, but first I truly want to wear my ring."

They were both kneeling in the dirt, facing one another, she in her riding outfit, he in his shirt and pants, and he slipped the ring on her finger just as several robins alighted on a nearby branch. "Red heart, red hair, red robins," she said, turning her hand back and forth in the mixture of sunlight and shadows that covered her fingers and her ring. Then she embraced him, even more ardently than before, and did not let up, she was certain, for a good half hour. Then she patted her fiancé on the cheek. "Let's ride along the ridgeline, my love."

It was late in the afternoon, but the day was still warm and the humidity had not relented, so it was a bit of a shock to emerge from the trees and the shade and feel the force of the summer heat. Crossing from the Round Tops, the two of them made their way along Cemetery Ridge. The sun was on their left shoulders as they walked their horses north toward town, looking below at the sparse number of wagons and riders on Emmitsburg Road, Taneytown Road, and, just past Taneytown and to the east, the Baltimore Pike. The orchard of peach trees and the field of wheat they'd ridden past earlier in the afternoon were green and lush on the valley floor.

"I was last up here during the winter," Clarissa said, smiling down at both the valley and the glitter of the ring on her finger. "You were still laid up with your wounds. I'm glad we could picnic on the big Round Top while you were in Gettysburg. Heaven knows if we'll get another opportunity. I'm sure time will fly by faster than a diving hawk."

"You told me you were up here frequently when you were a girl."

"Oh yes, Mother and I were up on this ridge every week once spring arrived."

"I should have hiked over from the seminary more often. It's a pleasant setting."

"This is the stone wall I'd pretend I was a mountain goat on. I did climb some of those oaks too."

"Ha. I never climbed them. I'd bring my Greek New Testament here with the best of intentions, but I'd always wind up dozing in their shade."

"And no one disturbed you? There are always people at the cemetery in the nicer weather, and families like to walk along the wall like my mother and I did."

"People are afraid of Lutheran ministers."

"Even sleeping ones?"

"Especially if the sleeping ones snore."

"Let's linger, Iain." Clarissa slipped out of her saddle and stood holding North Star's reins. "There's no one about, so you can hold me here among the oaks if you'd like."

"That, Miss Ross, is a capital idea."

"I'm grateful you think so, Mr. Kilgarlin." She gave him her widest and most dazzling smile as he climbed down from Plum Run, a man-slaying smile that, she reflected, she'd begun to practice in front of the mirror once she'd turned sixteen, but a smile that she had hardly ever used. "You've made me the happiest woman in Gettysburg today, oh, probably in all of Pennsylvania and the Union, and the Confederate states as well. There's not much to be happy about, North or South, but I'm happy that you love me and are coming back to marry me."

"I'm happy when I make you happy."

"Well, then, how happy we are." She stepped into the trees, leading her mare, and looked back over her shoulder, still smiling her long-practiced but rarely used larger-than-life smile. "Let's take each other in our arms, Iain Kilgarlin. Let's hold on tight and see if we can't make an improvement on the lack of happiness in our divided nation."

"I'm sure President Lincoln would thank us."

"I'd like to think everybody would thank us, Iain."

Chapter Fourteen

August
Christ's Church
Gettysburg

 sharp thunderclap resounded just as Clarissa reached the steps leading into Christ's Church, so she ran all the way up, just as she had done countless times as a child despite reprimands from her mother and father. The clouds burst and showered her the moment she opened the door and ducked inside. She shook her parasol and placed it on the floor in the entryway, leaving it open to dry. Then she readjusted her white bonnet and brushed the sleeves of her white dress with her fingers to get rid of the raindrops. And faced the wide central aisle of the small but beautiful sanctuary, the stained glass windows on either side now running with water from the summer storm.

Fifteen rows of pews. Two pews on each side of the main aisle. Two smaller aisles along the walls and windows. The pews where the gates opened to the main aisle cost more to rent. Her parents paid three dollars and fifty cents every six months. The family beside them, whose gate opened to the smaller aisle along the wall, paid perhaps half of that, she wasn't sure. Kyle Forrester had been expected to pay fifty cents per school term for a pew next to the west aisle, pews set aside especially for students. But he had often joined her family in their pew close to the front. She walked up the aisle to it, opened the small gate, and smiled. As a girl, she had often swung on the gate, which also got her into trouble, just like running up the church steps did. But nothing got her in so much trouble as the balcony or gallery.

She turned and looked back at it. *"Resolved, that the short pews on the left side of the gallery be assigned to people of color"*—a decision apparently set in stone in 1835 six years before she was born. How many times had she twisted about in the family pew and asked out loud why the "people of color" couldn't sit with everyone else and be close to the beautiful windows and the beautiful altar? Her mother hushed her. Adults seated in pews nearby hushed her.

But that was nothing compared to how she felt as a sixteen-year-old when she realized William could not sit with them at the front of the church but had to go to the balcony. "This is an outrage," she once said out loud, in a particularly fine redheaded mood. "His blood is no different than ours. I've seen it. No different than yours, Mr. Miller. Don't shush me, sir. It's a free country. Or perhaps it is not a free country. Are the people on the left side of the gallery free? I thought we were Christians, and that there was no slave or free once we were Christians, but all were one in Christ Jesus."

She had been asked to leave. Her parents were horrified, but she marched down the main aisle and out, quite happily, and attended the German-speaking Lutheran church on York that morning, St. James. She had enough of the heavenly tongue in her head to sing the hymns and follow the sermon. And when the decision was made to ban her from Christ's Church for a month, she took herself to the Catholic church as well, St. Francis Xavier, and three or four times to the German Reformed Church on High Street, where she often sat with Ginnie Wade and Ginnie's mother and younger brothers. She had made up her mind to return to Christ's Church if and when she was ready, not when the church leaders said she had their almighty permission. Thinking about the incident still made her simmer as she gazed up at the balcony. She had only rejoined her mother and father, in their seven-dollar-a-year pew, when the minister, whom she liked, had personally asked her to come back and when William had said he missed worshipping with her.

"You are not worshipping with me, William," she had retorted. "I might as well be a mile away."

"I am high and lifted up, Miss Ross," he had replied, smiling. "And though you may dwell far beneath my lofty status, I can see you very well indeed, and I pray when you pray, sing when you sing, bow my head when you bow yours, and listen to God's Word when you listen."

He had made her laugh. And she was back in the Ross pew that Sunday morning.

And working with the Underground Railroad before she was seventeen.

"We shall simply have to pray for you more than we ever have," her mother said in response to her hotheaded daughter's demand.

"Then that is a good thing for you both," Clarissa had replied, tossing her hair. "I have offered the two of you an opportunity to enjoy a closer walk with God."

She removed her sunbonnet, smoothed back her crimson hair she'd pinned up in a bun, and looked around her at the colorful windows—now radiating light with the sun's reappearance—as well as the baptismal font, the pulpit, and the pipe organ. And the altar. What would it be like to stand there with Iain and exchange vows? The church where, with all its flaws along with all its goodness, she had grown up? Where Iain, masquerading as Kyle Forrester, had preached his first sermon? *And what a sermon it had been.*

"What's going on in that pretty little head of yours?"

She smiled as Iain entered the church and came up the aisle. "More than your pretty little head could ever handle, sir."

"Do you hold that as a proven fact?"

"I do, sir." She held out her arms. "But who wants to quarrel with that pretty little man of mine? Especially when he's dressed up so fine."

"Your father and William helped me get into all this to begin with. Then your mother appeared to fuss over the details."

"As shall I. My chevalier."

They hugged, he gave her a kiss on the cheek, and then she stepped back to survey him.

"Kyle Forrester in a suit and tie. Liberty in a black hood. Iain Kilgarlin in a homespun cotton shirt and pants. And now this. Your latest incarnation—Captain Kilgarlin in the uniform of an officer in the United States Army. Where will it end?"

"In certain moods, Avery, you wouldn't have it end until I was commanding general of the Army of the Potomac."

She brushed lint off the epaulet on his left shoulder. "I may have to lower my aim. Once you join your regiment and square off against Thomas Jackson, the conflict may not extend far into '63."

"Wishful thinking."

"Very wishful."

She continued to scrutinize him. He wore a dark blue frock coat with a single row of nine brass buttons and two gold shoulder straps, pants that were lighter blue, a red sash with a large tassel tied under a wide black belt that held a gold buckle engraved with an eagle, a saber in a scabbard that hung off his left hip, a holster with a revolver on his right hip, a slouch hat with a gold band and a gold bugle—which she knew meant infantry—and the black boots her father had made for him. The boots were polished so brightly they looked like mirrors, which she had intended, since she was the one who had polished them the night before. She reached over and took his hat off his head. "You're in the house of God, sir."

"Thank you for reminding me. The stained glass windows ought to have been my first clue."

"Hmm. Of course, no kepi for you. You needed something jaunty."

"You don't like the slouch hat?"

"Actually, I do. I just don't want you to stand out, that's all."

"Plenty of officers wear slouch hats."

"So it might take awhile for the sharpshooters to get to you." She took another step back. "Turn around for me, please, Captain Kilgarlin."

"Your parents are waiting in the carriage outside."

"I expect they are."

"They reminded me we have just thirty minutes."

"And I want twenty-five of those. Did you already load Plum Run?"

"Yes."

"How was that?" Clarissa asked him.

"Capital." Iain grinned. "He took right to his stall and hay."

"*Capital.*" She grinned back, mimicking his voice. "Now turn around, please, sir."

He did as she wished.

"I thought so." She gave the tails of his frock coat a yank at the back. "I suspected they'd be bunched up."

"From the carriage, I'm sure."

"I'm sure. Remind me to straighten them out again at the depot. Where's your cloak? Your gloves? Your waistcoat?"

"With my luggage."

"Your gold epaulets? The round fancy ones?"

"Luggage."

She placed his hat on the floor and took his hands in hers. "I love thee."

"And I love thee."

"Are you bound to me?"

"For eternity," Iain responded.

"Do you take me to be your lawfully wedded wife?" she asked.

"I do."

"To have and to hold?"

"Yes."

"In sickness and health? For richer or poorer?"

"And till—" he began.

"No." She put her fingers to his mouth. "No."

Iain remained silent.

She snuggled into him and closed her eyes. "The only other thing that remains to be said is I take you to be my lawfully wedded husband."

"I'm glad to hear it."

"And. . .you may kiss the bride."

"I like that part."

The kiss, the first to bring their lips together, was soft, heartfelt, and brief. She placed her fingers on his cheek when he wanted to continue.

"When you come back," she said. "When you come back to me."

"I've waited this long. I can wait a little longer."

"I'm glad you feel comfortable waiting, sir. I don't."

"Then. . ."

"Hush. Once you return." She played with the brass buttons on his frock coat. "I take this seriously, you know."

"What?"

"Our little ceremony here by the altar. No minister, no witnesses, no Bible, but to me it's real, to me it's true, to me it just happened. You're my husband. My man."

"Avery. . ."

"Shh. Don't go all Union officer on me, please. When the day arrives, there will be flowers and a reverend and my parents, and maybe crossed swords we can walk under once we leave the church and head down the steps. It will be a magical day. But it won't be any more meaningful to me than this, right here, right now. So far as I'm concerned, something amazing happened in this church over the past few minutes. Amazing and eternal. God saw it. That's all I care about. I can't let you go without having this. Do you understand? I had to have this. I had to have you."

Iain nodded and stroked her hair. "I do understand. And it does matter to me."

"You'll be back, Iain Kilgarlin," she whispered, and her words had the quiet fervency of a quiet prayer. "You'll be back. There is no other possibility that I will accept."

December
Christ's Church
Gettysburg

$\mathcal{C}$larissa was bundled in her warmest cloak and bonnet and stood at the foot of the steps leading up to the doors into Christ's Church. Snow was falling thick and fast and silent, and the ink on the small envelope in her gloved hand began to smear with melted snowflakes. She had walked to the church specifically to open the letter addressed to her. But several things made her hesitate: there was blood on the three-cent postage stamp affixed to the envelope, the writing on the envelope was not Iain's or that of any of the three seminarians still serving with the Army of the Potomac, and the terrible slaughter of Union troops at Fredericksburg earlier in the month made her fear the worst.

His name had not appeared on the casualty lists in the Philadelphia or New York papers, but that didn't mean anything. Several Adams County families she knew had breathed a sigh of relief after fathers and sons and brothers and cousins did not end up on the lists after the vicious fight at Antietam in September, yet news had come in November, in the form of letters written by their commanding officers, that several of them had died in the battle or succumbed to their wounds in the hospital. She knew she should have asked her mother to be with her, that she should be opening the envelope at home and in the parlor by the fire, but if it was the most terrible news possible, she wanted to be at the church so that she could run inside to the altar and throw herself down to weep and pray.

It is the only spot in town that will afford me any comfort at all. God, have mercy. Lord, have mercy. September was bad enough. But Fredericksburg! What has become of my high hopes of ending the war and ending slavery? What has become of the man I wed, with God as my witness? This is too hard. War is too cruel.

Slowly, she peeled open the envelope.

Tugged out a sheet of paper that had been folded two or three times so that it would fit.

Spread it open.

The writing inside was not Iain's either.

She thought she was going to faint, but she gritted her teeth and, blinking her eyes against the fall of snow, forced herself to read the untidy scrawl.

> *Dear Miss Clarissa Avery Ross,*
> *You will forgive the tone of this here letter. But it's the best*
> *that can be done under the circumstances, Miss Ross.*
>
> *My name is Billy O'Malley and I am from Co. Derry.*
> *I came over with my family when I was four. We settled in*
> *Philadelphia. I joined the Philadelphia Brigade and here*
> *I am.*
>
> *The Captain ought to be writing this. But a Reb*
> *sharpshooter got him.*

"I said so!" cried Clarissa, tears bursting from her green eyes. "You and your slouch hat! Oh Iain!"

She dropped the hand that held the letter to her side. "I can't read anymore. I can't."

But she steeled herself and brought the letter up again.

The ink was running as the snow struck it.

She squinted and struggled to make out the words, tears ruining her sight.

> *His sword took a licking from the first ball, and the second bounced off the hilt and took some meat out of his hand. There was a third that plugged his fancy hat. But there weren't no more after that because Tim O'Hearne knocked that sharpshooter fellow out of the tree with a bullet of his own.*
>
> *That was the Captain's writing hand, so I am writing for him. I can say his hand is healing up right as rain and I guess he will do a January or Febr'y letter on his own. The boys all expect him to make Major. Merry Chris'mas and it was a pleasure meeting you, Miss Ross.*
>
> *O'Malley*

Clarissa dropped like a stone and sat on the church steps in the snowstorm, laughing and crying and thanking God all at the same time. Passersby picked up their pace once they saw her slumped there and heard her cries. She didn't notice them or the looks they gave her, and even if she had, she wouldn't have cared. There was a final paragraph at the bottom of the sheet of paper, where the handwriting was even worse than that which had preceded it. She was having a hard time deciphering the letters, but she was so full of happiness and relief now, she didn't care what the note said. Until she began to comprehend what she was reading and who had penned it.

> *I am heartily sick of Virginia weather and Virginia campaigns. Maryland fall weather was a respite—did you receive the letter I wrote in October? But now we are back*

to this soggy mess. The sky and the Rebs and the mud are the same color. Fred'burg was the devil's own, no doubt about it, but we shall prevail. I told the boys that we must, for I have marching orders from my belle to reach Richmond this July or August. I showed them the photographic image your mother gave me that was commissioned when you turned nineteen. Imagine, you are wearing a twelve-hoop dress. I didn't think you had such a creature in your wardrobe. Now the lads are all enchanted and wish to write you. I told them to write away. I warned them you were as redheaded as secesh cannon fire, and just as fiery, but they don't care. My hand is cramping. I will close and get this off. I love you, Avery, I love you to the extent no Reb bullet can kill me because you slew me long ago. All this to say, I am alive, Avery. Liberty is alive, Kyle Forrester is alive, and because of that, Iain Kilgarlin is alive too and in love, very much in love.

The minister left the church five minutes later and was startled to see a woman on the steps, hugging her knees and rocking and quoting verses from the Bible as if she were a child reciting her Sunday school lessons. He came down to her.

"Ma'am, are you all right?" he asked. "Is there something I can do?"

She turned her face to him, and although she looked to have been crying, her smile was so bright and her face so wet, he was certain it must have been melting snow and not tears.

"Reverend," she greeted him. "The Lord bless you."

"Miss Ross." Her features were unmistakable to him. "I trust I find you well? You must be chilled to the bone sitting here in the snow."

"Forgive me. I had a letter to open. It was urgent, so I just planted myself on the church steps to read it." She began to climb to her feet, he extended his hand, and she took it. "Please excuse me, Reverend."

"I hope the letter was welcome news, Miss Ross?"

"Oh, most welcome, Reverend." She laughed. "He's alive, he's alive, sir, he's so very much alive."

She hopped down the steps as if she were ten and half skipped, half walked along Chambersburg on her way to her house.

"Good day, Reverend," she called back. "Thank you."

"For what, my dear?"

"For your prayers. For your prayers for all the soldiers. God answers them, you know. Not all of them, I suppose, and not always the way we like, but today His response has been more than sufficient, and I take heart from that, and now I have an enormous appetite again, ha-ha."

The minister continued to watch her until she disappeared in swirling snow and top hats and black carriages with whirling wooden wheels. "The lark's on the wing," he heard her singing, "the snail's on the thorn; God's in His heaven—All's right with the world."

Chapter Sixteen

May and June 1863
The Ross House
Gettysburg

W hat news from Virginia, Father?"

Clarissa's father had employed three men at the beginning of the war to help meet the military's demands for his boots. Then he had added another four. Now, in the spring and summer of 1863, there were twelve workers, and he'd had to build another section to his shop, which was a block from the Ross house. It became the perfect place to hear news from Union officers about the war, often before papers ran the stories.

She never got enough letters from Iain to suit her, and as busy as she kept herself by earning money with her sewing, or learning to read the Greek New Testament, or even doing some of the fine stitching on the popular Ross cavalry boots, she would find her father in the parlor and ply him for information on troop movements, especially those that involved the Army of the Potomac and the Philadelphia Brigade. Once she got his attention, she always began with the same query: *"What news from Virginia, Father?"*

His responses, of course, were always different, and about the middle of May he replied, "Since Chancellorsville? Nothing, my girl, nothing. Lee may have won, but I am told his dead and wounded were as great in number as our own. A Pyrrhic victory, I would call it. So the armies are resting. Licking their wounds for a time."

"I've heard nothing from Iain."

"It's too soon for that."

"His name isn't on the casualty lists. He could be a prisoner."

"It's my understanding his brigade was not heavily involved in the fighting. Not like they were at Fredericksburg or Antietam. I am sure he's fine. You'll get a letter in June or July."

"What if. . .what if we keep losing the battles? What if we lose another one?"

"I've been following the reports from Vicksburg. It's too early to tell, but I think this General Grant may win the day yet. If he does, the Confederacy loses control of the Mississippi River. That will go hard on them."

"But. . .our battles here in the east. . .in Virginia. What if we keep getting beaten? What if Washington is threatened? What if Lee can't be stopped?"

"McClellan stopped him at Antietam, my dear—no matter how the Richmond papers howl that it was a draw. The Army of the Potomac fought Lee and his Army of Northern Virginia to a standstill. And then Lee withdrew. He retreated back to the South. Think about it: Lee invades Maryland, Lee is stopped, Lee retreats to Virginia. How is that a draw? He lost and then he skedaddled. He certainly didn't gain any ground, and he certainly didn't continue to press north, did he?"

"But Fredericksburg was a disaster for us."

"Yes. I won't argue that point."

"And Chancellorsville was another disaster."

"I won't argue that point either."

"What happens if we experience another defeat like Fredericksburg or Chancellorsville? What then?"

Her father shook his head, opened his book—*David Copperfield*—looked down, and began to read. "Then I suppose we would make peace. They would go their way and we ours."

"And they would keep their slaves and their cotton fields and their plantations."

Her father continued to read. "I imagine."

The conversation was over.

Iain had last written her in March and had talked about President Lincoln's Emancipation Proclamation. It had not made much of an impression on the Irishmen of his regiment. They fought because they hated the South and its plantation owners, aristocrats who reminded them of the cursed English nobility who had oppressed Ireland for hundreds of years. In fact, the English lords and ladies openly supported the South and its wealthy planters, so the lads of the Sixty-Ninth liked nothing better than ripping into the sons of the Southern nobility and putting them in their graves. That's why they fought. And for their new country, the United States of America. As for the slaves? Well, they didn't like others being enslaved any more than they liked seeing Irishmen enslaved by Englishmen. But they weren't fighting the war for the plantation slaves. And they didn't want them crowding north and taking their jobs, because freed slaves would work twice as hard for half the pay.

> *Abolition and emancipation have a long way to go yet, Avery. My boys don't sing the last verse of "The Battle Hymn of the Republic," the one about dying to set men free. So then, winning the war must be the first step. All the other steps will have to be fought for after that. Every single one. But the first fight to win will be this war. I reckon you will have to pray much harder for that. Everyone will.*

But the Army of the Potomac had lost again, Union prayers or not, and lost badly, little more than a month after she had received Iain's letter. In Chancellorsville. In Virginia. At the beginning of the month of May. She sensed Iain was still alive—she had no ominous feeling warring against that belief in her soul. But the stone had sunk again into the deep, dark pond of her heart. They were losing the conflict and all the dreams and visions of a free and beautiful America that went with that loss.

Yet there was William in Union blue. He had enlisted in the Fifty-Fourth Massachusetts—what they called a colored regiment—after reading a speech by Frederick Douglass in the *New York Times* that, as he put it, "has struck fire in my bosom and an almighty blaze in my soul." No one in the household dissuaded him. Clarissa agreed with Mr. Douglass that an armed freedman who fought bravely for the Republic would alter people's opinions of the African Americans and hasten the end of slavery in America, ensuring the slaves' freedom, citizenship, constitutional rights, and—down the line—enfranchisement, the liberty to vote their conscience.

"*Do you remember the night you rescued me from the slave catchers, Miss Ross?*"

She and her parents had stood with William on the railway platform in Gettysburg in early March. He wore a dark suit and a coat against the chill, a white shirt, a tie, and a hat with a low crown. The train to Boston was departing in ten minutes. If selected, his training would begin at Camp Meigs in Readville, just outside the city.

"*It wasn't just me, William.*" She smiled. "*About a dozen of us stopped those men in their tracks.*"

"*It's you I remember most of all. Though I thought you were a stocky old man then with a bone to pick with every person on earth.*"

Clarissa and her parents laughed.

"*Surely not me,*" teased Clarissa. "*Though I do have bones to pick with various people from time to time, I suppose. It's my constitutional right as a redhead.*"

William grinned. "*None of them argued with your pistol.*"

"*No. Nor with our shotguns.*"

His face sobered suddenly. "Lee and Jackson let their men scoop up any person of color they laid their hands on when they retreated from Antietam— freedmen, ex-slaves, men and women who'd been born free, those who had bought their freedom. . .it didn't matter."

"It was wrong," said Mr. Ross. "And the Union's General McClellan didn't care one whit. He'd have helped chain them up and deliver them to Lee as a parting gift, if he'd thought of it."

"They say the war isn't about slavery," Mrs. Ross spoke up. "Yet Generals Lee and Jackson countenance that sort of behavior from their troops. And the one a good Episcopalian and the other an upstanding Presbyterian. Clearly, enslavement matters."

"Of course it matters." Clarissa narrowed her eyes. "They can howl about states' rights in their newspapers all they like. What they ought to say is their most important right is the right to run their economy on the backs of those they hold in bondage. That's what they don't want anyone interfering with. 'You're trying to destroy our way of life.' Some way of life for those in fetters and under the whip." She turned her flashing green eyes on William. "You give it to them, William, do you hear? Don't you back down from a fight, sir. Give them your 'rows of burnished steel. Loose the fateful lightning of His terrible swift sword.' Show those sons of Mississippi and Georgia and Alabama how a freedman can march and shoot and bayonet. Show them."

She was seething, but she didn't care how contorted her face must look to others on the platform. Her Scottish was up, and she felt like traveling to Boston herself and enlisting in the Fifty-Fourth. Her mind raced with ideas on how to darken her skin and how to cover up her womanly form with a Union uniform that was three sizes too large. It could be done. She had done it on the Railroad. They had all thought she was a man. She could do it in the army.

William looked at her with wide eyes. "Pardon me, Miss Ross."

Clarissa blinked. "What is it, sir?"

"I'm not sure I heard you correctly, Miss Ross."

"Heard me correctly say what?"

William went silent.

Her mother put her hand on Clarissa's arm. "Um. You asked him how he thought you might look in Union blue and with skin as dark as his."

"Oh." Her face reddened. "I see." Recovering, she looked around at them all. "Well, sometimes I wish I could enlist. And I certainly don't have any qualms about exhibiting a skin darkened by the sun, instead of having one that is always burning and peeling if I don't protect it properly."

William recovered too and smiled. "I'm sure you would look fine, Miss Ross. With your ivory skin, you are as beautiful as the day. With a darker skin—"

"As dark as what they call French roast," she interrupted.

He laughed. "As dark as what they call French roast, Miss Ross. With a look as dark as that you would be as beautiful as the night sky. If I may say so." He glanced awkwardly at Mr. and Mrs. Ross. "I hope I don't offend."

"Oh William." Clarissa knew her emerald eyes were dancing with an unusual glitter, a glitter she had noticed in the mirror once, and an effect that occurred only when she fell into a merrier mood. "You do not offend. You make me happy."

He doffed his cap briefly. "You won me back the freedom I'd been born with, Miss Ross. A small compliment is the very least I can pay you in return."

The train whistle shrieked about then.

And she inclined her head toward William. "Vivere et mori liber gratis, *sir."*

He bowed his head in return. "Vivere et mori liber gratis, *Miss Ross."*

"My, my, so many scholars we have waiting on the train here today." Clarissa's mother smiled. "Perhaps you could let the rest of us in on your Latin secret."

"We used it as a code on the Railroad now and then," Clarissa responded. "You had to translate it properly for the response."

"Which was?" pressed her mother.

"Live free and die free."

William nodded and picked up his portmanteau. "Live free and die free," *he repeated. "I wish that was the motto of the Fifty-Fourth."*

"Live it, and in your heart, it shall be," Clarissa told him.

And he had left them, sitting stoically by a window, watching them as the locomotive pulled the passenger cars clear of the station, but never waving.

She had written Iain about William's departure and his successful selection and enlistment. She wrote Iain about everything and she wrote him every day, gathering up the pages and posting him a letter once a week on Monday mornings. It kept her sane. Just thinking about him day after day, not able to see him, not able to touch him, worrying that a secesh bullet might find him in his tall slouch hat, worrying about disease and gangrene and amputation, fretting over how the war was being lost and how it kept dragging on week after week, month after month—if she didn't keep pen and paper at hand and share with him all her thoughts, large and small, chat with him about her news, shed her tears onto the ink because she missed him so much, press her lips to the pages filled with her tidy handwriting, perfume it with her cologne, send him locks of her hair—and once, a cameo in ivory and Wedgewood blue of her exact profile—if she didn't do all those things and more, she might as well lie down and die, it hurt so much to be separated from him and to wrestle with thoughts of his death or crippling from Rebel shellfire or bullets. Sometimes she woke up in the night and she could hardly breathe because of the fear, thick as the smoke from ten thousand muskets, that suffocated her mind and dreams. Writing and prayer helped with all of that, so no day went by without her dipping her pen into its inkpot.

January had become March and then April, May, and June. How warm the weather had turned. How green the grass and blue the sky and silver the rain showers. How the apples and peaches ripened in the orchards. How the wheat grew tall in the fields, and the corn too. How the creeks and streams ran true. She told Iain all of it, painting a picture with every mailing of how the seasons were turning, and how lovely and peaceful Gettysburg was, and how sweet the air smelled, full of flowers, and how swiftly the birds flew, and how cheerful their songs were, never missing a note, never missing an opportunity to alight on a branch bright with leaves or to soar above clouds that resembled mare's tails, as free as God intended every creature should be, as free as the human heart.

> *I love thee,* she wrote. *And how do I love thee? Well, I shall ask Mrs. Elizabeth Barrett Browning to assist me. Hmm. Let me count the ways, my love, my Iain, my husband, oh yes, my lifetime, my heartbeat. I love thee to the depth and breadth and height my soul can reach. I love thee freely, as men like you strive for right. I love thee with the breath, smiles, tears of all my life.*

Once he wrote back, in a letter that looked as if a caisson full of ammunition had run over the sheet of paper four or five times, and told her:

> *Often enough I ride apart from the others in the evenings so that I can be with you and whisper your name—I love to hear your name rolling off my lips. And when we've gone into combat in Maryland and Virginia, despite the horrors of war—and, I tell you, the horrors are great—I've often thought how pleasant it would be to have you at my side. Not with the bullets in the air or the cannon belching fire, but to have you at my side to see the beauty of the places we've fought in. The hillsides, the woods, the brooks, the wildflowers, the tidy farms, miles of rail fencing, walls of rugged gray stone. I know you'd be enchanted by all of it. When the day is done and the shooting has stopped, I imagine you strolling with me at sunset and taking in the fields of hay, and the tall pines and oaks, and the meadows*

spangled with daisies—the dead are not there, nor the smashed wagons, nor the muskets strewn over the trampled grass. No, the war is not there. I walk with you as the shadows grow long and the colors become gold and purple and vermillion, and I feel your small hand in mine, breathe in the pure beauty of your face and scarlet hair, of the eyes that dazzle me, and I rejoice that you are my bride and wear my ring. I want you to know I mean to keep my promise and return. If any man ever had a reason to survive a war, I do. Amica mea reddam. *That's my personal regimental motto as this war rages: amica mea reddam—I shall return, my love.*

His letters were never as many as hers, so she read them over and over again, keeping them in a black leather Bible in her room. But that one—where he walked with her through fields of battle that were no longer fields of battle but fields of romance and tender devotion—that one she read every day, sometimes twice a day, and it always made her cry.

She had written back:

I don't want our love to be a dream. I don't want it to be miles apart. I don't want a lifetime of imagining it. I want to walk those fields with you. I want to feel your strength when you hold me or take my hand. I want to snuggle up against you when I'm tired or scared or empty. I want you. Not a fantasy. Not a hope. Not a wish. You, sir, in all your rugged manhood, your sweet, gentle spirit, in all your exceptional masculine beauty—yes, in all the power and glory the good Lord has given you. I am not content with words on a page, no matter how fine. Or pressing my lips to a sheet of paper, knowing you shall press your lips to the same spot. I am not satisfied with your news about a world far removed from me. I want to hear your whispers in my

*ear. I want to feel your lips eager against mine. I want your
world to be my world, and my world yours, and I want us
to be eternally present in that universe, sir, not absent from
one another but eternally present, in this life and the next. Is
all this so much to ask? Don't other couples have each other
every day? Don't they share all their meals and pour coffee
and tea into their cups and smile across the table? Oh Iain, I
love you so much I'm breaking in two. I know I'm a soldier's
wife. I know there are thousands of other women in my
shoes because of this war. I don't mean to sound selfish—after
all, I can't expect this war to be won by the sacrifice of other
families and never by my sacrifice, or yours, can I? I just
don't want you to remain as a thought in my head or as a
memory or a romance that only spans the miles in my dreams
and in my handwritten sentences tucked away in envelopes.
I don't just want good feelings or to perpetually read sweet
sentiments from you. I don't want an angel in heaven. I
want the man. I want the man I love. I want him real and
I want him here. Oh, my treasure, I love thee with every
ounce of blood in my heart and every light of spirit in my
soul. Without you I cannot live. With you I can never die.*

And just as he imagined her walking with him through battlefields
empty of battle and suffering and death, so she imagined him walking
with her through the town, a town also empty of battle and suffering
and death, one suffused with peace and light and warm blue sky, where
such guns as people possessed made no sound, but for the fall hunt. A
town where horses did not strain under harness to move cannons, where
wagons did not haul kegs of powder, or ambulances wounded men,
and where the uniform of the day was simply a suit and a tie, and any
smoke that filled the air was not from muskets but was just the smoke
of burning leaves and branches and dry grass that had been raked into
mounds. Iain was a wonderful companion for such leisurely strolls up

one street and down another, even as far as the seminary. Often enough she spread a blanket on the grass and nibbled at a cucumber sandwich, and he joined her on the blanket, hoping for some cold chicken or ham.

Her mother teased her gently when she returned from her walks with Iain, and always asked, "How is your beau today?"

Clarissa did not mind playing along. "He is right as rain."

"Did it rain?"

"No. The clouds moved on and we basked in the heat."

"Is he still the charmer?"

"Oh yes, Mother. That Southern boy is always the charmer."

"I thought he was Irish."

"He is Irish too."

"And American born."

"He is all three. And more."

Her mother would laugh. "Did you ever get all those men sorted out in your head? Liberty and Kyle Forrester and Iain Kilgarlin?"

"I did," Clarissa would reply.

"And which one did you choose?"

Clarissa would smile. "All three chose me and then, at my request, voted on it and decided to join and become one person, just so they could become one with me. Now everything is very merry."

"What a fortunate bride-to-be. To have three men at your feet all rolled into one."

"Aren't I?"

"And when will we see this amazing three-in-one man again?"

"He has assured me he'll be home for Christmas."

"Oh." Her mother would quiet. "I wish that were true."

So Clarissa's days and games and letter writing, and all ten thousand of her young woman's dreams, passed into the shimmering heat and silver showers of summer. On the last day of June, she found her father in his shop and blacking a new pair of riding boots she'd done the stitching on. "People say there is Union cavalry at the edge of town. I took a walk, but I couldn't spot them."

He grunted. "Just passing through. Probably on their way east to help wrest York away from Jubal Early and the Rebels."

"What news from Virginia, Father?"

"Nothing, my dear, nothing. But a battle will boil up soon enough. They say Lee is out and about and spoiling for a fight down Virginia way."

Chapter Seventeen

July 1 and 2
Gettysburg

The crack was distant, but it might as well have been at her elbow. She knew what it was. Instantly, her mind took her back to a Christmas Eve years before when Liberty had extended his right arm and fired shot after shot with his pistol.

A loud roar of gunfire followed the lone shot.

Tumbling into her brain right after that first image of Liberty, she saw herself shooting at slave catchers in Chester County as they pursued her and Iain along the road to Lancaster. She had emptied her revolver several times on that flight. And then her mind disgorged a memory of Iain covered in blood, and her hands covered in more of it, and how cold the night had suddenly become, and how cold her hands, and how dead her heart.

She had been weeding in their backyard garden and nibbling on a small carrot she'd yanked from the ground.

The musket fire swelled and no longer seemed distant.

Running into the house, she saw by the tall clock in the hall that it was just past seven thirty in the morning.

Wednesday.

"Mother!" she called.

"What is it?" Her mother came rushing out of the parlor where she'd been dusting. "What's wrong?"

The windows rattled.

They heard the boom of cannons.

The distant shriek of a shell.

The distant scream of horses.

And they clutched each other.

"What is it?" Clarissa stared into her mother's wide and frightened eyes. "What's going on?"

"It sounds. . .it sounds. . ." Mrs. Ross stuttered.

"Like a battle?"

Mrs. Ross nodded, eyes wild.

"It can't be," Clarissa said for both of them. "The troops are in Virginia. All of them."

More cannons. More shells. More explosions. More musket fire.

The glass panes shivered, and crockery on shelves bounced.

"I need to look," Clarissa said.

"No!" Her mother almost shouted. "Don't go outside. There will be stray bullets. Stray shells."

"How else can we know what's happening?"

"We know what's happening."

"Someone has to—"

The front door flew open.

"The Confederates!" Mr. Ross's face was red. "There are thousands of them!"

"What?" His wife fought for comprehension. "What?"

"Twice as many as we have. All we have are cavalry. I think just cavalry. The Rebs are coming in from the west. Maybe using Fairfield Road or Mummasburg. Or Chambersburg Street. Our boys are set up just outside of town. On Oak Ridge and McPherson Ridge, that's what it looks like to me."

"Why would you go out there to look?" Mrs. Ross was almost frantic. "It's too dangerous."

"The fighting is far away."

"It's not far away. Oak Ridge is hardly a mile out of town. That's not what I call far away. Not for a cannon ball."

"I don't think the Rebs have much artillery. I don't know."

"Then what do you know? Do you know why they're here? Do you know what they're fighting about?"

"No."

"What on earth is there to fight about in Gettysburg? What could the Confederate army possibly want in Gettysburg?"

"I don't have your answers." Mr. Ross turned to go. "It's no more than a skirmish. It's noisy, but don't fret. I'm sure it will be over in a few hours. One or the other will simply withdraw."

Mrs. Ross was still wound up. "How can you be sure of that?"

"You said it yourself. There's nothing of military importance here. Why stay?"

"I pray you're right."

"Yes. Pray." He stepped outside the door as thousands of muskets hammered at the summer morning. They were not letting up. He gave Clarissa a hard look. "Stay indoors. Both of you. I'm sure the fighting will not come into town. It will stay in the fields. There's nothing to battle over in the town."

Mrs. Ross was still looking at the door her husband had closed behind him several long seconds after his departure. "Fetch your Bible, Clarissa," she said, without turning around. "Begin reading the Psalms out loud to me. To both of us. I'll make us some tea. Are you hungry?"

Clarissa's stomach was in knots as tight as the ones she had experienced on the Underground Railroad during the worst crises. "No."

"Neither am I." She remained fixated on the door. The firing had become a constant thunder from the north and west of town. "I'll put the kettle on. We must pray."

"Yes, Mother."

"But first read to us from the Bible." She didn't move. "I'll put the kettle on."

"I won't be a minute." Clarissa ran up two flights of stairs to her bedroom in the garret. She snatched up her Bible, and several of Iain's letters fell to the floor. She bent to scoop them up, her mind whirling.

Iain. Are you out there? Are you shooting? No, no. You can't be. The Army of the Potomac isn't out there. The Philadelphia Brigade isn't out there. But who is?

Her mother had put the kettle to boil on the stove but had spilled a bag of tea. She was trying to pick up the leaves off the top of the stove and burning her fingers, wincing, thrusting them in her mouth, then plucking at the tea leaves again.

"Mother, stop."

"I've ruined the tea. I can save some of it if I'm quick enough."

"Never mind. We have lots of tea. Stop burning yourself."

"I can save it."

"Stop." She took her mother's hands. "Let me make the tea."

"No. No. I can do it. I'll put the kettle on."

"The kettle's on the stove. You put it there. It's almost at the boil. You did a perfect job, Mother. I'll do the rest. Can't you start reading the Bible for us?"

"I don't have a Bible."

"Here's mine. Use mine."

Her mother took the black leather Bible from her daughter's hand. "I confess I'm rattled, my dear. I don't know where to begin."

"Psalm 23. That would be a good place. Don't you think?"

"Twenty-three. I have that memorized."

"Then recite the Twenty-Third Psalm, Mother. Recite it for us while the tea steeps."

"What did you use?" her mother asked.

"Irish breakfast tea," she replied.

"Irish. Captain Kilgarlin would like that."

"Yes. Yes, he would."

The firing could not be ignored or dismissed, but her mother stood in the kitchen and gazed out a window at the garden, and her voice rose stronger and steadier over the distant crash of the muskets and cannons, still a mile away if Mr. Ross was correct.

" 'The Lord is my shepherd; I shall not want. He maketh me to lie down in green pastures: he leadeth me beside the still waters. He restoreth my soul: he leadeth me in the paths of righteousness for his name's sake. Yea, though I walk through the valley of the shadow of death, I will fear no evil: for thou art with me; thy rod and thy staff they comfort me. Thou preparest a table before me in the presence of mine enemies: thou anointest my head with oil; my cup runneth over. Surely goodness and mercy shall follow me all the days of my life: and I will dwell in the house of the Lord for ever.' "

" 'In the presence of mine enemies,' " repeated Clarissa. "Recite it again, Mother. Please. It calms my mind."

"Of course."

She did but stopped at "the valley of the shadow of death." Then repeated the whole line three or four times: " 'Yea, though I walk through the valley of the shadow of death, I will fear no evil: for thou art with me.' " She finally moved on to the rest of the psalm, and after that to Psalms 24, 25, and 26. Many psalms she repeated twice. The gunfire never stopped, so she kept reading, now and then stopping to sip tea that went from hot to warm to cold. Suddenly the clock in the hall struck noon. She paused, waiting for the twelfth gong. As soon as it did, a loud peal of thunder burst over their house and the town.

"It's going to rain," Mrs. Ross said.

Clarissa went to the window. "The sky is blue."

"Perhaps you can't see the thunderhead."

"I don't think it is a storm, Mother. It's too constant. I think it's a fresh battery of cannons. Maybe ours, maybe theirs."

"I wish your father would come home. What can he be doing at his boot shop? Surely he isn't getting his people to work through all this?"

He arrived ten minutes later when Clarissa had taken over the reading and was at Psalm 107. Mrs. Ross jumped up and threw her arms around him so tightly Clarissa saw her father wince. "It's all right," he kept saying to his wife, "it's all right."

"Why have you been gone so long? What on earth are you up to at your shop when there is a battle only a mile away?"

"Officers have come for boots. Some have had theirs shot to pieces. Others have been needing new ones for months and took the opportunity to come to the shop when there was a lull. It was a good thing we hadn't shipped the latest batch to Harrisburg." He released his wife gently and dropped into a chair. "We've whipped them. I believe we've whipped them. Hundreds of Rebel troops have surrendered by McPherson's Woods. The Iron Brigade is here, the Black Hats, and they've trounced a brigade or two. Yes, a good number of Union boys are here now. General Howard with Eleventh Corps. Reynolds with First Corps. But bad news there. Reynolds was killed this morning."

Mrs. Ross put a hand to her mouth. "Oh no."

"God rest his soul. But we've pushed the Rebels back, Ann. And captured General James Archer. That's the news I'm getting at my shop. I have everyone working like beavers. Boots are going out the door as if we were an ammunition cache. I think the Confederates will withdraw. They're getting a licking. Unless they plan to sink their teeth in and bring up more divisions. Then this fight could get out of control."

"We heard new cannon firing," Clarissa said. "At noon."

Her father nodded. "The Rebels have set up batteries on Oak Ridge."

"So then, they do intend to stick it."

He shrugged. "Or cover their retreat. Hard to say." He looked around. "Could I get a sandwich and some coffee? I need to get back."

"You must be careful, Benjamin," his wife admonished him. "Very careful."

"Officers from First or Eleventh Corps will keep me apprised of the situation when there's a lull."

"What if there is no lull?"

"Ann, I won't get caught if the battle moves south through the town. I'll know. I have my new boy, Gilbert, staying abreast of the situation."

"How?"

"I've sent him up to the cupola at the seminary twice. I've let him ride Rosebuds. She's gentle and swift and never panics."

Ann Ross listened and finally nodded. "I will fix you something." She went to the kitchen. "You just rest yourself there."

Clarissa followed her. "I can do that, Mother."

"You can help. But you're not doing it all."

"I. . ."

"Don't coddle me, Clarissa Avery. I'll find my rhythm. I'm fine."

After Mr. Ross had returned to his shop—the volume of firing increased noticeably the brief moment he held the front door open—Clarissa and her mother prayed together for a half hour and resumed reading the Psalms once more, now and then hearing the welcome clatter of rain on the roof and windows, doubly welcome because it deadened the sound of the fighting. After Psalm 150, they began again with the Twenty-Third. Just after two o'clock, there was a pronounced explosion of muskets and cannons that grew without stopping. The windowpanes began quivering again. Crockery moved around. Something broke with a loud crack somewhere in the house.

It makes it sound as if the house is haunted. As if we have ghosts. Do we? Do we have ghosts?

They tried to keep reading, but the battle roar was harsh and incessant. At a quarter to four, Clarissa glanced at the clock and then the window and saw horses and riders in blue moving quickly past their house toward Seminary Ridge. Two or three became ten or twelve and then scores. She got up and looked. Horses pulling cannons and caissons pounded past. Some of the horses were bleeding. Then came the men on foot. Hundreds of them. Running. Limping. Being helped by fellow soldiers. Turning and shooting behind them. As she watched—her mother begging her to return to her seat—an infantryman was struck a blow out of thin air and spun around. Blood was on his chest. He fell. Other men ran frantically over him as he lay in the street. So did several limbers hauling large artillery pieces, the horses rearing and plunging and stamping their hooves as their drivers whipped them. And then there were more soldiers in blue running. And more.

"We're routed." Clarissa spoke so softly her mother said she could not hear what she'd said. She repeated herself in a stronger voice: "Our boys are running. They're running as if all the devils of hell were after them."

"Oh no. Oh no. And where is your father?"

Clarissa did not sit back down, though she knew she should have because she could hear the crackle of musket fire right outside their door and saw the smoke and muzzle flashes. She simply couldn't pull herself away from the frightening spectacle of the Union retreat. It was sheer pandemonium. And then there were gray uniforms. So many there was no point in counting the number of secesh infantrymen. "A lot, Mother," would have to suffice. They were streaming in the direction of the seminary. She ran up the stairs to her third-floor room, where a window faced the Lutheran seminary and she could see the building and the grounds. Her mother followed her, moving almost as nimbly as her daughter.

The tall brick seminary building was smothered in dark gray smoke from thousands of muskets. Flames flickered and leaped as if trees and bushes were burning. The Union held the high ground, but the Rebels had the numbers, and they swarmed up to the ridge screaming and shrieking. Bayonets. Muskets. Cap-and-ball pistols. Cannons. Horses running and falling. Men rolling down the slope and not getting up. The red Confederate battle flag. The Stars and Stripes. Regimental banners of all colors. Some riddled with holes from bullets and shrapnel. Falling, rising, falling, rising—as soon as one flag bearer was shot, Union or

Confederate, another took his place and lifted up the staff, holding it high until he too was shot.

"They are breaking." Clarissa was whispering into her fist. "Mercy, Lord, mercy. Our boys are breaking."

The Union troops began to retreat again. This time heading toward Cemetery Ridge. Where Clarissa's stone wall stood. And the Round Tops. And the chestnut oaks she and Iain loved.

Not all the boys in blue were panicking as they withdrew. Clarissa and her mother watched a formation of Black Hats turn, fire, reload, march off as if they had all the time in the world, turn again, fire as one again—their fire scything through Confederate ranks like a sharp-edged farm tool—reload, and continue their march toward the second ridge.

"They will cross the valley," Clarissa said out loud. "Maybe ford one of the little streams that will barely wet their boots. Climb the fence onto Emmitsburg Road. Climb another to get off Emmitsburg Road. Run or limp or march up the slope to the stone wall. It's not much of a slope. And it's not much of a walk. Most of them will get from the seminary to the top of Cemetery Ridge in twenty to thirty minutes."

"And then what?" asked her mother.

"I don't know. I expect they will stand and fight until they are overwhelmed. They are vastly outnumbered. Just those two corps and it looks like the Rebels practically have an army in Gettysburg. Why? I don't understand why they are here."

"Maybe. . .maybe our boys should just surrender and be done with it."

"If Iain were here with Second Corps, he wouldn't surrender."

The front door banged open downstairs.

"Ann! Clarissa!"

"We're in my room, Father!" Clarissa called.

"Get down! Get down to the root cellar! There are thousands more Rebels coming. Who knows what they'll do? Who knows what they're aiming at when they shoot? We need to get out of sight. Hurry."

They followed him through the trapdoor located in the pantry off the kitchen, stepping carefully down the ladder to sit in the dark among sacks of last year's potatoes and carrots and apples and turnips. The thump of cannons and bursting shells and the hail-on-a-tin-roof rattle of musket fire was still distinct. Once they heard boots stamping through the house, a man shouted, glass broke, and there were several loud musket shots. Then no more sounds. Clarissa looked at her father and raised her eyebrows. He shook his head and consulted his pocket watch in the light of a small candle they had lit.

"It is just after six o'clock," he said.

The gunfire continued, but as Clarissa counted to one hundred for the fifth time, she could tell it was decreasing. Then it was sporadic. By the time her father announced it was six thirty-five, there was no firing at all. No sound from the street. No shriek of shells over the rooftop. No horses' hooves. There was nothing. Still, they waited, silent, listening. At eight, Mr. Ross nodded and went to the two doors that opened to the backyard and the garden.

The doors were on a slant and locked from the inside. He opened them slowly. The rush of evening air felt as good as cool water on her face to Clarissa. Her father walked up the ramp and went out into the backyard. After a minute, he called softly for his wife and daughter to join him. They stood together and looked at the houses near theirs. Many were dark. On the air, Clarissa caught the smell of burnt powder, still floating about from all the fighting that day. Everything was etched in silver, and the night sky was luminous—the moon hung enormous and round in what darkness it had not burned away.

"We won't light any lamps indoors," her father told them. "It's best to be prudent at this point. The fight could be over and either the Rebs or the Union troops will withdraw tomorrow morning. Or Thursday might see them clash again."

"Is the rest of the Army of the Potomac coming, Father?" asked Clarissa. "Did you hear?"

"I received no reliable news on that."

After a few more minutes, they went around to the front and entered their house. A window had been smashed and three or four percussion caps from a musket littered the floor. There were boot prints of dried mud. That was all. Her father prayed with them, and they went to their rooms. Once she had changed into her cotton nightgown, Clarissa opened the curtains and let the moonlight flood her room. It was as if she'd lit twenty or thirty candles.

She stood at the window and saw campfires flaring around the Lutheran seminary. Now and then a body would pass in front of them, man or horse, and the silhouette would be obvious. She watched and prayed a long time. Then she went to a window that faced east and whispered, "Come to me, my love. Come with the army and fight here. Come and be by my side. Please, won't you come? Then I can keep you safe. Then my faith and hope and presence can better protect you. If there must be a battle here, then you must be in it, and if you are, then so must I."

She thought she did not sleep but realized she must have, for there were creases on her face from her pillow, and she recalled part of a dream where she had been riding her horse on Seminary or Cemetery Ridge. The dream had not been unpleasant, and as her thoughts began to crowd in upon her, her stomach quickly tightened. War had come to her peaceful town, and she knew nothing would be the same in its streets or hilltops or fields again. Blood had been spilled, and it would be in the soil forever. She just knew it. As if a murder had been committed in a lovely home and now no one could enter that home, no matter how dressed up it was, without thinking about what had happened there.

We're going to have ghosts. And forever and a day, when people come here, they're going to come looking for those ghosts: loved ones, fathers, brothers, fiancés. People will come looking for the dead. Just like at Sharpsburg or Fredericksburg or Shiloh.

"But if they break off now," she said out loud, "if both armies leave off now and go their separate ways, perhaps it will not be so bad; perhaps we will not be remembered for the one-day fight, but for better things."

You just prayed Iain would come.

Only if there's more fighting here. Then he must come and make a differ-ence. But I'd just as soon all the soldiers went away and left us to our wheat fields and orchards and unblemished meadows and ridges. I just want our town to be known for its beauty. Not warfare and death.

You can't control fate.

I don't believe in fate. But I am certainly aware I can't control generals or battalions or history. Or the ways of God. I can only wish and pray. And then, whatever comes, act as I see fit as a Christian woman.

Clarissa's father rose before dawn, and the three of them ate a break-fast of toast and oatmeal together. From their windows they could see Rebel soldiers roaming the streets, cannons drawn by horses thunder-ing past, and officers on horseback moving to and fro. Finally, at nine, her father left for the shop. Clarissa and her mother decided to read a Gospel—they chose Luke—and took turns reading chapters out loud. The cracks of whips made them cringe, thinking thousands of muskets were about to open fire again, but the morning remained quiet. Mr. Ross returned promptly at noon, took off his hat, and fell heavily into a chair.

"What's going on, Ben?" asked his wife.

"What news, Father?" asked Clarissa, trying not to push him. "What have you found out? Are the Confederate soldiers leaving?"

He blew out a lungful of air. "Where do I begin? Well, first of all, no, the Rebs aren't going anywhere. Lee is here. Has been here since yes-terday afternoon. He means to finish the fight. That's what the Confed-erate officers think. No one has been given instructions to withdraw. A number of them have congregated at my shop. Some of it was ransacked overnight, but they didn't find my cache of finished, or almost finished, boots and shoes. Those were well hidden under a trapdoor. Or, had been well hidden. A Reb major had just uncovered it before I walked in, and they were busy sorting through the pile. They said they would pay me, and so they did—in Confederate dollars. Which will be useful if we ever head down to Richmond to purchase supplies. Another promised to get me Yankee dollars if he got his hands on any. And one colonel did come by when he found out what was going on and gave me two gold pieces." He lifted his hands in resignation. "Yesterday I outfitted Union troops. Today, Rebel troops."

"There is nothing you can do about that," his wife responded.

"Indeed not. Shortly after all this, the sexton came by expressly to tell me our church had been turned into a hospital. I went quickly along Chambersburg, and sure enough, the pews were packed with wounded. Union and Confederate both. Some were lying, some sitting, some were on the floor. I will tell you there was already a small stack of hands and feet, yes, and legs and arms, outside at the back. I understand the seminary has been turned into a hospital as well, oh, and the other churches in town too. But Christ's Church couldn't be busier. They badly need more help to clean and bandage wounds and feed the soldiers."

"I will go," said Clarissa.

"Well, you are not going alone." Ann Ross sat upright. "We'll both help."

Ben Ross held up a hand. "All three of us will help. I see no danger to moving about the town this afternoon. Most of the troops are away off toward Seminary Ridge. I expect there will be an action, but heaven knows when. It is getting on to one o'clock. In any case, I must tell you, I borrowed a brass scope from the reverend and went up to the church's cupola. I had never been up there before. With the trees in full bloom, I could not see much. I did spy the seminary and see some large Rebel troop movements. No cavalry, which I find odd, given that I was told the whole Army of Northern Virginia has been ordered to concentrate in Gettysburg."

"But why?" demanded Ann. "Why? What do we have here that Lee wants?"

"Right now? The Army of the Potomac. Meade has brought his men here. He is going to fight. And Lee wants to fight too. And destroy him. So that is that. No one appears to be budging. I took Rosebuds from

Gilbert and walked her wherever the Rebs would let me. I must tell you, they were most polite and obliging. A Mississippian officer escorted me as far forward as I was permitted. He recognized me from the shop and called me the Boot General."

"So, Iain's Mississippi is here," said Clarissa.

"It is." Her father locked his gray eyes on her. "And so is he."

Her heart stammered in her chest, as if it could not catch its rhythm properly. "You're sure?"

"Most of the Army of the Potomac is here now, my girl. Dug in on Cemetery Ridge. From the graveyard to the stone wall and the copse of chestnut oaks, and all the way south to the Round Tops, though even with my scope I could discern no Union troops on those two hills. However, I did pick out something else—a green flag here, a green flag there. Now, I realize there are other Irish regiments in the army that fly green flags. I don't know how many. But it's safe to bet, if I were a betting man, that one of the flags I spotted is part of the colors of the Sixty-Ninth."

"I see." Clarissa had been holding her breath and suddenly expelled it in a rush. "Where. . .where do you think his regiment is located?"

"I can't say. Perhaps more toward the trees? Those chestnut oaks of yours? If the flag I saw in that area is, in fact, theirs. As for Lee, well, he has Mary Thompson's farmhouse on Seminary Ridge."

"What?" Ann Ross stared. "Widow Thompson's?"

"Yes."

"Where is she?"

"I have no idea. Perhaps still in her home? Lee is a gentleman and will afford her every consideration. Oddly enough, I was told Meade has made his headquarters at Lydia Leister's farm on Taneytown Road. Just back of Cemetery Ridge."

"Another widow. With six children."

He nodded. "Meade is there. If the information I received is correct. One of the Union wounded at Christ's Church said it was so. Who knows? Wednesday was confusing for everyone it seems, soldiers and civilians and generals alike." The clock struck one. "There. Time is getting on. Still quiet. No cannons. Nothing at all. Let's have ourselves a meal and head along to the church. Ambulances continue to bring in casualties from yesterday's fighting."

For Clarissa—once they arrived at Christ's Church—looking at the soldiers' bullet wounds, Federal or Confederate, was like staring down at Iain's wounds again. Her stomach and mind rebelled, and the stench in the sanctuary assailed her nose as well, but she fought it all down, just as she had fought it down when Iain lay half dead in the dust of the roadway. Whatever she was asked to do, she did. Washing wounds and bodies, trying to cheer up those who were aware and alert, fetching items for the surgeons—those were the things that took up most of her time. She thought about little else, not even Iain up on the ridgeline, until the loud crash of musket fire and artillery made everyone in the church jump.

She was free to rush to the door and look outside. Smoke was rising between Seminary Ridge and Cemetery Ridge, that beautiful valley where so much grew so well, and it only became darker and thicker, as if a storm cloud had fallen to earth. The din did not stop. She had hoped, *Oh, only a skirmish, please, a skirmish,* but she knew it was the sound of full-out battle. Did she hear men shrieking? Was that the awful Rebel yell? The same sort of wild and angry screaming she had heard for the first time the day before?

"Lee's got you Yankees now," she heard a soldier on crutches croak at her elbow. "Sorry to say it—you all have been mighty kind—but Lee will have at your blue-bellies this afternoon. They will be on a tear for Washington an hour from now. I 'spect they will outrun their horses again."

"They didn't run for Washington yesterday, sir," she retorted.

"Probably too shell-shocked. Another dose of Dixie cannon and musket oughta set 'em running flat-out. All they'll need now is someone to help point 'em east. Wouldn't want 'em getting that messed up and have 'em running straight at us, no ma'am. Why, we'd shoot and gut the whole barrelful."

She turned quickly and went back into the church, refusing to listen to any more of his taunting, and refusing to get into an argument with a wounded soldier, Rebel or not. Someone propped open the doors to improve the circulation of air in the building, so the roar of combat followed her wherever she went. Now she could not stop thinking of Iain, certain Lee had his men assaulting Cemetery Ridge. What had he called it when he wrote her after Antietam? *"I've seen the elephant."*

Well, she certainly couldn't claim to have seen the whole elephant from the church steps just now, or from her bedroom window the day before, but she'd definitely caught a flash of its tusks, and it put a huge weight on her heart. She felt she could not get her breath. Rain showers that came and went all afternoon helped a bit because they brought a small measure of coolness and moisture. Once she went outside just to get her face and hair wet. Ten minutes later, the only wetness on her skin and dress was from the perspiration she could not control. It seemed that all she had left in her was prayer.

God, keep him safe. Please, please, have mercy.

How many women, she wondered, biting her lip, *both North and South, have prayed that very same prayer a million times over since Fort Sumter?*

An hour later, the noise of war had not diminished; if anything, it had increased and seemed wilder and more frenzied. Or was it just she herself who felt wilder and more frenzied? She swiped the back of her hand across her brow. Even with the doors open, the church was impossibly hot. How would the pitiless summer sun feel to the men fighting under it, canteens empty, faces grimed black from burnt powder, voices hoarse from shouting? How did Iain feel, with the bull elephant thundering at him, tusks bared, bellowing, kicking up acres of dust and dirt? Did he even think about the heat? Or was he too busy trying to kill the men who were trying to kill him to think about anything except aim, shoot, reload, aim, shoot, reload?

At five thirty, glancing at the spare watch her father had thrust into the pocket of the blood-spattered apron she had thrown on over her dress, she could sense that something more was going on, that suddenly more guns were engaged, more muskets were firing, more men were hollering than before. She couldn't stand it—Iain was under attack; his life was at stake. She was helping other soldiers, and she was grateful she could help them, but she couldn't do a thing for him. From one moment to the next, as the sound of firing swelled to a roar like wind in all the great oak trees of Gettysburg, or a hailstorm pounding against a thousand rooftops, or a tempest exploding in huge whitecaps off Boston Harbor, she thought she'd lose her mind imagining what might be happening at Cemetery Ridge—muskets, bayonets, broken bodies, death. The busier she could make herself, the better. It was the only thing, she knew, that kept her sane, that and the constant prayers she was hurling to heaven. Others took breaks. Her mother implored her to take a few minutes, get off her feet, and drink some hot coffee or tea. But she gave her mother what she knew must be her wild-eyed look, red hair unraveling over her face, every strand dripping with sweat, pushed back again and again by hands smeared with the blood of a hundred soldiers, blue and gray: "I can't stop, Mother, I can't. If I stop doing something for my man by helping these men, I'll die. I swear, I'll drop to the floor stone dead. Let me be, please, let me be."

Five thirty was soon seven thirty, and the shooting had not stopped. When she went to the door at nine and looked out at a sun dropping down to the horizon, the crackle of muskets continued, and as dusk came on, huge flashes of gunfire were vivid just outside town to the south. Only toward ten, when she stepped out again as it grew dark and the moon was a massive ball of red and gold at the eastern rim of Gettysburg, did she sense the fighting was petering out, that thousands of muskets had become hundreds, then twenty or thirty, and finally, none. A breeze carried the rotten-egg stink of black powder to her nostrils, and she placed a hand over her nose.

At the same time as she stood there, a company of Rebel troops came marching along Chambersburg Street and passed by in front of her. For a flicker of a second, one of the soldiers glanced her way and their eyes locked. Clarissa instantly recognized that she was looking into a woman's eyes and face, even though the woman was disguised as a man. The woman knew she knew. And it felt to Clarissa, as the female soldier marched down the street with her comrades, that she fired a brief plea Clarissa's way not to reveal her secret.

"I won't," Clarissa murmured. "I don't know your reasons, but my lips are sealed. And, if it's for love, I understand. Believe me."

"Miss?"

Startled, she turned to face a Rebel officer. "Sir?"

"I've noticed how hard you've worked in this hospital here. Even with my own men. I realize you must be exhausted at this point, but I wonder if I might beg a favor?"

"What is it, Major?"

"The day is at an end. And the day's fighting. I'm sending several ambulances out to the battlefield to gather up wounded and bring them water since we won't be able to collect every man at once. You are young and strong and have the good eyes and ears that go with your youth. You may find wounded the ambulance drivers would miss." When she did not respond, he added, "There is a truce right now. Both sides will be looking for any comrades who might still be alive. No harm will come to you. No one will shoot. And my men will treat you with honor and respect—you have my word. There will be other nurses on the field as well. But with your zeal, the zeal I have personally witnessed in the church this afternoon, and your attention to detail, I believe you can help us save lives. Might I prevail upon you?"

"Yes." She nodded. "Yes, Major. Of course I'll help. It would be my Christian duty to assist you and the ambulances. It would also be my duty as a human being. A human being made in the image of God. As every man, woman, and child is."

He inclined his head. "The ambulances are just over here."

"I will let my parents know."

"Very well."

She anticipated the arguments of her mother and father, and she reminded them how long she had worked with the Underground

Railroad and of the dangers she had faced. Brought home the point it was her Christian duty to respond to the enemy officer's request. Made the case that a truce to gather up the wounded and suffering would be honored by both Lee and Meade, as it had been in many battles before this one, and no one would be taking shots at her in the dark. Got them to admit she might well make a difference and find soldiers the others did not. And was soon seated next to a sergeant from Alabama and a driver from Georgia as her ambulance made its way to the valley between the two ridges and out among the grasses close to the south-western end of Cemetery Ridge. What she saw was the Union army's left flank, the Confederate army's right. Lanterns floated all over the field like fireflies. As the moon rose and painted the land and the soldiers, dead and living, in silver, it seemed as if the lanterns were no longer necessary, though Clarissa still lit the candle in hers and carried it by one hand.

Immediately as she stepped down from the ambulance, the Alabama sergeant offering his hand, the cries and groans, even screams, of the wounded struck her ears and her heart and made her flinch. But she moved ahead, found a man at her feet with one arm twisted at an impossible angle to his body, directed the sergeant and driver to lift him carefully onto the stretcher—something she bent to help with even though both protested—and carried on while they were settling the wounded soldier into the back of the ambulance. She found another and another and another, and while at first she noticed which were Union and which Confederate, after an hour, the ambulance full, they were all simply soldiers to her—and sometimes, in her thoughts, not even soldiers but damaged souls—Americans, ordinary men who would die if she and the sergeant and driver did not get them into Gettysburg or up to the seminary.

She traveled back to Christ's Church with them once, but the second time she refused because she had begun to go about with five or six canteens, giving the wounded she found a drink—"Even a sip of water will save some, Sergeant, so you can't expect me to keep popping up and down from Gettysburg as a passenger when I could be here in the field rescuing a family's father or brother. I won't stray far, and it will be easy enough for you to find me again in this full moon." They did not have any trouble making their way to her again, and when they did, she was holding a Rebel captain's hand as he died, trapped under his dead horse, his chest crushed. She knew the sergeant saw the tears in her eyes; she did not brush them away in time. "I prayed the Lord's Prayer with him," was all she said. "He asked me for that."

Often enough, she passed by Union troops with lanterns who were peering down at upturned faces already illumined by the moon. And, often enough, when the sergeant was not nearby, she asked the Union men if they knew the position of the Sixty-Ninth Pennsylvania. None ever did. Until eleven, when one lieutenant pointed back at Cemetery Ridge: "I don't know how familiar you are with this place, miss, but the Pennsylvanians are just yonder, by a stone wall. There is a big bunch of trees. I think the Sixty-Ninth or Seventy-First are there." And she looked up and to her left, to the north, and thought she could glimpse the line of the wall under the moon and the oak chestnuts back of it, but she wasn't sure.

The truce was due to end after midnight. They were going to do one more collection of wounded. "The pickets will get almighty jumpy after that," the sergeant said. As he climbed up to sit beside the driver, the ambulance full of soldiers, Clarissa handed him a piece of paper she had folded twice: "Please give this note to my mother."

He leaned down and took it. "You'll be seeing her again shortly. The truce is almost over and the pickets will be active. We'll need to clear the field."

"It's something she'll want to know about sooner than that. Thank you, Sergeant."

He touched his cap. "My pleasure. We'll be back for you and our final batch of wounded."

"Of course you will."

The ravaged peach orchard, its fruit trees riddled with bullets, made her feel like crying as she moved toward the ridge, frequently stopping and going to one knee to give soldiers water from her last two canteens. The crushed and bloodied stalks in the wheat field, its summer crop thick with mangled bodies, only added to the pain she was already feeling over the dead and wounded, while her anguish from the day before fastened into her heart like the claws of a bird of prey—a second afternoon of vicious fighting made it almost certain, in her mind, that from now on her beautiful town and its farms would be known for killing and destruction and as the place where two armies had blasted one another to pieces. Even if Lee or Meade withdrew Friday morning. But she knew in her bones neither of them would withdraw. The battle had not been settled. Two days of slaughter and the battle had not been settled. A man reached out with his stub of an arm as she came near, and begged for water, and she quickly went to his side.

Once the sergeant and driver left, Clarissa had waited until they were well gone then began her drift from the peach orchard and wheat field, to the right and to the south, until she was closer to Union lines, though she saw Rebel soldiers watching her, with her lantern and canteens, from the huge pile of boulders she recognized as the Devil's Den. She avoided contact with them and walked to her left. About a hundred yards away, picking her way through twisted and rigid bodies as she searched for the living, she found a Union corporal gasping for breath and knelt. He took the water from her canteen greedily and asked her not to leave.

"I won't," she told him. "I promise."

And she sat for ten or fifteen minutes with the dying corporal, the two of them hidden away among scrub and rocks, the spot where he had fallen that evening. They talked. At some point, without scarcely thinking it over, she asked if she might borrow part of his uniform, perhaps his kepi and his frock coat, so that she could join her husband on the heights and hold him in her arms and, if the battle continued in the morning, fight beside him.

"I would like that," he whispered, struggling for breath. "The thought of me. . .fighting on after I'm dead appeals. And then, if you would, send my. . .uniform home. The address is sewn into the pocket of my tunic. Right. . .by the bullet hole. Can't miss it." He laughed, choking. "The Rebs didn't." He grasped her hand more tightly. "Sam Rutgers."

"Mrs. Clarissa Avery Ross. . .well, Kilgarlin, it is, Mrs. Clarissa Ross Kilgarlin."

"I'm the fool who goes into battle with his pack on. It's hereabouts somewheres. Got a. . .spare tunic and pants stashed in it. Belt too. That's how I've always. . .done things. Use those. Don't be afraid. You have my blessing. Win this. . .fight, my girl. You and the boys, you gotta win this fight. You know. . .you know how to shoot, Mrs. Kilgarlin?"

"Yes, Corporal Rutgers."

"Reload?"

"Yes."

"Do me proud. Do my unit proud."

"I will. Tell me what it is, Sam."

"The 124th New York. Fine boys. Proud boys. We held the Rebs back. Bought the army's left flank time. Bought those hilltops up there time. We got shot all to pieces. Lost Major Cromwell. . .and Colonel Ellis. . . . They wouldn't get down off their mounts. . . . Wanted us to see 'em and fight harder. . . . And we did, we surely did, Mrs. Kilgarlin."

"I know you did, Sam. I won't disgrace your uniform. I won't. If Lee attacks tomorrow, I'll fight for you. Just like you fought today. The 124th will be on Cemetery Ridge. You'll be there."

"Wish I could stick to see you. Wish I could. But. . .thank ye. Thank ye, missus."

She prayed over him after he had passed, and let a tear cut down a cheek stained with dried blood and sweat and death. Then found his pack a few feet away and the clean uniform inside with its two chevrons, extinguished her lantern with her fingertips, and quickly stripped off her apron and dress. She folded her apron several times and bound it tightly over her chest. After that she slipped the tunic over her arms—it was several sizes too large and hung off her like a sack—and pulled on the pants, stuffing the extra length into her military-style boots and cinching the belt around her slender waist until it held up the pants. They were still loose, but she knew she could make it work. His bayonet was on his hip, and she took it and hacked at her hair until it was well above her ears. It was far easier than she'd thought it might be because he had kept it razor sharp—he'd been a well-organized and meticulous man. And now she was him as well as being Clarissa. The same way Iain had once been so many persons rolled into one.

Finding the address sewn into his tunic, she ripped it free, pocketing it. Then she took several minutes to arrange his body, as if for a viewing, and tied a kerchief under his jaw so it would not hang open. She found a twist of tobacco in his pack and decided it would help disguise her voice. Biting off a piece, she had hardly begun to chew before she gagged and needed to spit. "Sam! What draws men to this habit? Oh my!" Determined, she kept at it, grimacing at the taste. She managed to chew away for a full minute before spitting again.

I will succeed at this subterfuge. I did it on the Railroad with my old man outfit; I can be a Union corporal in the dark on Cemetery Ridge.

She knelt and rubbed handfuls of dirt all over her uniform. Then she scrubbed it into her face and hair. She kept her nails short, so there was no need to do anything there except get more grime under them. She even nicked her cheek with the tip of the bayonet and let the blood dribble down her cheek. She spread some of it around her jaw and smeared it over her eyebrows and eyelashes and the bridge of her nose. And then ground it into her chopped and ragged hair. *I must look a fright. Good. The uglier, the better.*

"Wish me luck, Sam Rutgers," she said to the dead corporal. "It wouldn't do to get shot by a picket right off."

She kissed his forehead. He was still warm. Then she took up his musket and cartridge pouch, attached the bayonet to the muzzle with a click of steel on steel, and began to walk up the short slope to the ridge. The moon made it easy to see where she was going. Union soldiers and officers didn't so much as glance at her as she went past. Until she came within fifty yards of where the troops were dug in.

"Who's that?" A picket challenged her as she approached the ridge-line, lifting his musket.

Her heart thumped in her chest and ears. "Corporal Rutgers." She growled as darkly as she could, chewed as hard as she could, and spat. "Who're you?"

"Sorry, Corp. How'd it go for ya out there? Find who ya were looking for?"

Clarissa spat again. "I found him. Stone dead."

The picket grunted. "What unit?"

"New York."

"We're New York. The Fifty-Ninth."

"The 124th."

"You gave it to 'em today. But you got hit, ya got hit rough." The picket lowered his musket. "Looks like ya got the raw kick of the mule ya'self." He looked Clarissa up and down. "Any chance I could have a chaw o' that, Corp?"

"Sure enough." She tugged the pack off her back and dug out the long twist. "Take what you need, soldier. I reckon it will be a long night."

"And a longer day tomorrow. Ya think Lee'll hit us again, Corp?"

"Well, he sure ain't pulling out, is he?"

"No, Corp, no sign o' that. Hood's Texans are still in that pile of rocks down there, that Devil's Den, the locals call it." The picket began to chew vigorously and handed back the twist. "Thank ya."

She slung the pack and began to move to her left, toward the copse of trees and, she hoped, Iain's position. "None of the regiments have shifted over the past two hours, have they, soldier?"

"Not to my knowledge, Corp. Ya looking for your boys? Ya know they pulled 'em right back and out of it."

"I know. But I want to find a friend. He's with the Pennsylvanians."

"Tight on our right flank, Corp. The Sixty-Ninth and the Seventy-First are stacked on our right flank."

"Much obliged, soldier." She spat a huge stream of juice and was glad to get rid of it. "Luck."

"Thank ya, Corp."

She made her way along the line, canteens still dangling from her shoulders, musket in her left hand. No one paid her any attention. She knew the ground and didn't have any trouble finding her way. It took a while, but she finally saw the trees and a stand of colors—one flag was the Stars and Stripes, the other had a harp. She spat, making a few soldiers near her look up with frowns on their faces, since she'd almost hit one with her stream.

I'm not very good at this, soldier.

"What're ye doing, boyo?" The one she'd nearly hit looked like he wouldn't mind a fight. "Go spit on Lee. Not on me. Unless you meant to spit on me, and we can blow off a bit of steam and settle accounts. Whaddya say to that?"

"Pat, he's a corporal."

Pat snorted. "Spit is spit no matter who's dishin' it."

The Irish accents were thick as wheel grease.

"You lads like a chaw, you're welcome to it." She reached in her pack and tossed Pat the twist. "I'm lookin' for Major Kilgarlin."

Pat bit off a plug of tobacco. "You a courier from Meade then?"

"Maybe."

"Why'd they send a corporal and not an officer?"

"The captains and lieutenants are in short supply after this evening's disagreement down below." She chewed and let her cheeks bulge so much her voice was distorted. "Is this the Sixty-Ninth?"

"Aye."

"Is Kilgarlin here or not?"

Pat spat a dark stream near her boots. Then raised his voice: "Major Kilgarlin, darlin'! Some leftovers o' today's brawl come to pay their respects, sir!"

A moment later a voice shot back, "None of your pranks, Pat. I'm busy."

She knew the voice. And felt wonderful.

For a few moments.

Till she heard Pat's voice again.

"And so am I, Major Kilgarlin, darlin'. This corporal from Meade is tiny as a mouse now, but he roars like a lion. Best come quick before the two of us get into it and I turn him into a mess o' busted bones."

Clarissa's temper found her with a burst of heat. "Try it, wee little man. Your own mother will only recognize you from the dirt between your toes."

Pat laughed. "He's a rare one."

"Leave it be, O'Shea." Iain's voice. "I don't want you in the brig when Granny Lee comes calling. Send him over."

"Away with ye, lad." Pat laughed. "I'll be here if ye feel the need to finish spittin' on me."

Clarissa wanted to say more but moved on through the dark and silver mixture the moon and night had created to where a tall man in uniform was brushing his horse. Her whole body lit up inside as if someone had placed a hundred candles.

He heard her footsteps. And continued brushing Plum Run. "What is it, Corporal? Are you truly from General Meade?"

She spat to clear her mouth.

He turned around, eyes narrowing. "Pardon me?"

She fought to clear her throat of tobacco juice.

He was not impressed and his eyes were like bayonets. "You're a sorry excuse for a soldier, Corporal. The fighting's been over for hours. You could've at least cleaned up in a horse's trough."

She couldn't move or speak.

"Well?" He put his hands on his hips, one still gripping the brush he was using on his horse. "Don't stand there as if you've been struck by lightning, Corporal. Speak your piece and get back to headquarters."

She exhaled. "Iain."

But forgot to change her voice.

"Iain?" Anger crowded his handsome face. "What do ya mean by calling me by my Christian name, Corporal? Address me properly. I'm Major Kilgarlin. Let me hear you say it."

"Iain," she said again.

He stared at her, unsure now. "Corporal? What are—"

"Liberty." She wiped a hand over her face, taking away some of the blood and grime. "Kyle Forrester."

His face looked as if she'd punched him. "What?"

"Iain Kerry Kilgarlin." She wiped away more of the dirt. And smiled her smile. "I love you."

Chapter Eighteen

July 3
Morning
Cemetery Ridge
Gettysburg

Clarissa knew she slept. She knew she dreamed. But she couldn't remember her dreams. And every twenty or thirty minutes a *pop-pop-pop* made her stir and he would say, in his softest voice, "It's all right. It's just that the pickets are jumpy on both sides. Sleep." And she would drift back into the dreams she would not recall once dawn came. And his arm was around her, so strong, so good, and her head was on his chest, and he was the best pillow and the best blanket and the best sleep, war or no war.

She had absolutely stunned him. And she enjoyed seeing the effect of that on his face. He had hauled her back behind the ridgeline, into a dark area where there were dozens of horses tethered but no soldiers within a hundred yards, and kissed her so deeply and so powerfully and with so much passion, she felt as if she were suspended in the silvery night air and spinning around and around. He complained once that she tasted like a cigar. But that did not stop him from kissing her as if he had been wanting to kiss her for a hundred years. And he complained another time that she tasted like a spittoon. And she'd responded by asking him when he had last kissed a spittoon. They'd both laughed about that. And then he had kept right on kissing her with more ardor and outright intensity than she had ever experienced in her life. The taste of her mouth, apparently, was not the most important thing when it came to Major Iain Kerry Kilgarlin loving Clarissa Avery Ross. For that she was grateful. Because she was aware that her lips and mouth and teeth were all stained brown from the tobacco she'd used to roughen up her voice, and she knew she probably did taste like some smelly old officer's pipe. *C'est la guerre.*

Of course, the scolding eventually occurred, which was something she'd been bracing herself for, even while they gripped one another as if they were dying and a kiss was their last chance at life and air.

Didn't she appreciate how dangerous a battlefield was? Her experiences on the Underground Railroad were not sufficient preparation for facing screaming Rebels and blazing cannons. How did she manage to get onto the ridge without getting shot? Did her mother and father know where she was? Where did she pick up a Union uniform? How did she cut her cheek? What on earth had happened to her beautiful hair? And what was he supposed to do now? Put her on the front line when everyone was certain there'd be another attack from Lee on Friday?

All this with her head nestled on his chest.

She smiled at his tantrum because it showed her, once again, how much he cared about her. And every now and then, as he raved, she would place a hand on his beautiful face and guide it back down to her lips. Which quieted him considerably for several minutes. Once released from her spell, however, he would launch back into his tirade, as if he were dressing down one of his soldiers. But this made her chuckle. *Oh, but he is so sweet.*

When he began to just simmer, instead of boil over, she calmly began to explain everything to him, throwing in more of what she called her deep-dish-apple-pie kisses on the way to keep him soothed. *Honestly,* she giggled to herself so that he couldn't see, *it's like reining in a spirited horse with the delicious red apples in my dress pocket.*

Her parents knew where she was—not that the knowledge would necessarily bless them that much, since her being on a battlefield was not likely to grant them peace of mind—for she had sent them a note through the good graces of a Rebel sergeant from Alabama.

She had been giving water to the wounded and helping find soldiers to take back to the hospital at Christ's Church in an ambulance, so that had given her freedom to roam the valley between Seminary Ridge and Cemetery Ridge, canteens on her shoulder, a lantern in her hand.

Soldiers on both sides had treated her with utmost consideration and respect. She had never felt she was in any danger during the brief truce.

She had sat with a dying corporal from the 124th New York, and he had been pleased to know he would fight on in her spirit. He had offered her the spare tunic and pants in his pack, and she had accepted. He'd wanted her to take his name and rank, and she had. That's all there was to that. Well, except that she'd used his bayonet to cut her hair short and nick her cheek, and chewed his tobacco to disguise her voice. She was getting better at spitting.

There was no fear of Bobby Lee or his minions in her heart, Clarissa told Iain. She could see clearly and shoot straight. The Railroad had been better training in dealing with dangerous men than he gave it credit for. What was worse—a bunch of snarling slave catchers from Georgia or a bunch of snarling graycoats from the same place? She had handled one mob, her Navy Six smoking in her fist, and she could handle the other. She was not some dainty Gettysburg belle. She was a big, strong, knows-her-business Yankee woman. Well, maybe not big. But big enough to handle anyone from any state in the Confederacy and make them turn tail and run for their lives.

What was he going to do with her? That was his problem. But she was Corporal Samuel Rutgers of the 124th New York, and Major Iain Kilgarlin had better treat Sam Rutgers right. Iain was an officer and a gentleman, wasn't he? So then, he was bound by honor to use Corporal Rutgers in his capacity as a noncommissioned officer to help stave off defeat in the conflict before them. Was the issue resolved between Meade and Lee? No it was not. Was a victory for the North still hanging in the balance? Yes it was. Therefore, Iain had better not toss Sam Rutgers aside instead of letting him fight. Sam might make the difference, as much difference as Pat O'Shea, that was for sure.

Of all the places she could be, this was exactly where she wanted to be, right at his side, regardless of the danger. And she could do battle as well as any man. Just because they were taller and stronger than her didn't make them better than her.

"Do you want me to go?" she had finally asked him, pouting and thrusting out her lower lip as far as she could.

"No," he had replied. "It's too dangerous to send you anywhere now."

"Good. Because I'm not going anywhere anyways."

And then had come more wonderful kissing and hugging and being held in those strong, sturdy arms of his, the moon drifting past overhead and the stars appearing in its wake with the extra shadow of darkness now afforded them. The night air was softer than cotton or velvet, and his regular breathing and his heartbeat were gifts of God she had been starved for since August of the summer before. Maybe she couldn't remember the dreams from her sleep, but she could remember this dream, this God dream, this man dream—Iain Kerry Kilgarlin. The groom at the altar. The wedding ceremony only the Lord had witnessed. But the Lord was enough.

Everything dreamy and sweet broke apart and splintered at four thirty Friday morning when a racket of firing made her sit up, bewildered and frightened. The horses whinnied and stamped their hooves and tugged on the lines that tethered them. Iain was not there but had wrapped his frock coat around her. She pulled it tighter as the firing increased. It was off behind her and toward town. Was Lee coming at them from the back of the ridge? She sat in the dark and scarcely moved. The moon was gone and the sun had not yet returned. Now she wondered if she truly was ready for everything hateful the day might bring.

"Our Father which art in heaven, hallowed be Thy name."

"Are you all right?"

Iain was back at her side.

Clarissa immediately leaned into him. "Yes, I'm all right."

"I just wanted the boys to be ready in case the fighting moved this way. It's at Culp's Hill. Again. They've been at it for days. Only the night sky makes them stop."

"When's sunrise?" she asked.

"Not for a while yet," he told her. "Can you sleep some more?"

"No."

"Then let's walk some. Stretching your legs will be good for Avery Ross."

"Avery Ross Kilgarlin."

"All right. Good for Avery Ross Kilgarlin."

"And Sam Rutgers too. Don't forget him."

He laughed. "My beauty, I don't think I'll forget Sam Rutgers as long as I live."

"I'm glad to hear it. Because he is Avery and Avery is him."

They walked among horses and commissary wagons. For a while they held hands, and she loved it. It felt incredible to be in uniform and near a battlefield and, in spite of the danger, holding hands with the man she cherished. It was something new, a beautiful new, and she reveled in it. The shooting continued, but she ignored the rough and ragged sound. They walked and chatted and walked some more, always avoiding concentrations of troops. It was five, five thirty, six. Every fifteen minutes, he left her and went back to the line to check on his men. Once he was gone for half an hour. The west silvered. As soon as he got back, he reached for her hand, held it a minute, then took his away.

"We're going to start running into soldiers everywhere now," he said.

"I understand."

"I want people to look at us and think of you as my adjutant."

"I'll make a perfect adjutant."

"I have no doubt of that. That's how I'll explain your ongoing presence with my men too. Which won't make a lot of sense to them because they'll wonder why I don't pick someone from the Sixty-Ninth."

"Did you have an adjutant?" she asked.

"He was killed yesterday," Iain replied. "The Georgia boys attacked us at the stone wall here. It was a brisk fight. He fell."

"I'm sorry."

"A bright lad. I miss him."

"I'll be sure not to disappoint you."

"You can't be harmed. Ever. In any way. That's an order."

She arched an eyebrow and saluted. Several others saw the salute and snapped their hands to their foreheads for Major Kilgarlin. He rolled his eyes at her and returned her salute, and the salute of the other soldiers and lieutenants and captains. "You do beat all," he hissed.

"Of course I beat all. That's why I'm the woman standing by your side this morning."

"Let's go watch the sunrise."

"That will start your men's tongues wagging."

"I'm sure. 'Who is this corporal from the 124th New York? And why is Kilgarlin settling for a corporal when he should have a captain or a lieutenant?' But we'll save that gossip for later. I don't want the sunrise disturbed. We'll watch it with the Seventy-First Pennsylvania or the Fourteenth Connecticut. They're on our right flank."

They made their way on horseback. He mounted Plum Run and gave her the dead adjutant's horse—he had been an officer.

"What's the mare's name?" she asked, holding the horse's reins.

"Stranorlar. It's a town in County Donegal in Ireland."

"Stran-lar." She quickly picked up on the pronunciation. "That's quite pretty. And strong at the same time."

"Well, she's your horse now, Corporal. Treat her well."

"I shall, Major."

Clarissa rubbed dirt back onto her face and mouth until Iain admitted she was repelling. Then she hung the bayonet on her belt, slung the pack off the side of the horse, and placed her musket astride the saddle as she rode. She and the mare adjusted to each other readily enough, and the ride was easy. Clarissa was sure there was no more unkempt adjutant riding the ridgeline than her that morning. But the filth and grime and dried blood, and the baggy uniform, served to utterly obscure her femininity, and that was what mattered. Her appearance could be chalked up to fighting with the 124th New York the evening before. It was an excuse no one would argue with. Especially since the Sixty-Ninth had seen hard fighting at the stone wall on Thursday. Her disheveled appearance was not out of line with that of many in Iain's regiment.

The pair embedded themselves with the Seventy-First Pennsylvania and waited for the dawn. When it came, it was an extraordinary display. Too good and too wonderful, she thought, for a battlefield, even though it was really her beautiful valley, with its fruit trees and crops of grain and the greenest green grass, which the July sun was pouring its rich golden light over. She had never watched sunrise from Cemetery Ridge. She had never even watched it from the seminary. But now she saw the sun move higher and higher into a sky that was a perfect azure, as bright and flawless as a sapphire she'd once held, and she was at the stone wall and on horseback with the man she loved only a few feet away. What an amazing thing that her first sunrise on the high ridge over Gettysburg should be like that. Yet it was also disturbing that it was the only morning, ever, that the bodies of horses and men had been strewn lifeless at the foot of the green ridge, the only morning that the landscape the sun touched was thick with the blood of hundreds of souls. It made her shiver.

Iain glanced at her. "Are you chilled?"

She didn't answer his question. "You're positive Lee will fight for a third day?"

"It's his nature. He will not withdraw without trying to finish the battle."

"He withdrew at Antietam."

Iain nodded. "But now he's had his successes at Fredericksburg and

Chancellorsville. Now he's been fighting in Gettysburg for two days. He won't withdraw."

"My valley has already been despoiled. Must it be the site of even more death and disaster?"

Iain had been wearing his slouch hat. Now he removed it. "Lee and Longstreet will come at us on the flanks or up the middle. If they can win, after half a week of battle, they can alter the course of the war. Even if General Grant takes Vicksburg and the Mississippi from them, they can crush the Army of the Potomac and put their sword to Washington's throat. Any truce will be on their terms. And their terms will be complete and unfettered independence for the Confederate States of America."

"Unfettered for white men."

Squinting from the cut of the sunlight, Iain put his hat back on and tugged down the brim. "Growing up in Mississippi and going downriver to New Orleans and Louisiana so often, I found out early on that there were freedmen who owned slaves and who used them to work their plantations. Those men were rich in cotton and sugarcane. Those same men have joined other freedmen in the South to fight for the Confederacy."

She stared at him. "You never told me this before."

"I'm telling you now so that you realize how much we are up against here today. We aren't just battling rich white slave owners. Or white men who never want the Southern way of life to change. We're wrestling with a whole part of the human race, one color or another, who see nothing wrong with oppression if it works to their advantage. And they do not call it tyranny."

"I know that terrible spirit is not just in the South."

"No, it isn't a white thing or a Southern thing. It's a human thing. But if we don't block it in the South, the enslavement of others will spread as far as the Confederate nation spreads and become pervasive on this continent. The Rebels are not demons. This is just the way they think and believe. And they will fight for their beliefs with fire and steel. So we fight back with fire and steel to give this country the chance to be a haven of freedom for all people for all time. That's the hope. Every generation will have to fight to gain or maintain their liberties, believe me. But this is our fight. Here. Today. It's the South's day to fight too. But if you and I want to see slavery end, that can only begin to happen if we win this war." He paused. "And we'll lose this war if we don't win today."

She sat silently on her mare for a few minutes. Gunfire continued to erupt on their right as the sun made the world around them ignite with acres of light. "The grass was always so green and untrampled here. The wheat always so tall. All you ever heard were honeybees and meadowlarks."

"It will be that way again."

"I pray to God you and I will live to see it. I pray to God we'll live to see it in a free country."

"Amen." He looked to his left. "I need to get back to my men. Are you ready to be Corporal Rutgers again?"

"I never stopped being him." She struck at several tears before anyone would notice. "Or Clarissa Ross Kilgarlin."

As they walked their horses back down the line to the Sixty-Ninth and the cluster of chestnut oaks, Iain asked, "Do you have any more of that tobacco?"

"Why? Do you want a chaw?"

"Not me. But you need a plug to help your voice along. And make those lips of yours look more revolting than they already are."

"Why, thank you very much for those kind words, sir. There's another twist in my pack."

"Start working on it, Corporal."

He had managed to tug a smile out of her. "Yes, sir, Major, sir. Anything to help the Union."

The men didn't have much to say about the return of Corporal Rutgers. Except Pat O'Shea, who spat near her mare's front hooves. She pretended not to notice but spewed a thick stream that just missed his head. It went exactly where she wanted it to and had the desired effect of riling O'Shea mightily, so she was quite proud of herself.

"You're getting good at that," Iain said.

"So I am too, and no mistake," she replied, imitating Irish jargon with a voice as thick as mud. "I am, however, a spittoon again, I'm afraid."

"It doesn't matter. There'll be no more romance until it's all over."

"That's disappointing, sir."

"Once the sun sets, Corporal."

"Sure, I'll be counting the hours, Major."

"Keep up with that Irish blather and I'll call you Killarney for the rest of your life."

Clarissa marveled that she and Iain could be talking about the future of the Republic and about fighting tooth and nail to preserve it, as well as to bring an end to slavery, in one breath, and in the next breath, banter with one another, spit tobacco juice, and look forward to being wrapped in each other's arms again that night. How did they know they'd even survive to see the night? What if they lost the battle and were in full retreat? What if they were prisoners of a victorious Rebel army? What if Vicksburg didn't fall to General Grant after all and, with the Gettysburg win under its belt, Richmond telegrammed Washington to accept its peace terms and the Confederacy's independence?

The shooting at Culp's Hill petered out just after eleven. At noon she and Iain dismounted and stood under the trees several minutes while he spoke with the regimental commander, Colonel O'Kane, as well as with officers he briefly introduced as Lieutenant Colonel Tschudy and Major Duffy. She barely listened. Their concern was that Lee might come straight at them and ignore the flanks, hurling all available men and resources at the center of the line. She swatted away flies and looked at the other adjutants, all of them officers and in much better condition than her, and they looked back, impassive.

"Are you hungry?" Iain asked her once the others had ridden away.

"I'm always hungry," she said. "I mean, usually I would be hungry. But is Lee going to attack? Is he not going to attack? If he does attack, is he going to attack us right here at the trees? Or what is he going to do? I confess it makes me a bit jumpy. And when I'm a bit jumpy, I don't eat much."

"Good. Because there isn't much to be had. Meade's concern was getting cannons and ammunition to Gettysburg. Not vittles. Are there any biscuits in your pack. . .Corporal Rutgers?"

"I guess there are some. But they're hard as rock."

"Mm. Let's fetch some coffee. You can dip the hardtack in that to soften them up."

"That's probably all I can handle right now."

"Don't worry. Once the shooting starts, any butterflies you have in your stomach will fly away."

"You're sure about that?"

"I am." He nodded. "But you won't be on that horse. You'll be flat on the ground and far back from the wall."

"And I suppose you'll stay on Plum Run even with bullets whizzing around you?"

"Of course. I'm an officer."

"And I'm the officer's adjutant. Where you go, I go. Where you are, I am."

Iain frowned. "Huh. We'll see about that."

"We will indeed. Why do you think I went to all the trouble of slipping away from town and disguising myself and hooking up with your regiment, sir? Just so I could watch you get yourself shot? If I'm going to do anything up here, I'll be making every effort to keep you alive. So don't try and put me five miles behind the battle line, sir. It won't work. Even a cage wouldn't hold me."

His hands were on his hips. "Are you finished?"

"I'm giving you your orders, Major. That's all."

He rolled his eyes. "My orders?"

She smiled. "I outrank Colonel O' Kane. I even outrank General Meade."

"What about Lincoln?"

"I outrank him too. You have no choice but to obey me. Sir."

She was going to add something else when a cannon boomed from Seminary Ridge. They both looked. Another cannon fired. Then there was silence.

"What was that?" she asked Iain.

Confederate artillery erupted in smoke and flame all along the heights. The sound came moments later. A huge roar of cannon fire. Shells began screaming over the ridge and exploding in the rear, pulverizing wagons and killing horses. Iain shoved her to the ground.

"Stay here!" he ordered. "Don't move!"

"Where are you going?"

"I need to ride the line."

"Then I need to ride with you."

"No!" barked Iain. "That's an order!"

"Yes!" she barked back, the crash of artillery rounds blotting out their voices to others. "That's my order! Sir!"

Chapter Nineteen

July 3
Afternoon
Cemetery Ridge and the Angle
Gettysburg

For two hours she raced along beside Iain, the cannon fire never relenting, explosions hurling mud and stone into the blue sky. The only reason she felt both of them survived the bombardment was because the Rebel cannons were not on target. She supposed they had meant to blast apart the Union defenses along the stone wall, but it was men and horses and wagons and limbers, far back from the wall and ridgeline, that took the brunt of the punishment.

Iain kept shouting at her to take cover, and she kept shouting back she was taking cover—right next to him. He was furious, but there was nothing he could do. The fight was on and he was stuck with her. He eventually realized he did need an adjutant and began sending her off at full gallop with messages to Colonel O'Kane, or Lieutenant Colonel Tschudy, or Major Duffy, and once to Major General Hancock, the commander of the Second Corps of the Army of the Potomac. It seemed to her that Hancock liked to sit high on his horse, with deadly shell fragments cutting the air, as much as her husband did. She could not resist urging him to get out of the saddle: "Will the general take cover, sir? We'll require your leadership once the Rebel infantry commence their attack."

He had shaken his head at her, as if he were getting rid of wasps or bluebottle flies. "The men need to see me during artillery fire as fierce as this. It keeps the blood in 'em." Then he'd grinned a savage grin at her. "You like your tobacco, Corporal?"

"I do, sir. Calms the nerves."

"I find that action calms mine." He scribbled a note on the back of Iain's message. "My compliments to Major Kilgarlin of the Sixty-Ninth. If the Rebel infantry come straight on—and I believe they must do, for that is where their artillery is concentrating its fire—he and his men will be in the thick of it. I'm certain the Reb gunners are using that copse of trees to sight their fieldpieces. And if the artillery is using those trees to send their shots where they want 'em, the infantry brigades will use those trees to send their men where they want 'em too."

"Major Kilgarlin won't break, sir. And neither will the Sixty-Ninth." She snapped him a salute. "Good luck, sir. God bless you."

Hancock returned the salute as another shell whistled over their heads. "Stick it to 'em, Corporal."

She realized that riding was the best thing for her to do as artillery fire rained down on the ridge. It was something she knew and something she could concentrate her thoughts on. Fear was not able to dominate her while she bent over her mare's neck. Shells were howling through the sky and ripping apart the ground. Men and horses were crying out. Rebel cannons were blazing and Union cannons were blazing back. . . . She rode through a hurricane of shrapnel and steel, yet she was as calm inside as a forest pond, as solid in her mind as a mountain. All around her was a storm that shattered the rocks to pieces, but it did not faze or intimidate her. She was at full gallop, the sorrel's mane whipping her face, and she was grinning a grin that didn't fit the circumstances—it was as if she'd been asked to dance by the handsomest officer at the ball.

In a way she had, and being his courier on a battlefield was the dance he'd offered, and she'd taken his hand, and the reins of the horse he gave her, and accepted.

It was on her gallop back to Iain, who told her she would find him by the regiment's colors, that a final shell exploded off her shoulder, spraying her with stones and slicing open her hand and cheek. After that, the firing stopped. She could suddenly hear the loud thumping of her heart and the harsh gasping of her breath. Her pace did not slacken, and once she spotted the green flag with its cloud and sun and harp, she kicked in her heels and arrived at Iain's side in a clatter of hooves and rocks. A captain was with him.

"You ride like a demon," the captain said to her. "I wish we had time for horse races. I'd bet money on you."

She saluted. "Yes, sir. Thank you, sir." Her mouth was full of tobacco juice, but she wasn't going to spit with him there.

"Do you fight like a demon too, Corporal?"

She grinned, knowing full well the effect was gruesome, for in addition to a muddy, lacerated face and her matted hair, stiff with dried blood, she was confident half her teeth were black with tobacco stains. The way the captain practically winced when she bared her teeth confirmed this opinion. He shook his head as if he might shake off a bad dream when waking up.

"You are a sight to behold, Corporal," he managed to get out.

"Thank you, sir." She kept grinning.

"I don't know how the enemy will feel. But you frighten the dickens out of me." He turned in his saddle to face Iain and snapped a salute. "All the best, sir."

Iain returned the salute. "Give it to them, Captain."

Iain looked at Corporal Sam Rutgers, also known as Clarissa, as the captain rode off. "You do look scary."

"Do I scare you?"

"You've never scared me, Corporal."

"Not even when I look like this? Like some sort of hag from the pit?"

"I rather like the look of my hag from the pit." He glanced at Seminary Ridge. There was no more cannon smoke. "What did Hancock say?"

She handed him the piece of paper. "He believes the infantry are going to sight on the chestnut oaks here, sir. That the Rebs are going to come straight at our position on the wall."

"Huh." Iain unfolded the note and scanned it. "Well, we're ready for them. I have cannons and muskets and a hag from the pit to stonewall those graycoats with."

"I suppose you could probably use a few more of me, sir."

He laughed, eyes still on the note. "One's enough for me, Corporal Beautiful. And if it's enough for me, it's enough for Lee."

"Beautiful?" She latched on to his use of the word. "You can't be such a romantic as to find me beautiful right now."

"I can see your soul, Corporal. They can't."

She was sure she blushed under all the grime and filth on her face. "How can you see my soul, sir?"

"It's in your eyes, Corporal. I don't care what else you or good Pennsylvania dirt or war does to your face. It's in your eyes—your dancing green eyes."

Always so quick with a comeback, Clarissa had no words. She opened her mouth but nothing came out because she could not form any sentences in her mind. Finally, she stammered, "I think. . .I'm sure. . .I mean, I know, sir, that. . ."

"HERE THEY COME!"

The shout rose from a hundred places up and down the line.

Clarissa looked and saw red flags with crosses of stars, sunlight shining on thousands of bayonets, men in gray and butternut marching out of the woods on the other side of the valley. She estimated the Rebel infantry to be spread out, shoulder to shoulder, for over a mile. The image excited her and frightened her at the same time. She watched them come over her perfect valley with its perfect green grass and approach the Emmitsburg Road. It would not take them long to reach the ridge. Perhaps twenty or thirty minutes. No more. She glanced down and saw that her knuckles had whitened as she gripped her reins more tightly. When she glanced up again, Union artillery was firing, and the marching men had begun to disappear in clouds of dust and red mist. As she watched, dozens of men. . .no, hundreds. . .vanished in smoke and fire, to be replaced by hundreds more who stepped into the gaps torn in their battle lines. The cannon fire increased and more men fell. And more. Still, the Rebels marched on toward the ridge where Clarissa and Iain sat astride their mounts. Then they reached the first high fence that barred them from Emmitsburg Road. They began to climb over in gray swarms. Hidden cannons erupted and threshed them, she thought, like human wheat. She shuddered. But the Rebels would not stop.

"How brave they are," she said in a quiet voice.

Iain barely heard her with cannons beginning to bark a few feet away. "They are fighting for what they believe. As are we. So we must be brave too."

"Yes, sir."

"At every moment in the history of our republic, there have been many Americas jostling with one another for the right to define the one true America. It all depends upon which vision prevails during any given generation. Today, right now, we're battling for our vision."

"And so are they."

"Yes. So are they."

The Confederates ran across the road and began to clamber over the second fence. Shells cut many of them in half. Clarissa looked away. She knew that once over the second fence they would start across the last stretch of field. She could tell that even more artillery had opened fire on them. She realized the Confederate infantry would not stop even if there were only a handful of them left. A count began in her head. It would not take more than ten minutes now. Ten minutes for them to reach the stone wall, the chestnut oaks, the zigzag angle in the wall, her and Iain, and the Sixty-Ninth. The colors were at the long line of stones now. The Stars and Stripes and the vivid green flag with its Irish harp.

Horses' hooves hammered the ground behind her. A voice bellowed not to fire until they could make out the whites of the enemy's eyes. Twenty or thirty paces. Did they remember the regiment's motto? *Riamh Nar Dhruid O Spairn Iann?* "Who never retreated from the clash of spears"? There could be no retreat. The regiment would stand its ground. The Irish would stand their ground. The Republic would stand its ground. They would die here, if they must, but they would not yield an inch of high ground to the enemy. It all came down to this—this minute, this hour, this destiny. The Irishmen would hold. The Americans would hold. There would be no surrender.

She turned to look.

Colonel O'Kane thundered off down the line with his retinue in pursuit.

She looked back at the field. Her green field. The Rebels were close. So close she could see faces, could see eyes and noses and mouths, and the grip of their hands on their muskets. She saw puffs of smoke and cuts of flame as they began to shoot. Five minutes. Four minutes. Two. Artillery blasts continued to slash them to pieces. Still they came. Running now. Charging. Yelling. Shrieking. Coming at her. Coming at Iain. Coming at the wall.

"FIRE! OPEN FIRE! FIRE!"

Union muskets roared all along the wall in a burst of dirty smoke and jagged flame.

The Rebels fell in rows.

In row after row after row.

And still they attacked.

"FIRE! FIRE!"

The Union line flashed like sheet lightning.

Rebels were ripped to pieces.

But other Rebels kept coming on.

Shooting, hollering, waving their red battle flags.

"The Fifty-Ninth has run!" came the shout along the line. "The Fifty-Ninth New York has broken and run! We are open on the left!"

Another shout rose up from the right. "The Seventy-First Pennsylvania has fled the field! The Seventy-First has pulled back! They're in retreat! No one has our right flank!"

"Hold!" Iain spurred his horse along the wall. "It all comes down to this! Hold the line! Do not break! We do not break! You're Americans now! You all are! Donegal, Kerry, Connemara—you're Americans! Fight like it! We will maintain our left and right flanks on our own! We will hold this line! We do not break, and we do not run!" He pointed with his sword, the fine sword Clarissa's father had bought him. "Close the gap! Get to that angle in the wall and close the gap! Lift the colors! The South do not take the day! Others run—we never shall! Push them back! Push them!"

Clarissa saw two things happen at once—Rebels pouring over the gray wall, covered in clouds of musket smoke, and a bullet striking Iain and hurling him from his horse. She froze. Could not think, could not move. Until a bullet cut open the skin on her forehead and blood spurted into her eyes. She swiped it away with her hand and realized she was screaming: "No, Iain! Not a second time! No!"

She galloped her mare to where he had fallen, and jumped from the saddle. Rebels raged toward her, howling, muskets and bayonets pointed. Bullets sliced past her head. She tore Iain's revolver from its holster, aimed, and fired.

"You will not take him! You will not take my country! My dream is as strong as yours! Stronger!"

She saw Rebels pitch to the ground and continued to squeeze the trigger. The pistol was empty. She knew Iain kept a second one tucked in his belt and yanked it loose. A Rebel officer lunged, swinging his saber. It had blood on it. She fired point-blank. He went down. Three men came over the stone wall behind him, right over the crazy zigzag angle, shrieking, thrusting with their bayonets at Corporal Sam Rutgers, at Major Iain Kilgarlin, at all Clarissa Avery's hopes and prayers. She kept firing. She could not stop. The soldiers fell one after another, and still her finger was on the trigger.

She glimpsed a Rebel officer—with his black hat on the tip of his sword, swinging it and yelling—and took aim, but he was already hit and collapsing. She saw the regiment's green flag and the red flags of the rebellion, the Confederate stars on their cross and the American stars on their patch of blue, men in blue and gray striking one another with the butts of their muskets, saw bayonets pierce chests, soldiers rolling in the dirt and hitting each other with their fists, saw them biting, kicking, choking.

Somehow, in all the shooting and screaming, Clarissa had the presence of mind to cry out to God. A Rebel officer leveled his pistol at Pat O'Shea's face. She fired. The officer was thrown backward by the force of the bullet strike. O'Shea saw it was her. She had no more bullets for the second Rebel who put his bayonet into O'Shea's body.

"Fredericksburg! Fredericksburg! Fredericksburg!"

The shout went up all along the wall.

Men hollered and cheered.

The Rebels that were not on the ground twisted and broken and dying were gone.

They were gone.

She could hardly see through the thick battle smoke. It made her eyes sting; it filled her nostrils with its stench. She blinked and ran a hand over her eyes and was not sure if she was seeing right, was not sure of anything. She had to climb to her feet and look again.

The Rebels lay on her rich July grass.

They hung draped over her wall.

They were bent into the posture they had held in the womb, only now they were bent and dead in the stone angle a farmer had built long ago.

Her stone angle.

She saw the few Rebels that were left limping back across her green valley to the Confederate lines, a dozen here, a hundred there.

Leaving their red flags scattered on the ground.

She saw that reinforcements had swelled the blue ranks on her left and on her right.

She took everything in, all the time tightening Iain's belt above the wound in his leg that kept bleeding and bleeding.

His eyes flickered open. "It's so quiet."

"Yes," she told him. "It's over and done, my love."

"Where are the Rebels?"

"Gone."

"And we still hold the ridge?"

She smoothed back his hair. "We hold it. We never lost it. And your men never ran, sir. They never broke."

He exhaled noisily. "Then the battle's over. Maybe the war, in due time."

"Lee will attack again tomorrow."

Iain shook his head. "You saw what the cannon fire did. There is nothing for Lee to attack with. He left the Confederacy on the summer fields of Pennsylvania. He left it in your beautiful valley between the two ridges."

The blood had not stopped flowing, so Clarissa tightened the belt again. She knew it must hurt, the wound and the tourniquet both, but Iain did not complain. She looked over the wall at the retreating soldiers once more. Many used their muskets for crutches. Or leaned on their comrades. They moved along slowly. No one was firing at them anymore.

"What do you see?" Iain asked her. "What are you looking at?"

"I'm looking at Gettysburg," she replied. "My Gettysburg. The Gettysburg that was and the Gettysburg that has just been born. Born in blood. Like all births."

"In time, it will be washed, Clarissa, just as newborns are."

"It may be washed, sir. Yes, over time it may be washed and it may shine. But it will never be clean. It will never be what it once was. It has lost its innocence. We all have. However little of it we had left."

"Do you have your dream?" His voice was growing weaker. "Is my dreamer still holding on to her dream of a free country and an end to slavery?"

She squeezed his hand. "She is. It's ragged now, her dream, like one of these battle flags that have been shot through a hundred times. Tear-stained. Frayed. But its colors are still true. And I can't throw it away. No, I will never throw it away. It's more real now than it has ever been before."

Chapter Twenty

July–November
Gettysburg

The heavens broke to pieces on Saturday, and neither army budged as rain struck like knives. Until the evening. On the evening of July 4, Lee began to retreat from Gettysburg. And Clarissa thanked God.

She did not trust Iain to the surgeons. They were "saw happy." She had prayed all day that Lee would swallow his pride and give the order to return to the South. Once the Army of Northern Virginia had fully cleared Seminary Ridge and trudged past the Union army on the roads leading south—it took hours—Clarissa, still looking for all the world like a ragged, tobacco-spitting Yankee corporal who had been kicked and trampled by cranky Rebel mules, made her way in the dark along Taneytown Road to Gettysburg. She had Iain on the saddle in front of her as Stranorlar trotted through the rain. Plum Run followed without being tethered.

She'd told the Sixty-Ninth that, as his adjutant, she was getting Major Kilgarlin to the hospital in the seminary or, if that was over-flowing, to the hospital at Christ's Church, or St. Xavier's, or St. James. In fact, she had only one intention, to get Iain to her own house, make peace with her parents, and nurse him back to health there. All of which she did. But she knew better than anyone that she poured the pain of her ten minutes of battle on Cemetery Ridge into dressing Iain's wound—from which the minié ball had been removed Friday night—cooling his fevers, washing the sweat and corruption off his body, soothing his spirits and telling him that he would make it, he had to make it, and that she refused to let army surgeons remove his leg and toss it in a tin bucket.

During the Saturday rainstorm, with Iain dry in a tent along with other wounded men, Clarissa had helped move the bodies at the stone wall and at the angle. She'd found Pat O'Shea there and had closed his eyes and said a prayer over him. Not ten feet from O'Shea, she found the Confederate female soldier she'd spotted marching by the church Thursday night. She had been part of General Pickett's division. Her hair had not been cut, like Clarissa had cut hers, but pinned rigidly under her hat and even pinned to it. Bullets had made rags of the broad-brimmed hat and ripped the pins loose. Her hair tumbled long and ragged over her shoulders and chest.

A redhead, just like me.

Seeing her broke something in Clarissa. She sat on the stone wall in the rain and wept, her body shaking uncontrollably. No one bothered her. She guessed they simply thought she was worn out, leaning over with her head buried in her hands, the dead at her feet and all around, the deluge drenching everyone. After a few minutes, she got back up, arranged the woman's body much as she'd arranged the body of Sam Rutgers, with more dignity than raw battlefield conditions usually permitted, wrapped her gently in a blanket, and got a private to help carry her to a wet grave.

Goodbye, daughter of Virginia.

The Mississippians never met up with Iain Kerry Kilgarlin of Natchez. Clarissa found out that Mississippi regiments like the Eighteenth, Thirteenth, and Seventeenth had clashed with New York troops far to the left of Iain and the Sixty-Ninth's fight with the Georgians on Thursday. And that other New York units had battled the Second,

Forty-Second, and Eleventh Mississippi on Friday as the Rebels clawed their way to Cemetery Ridge, but that had taken place far off on the right flank, nowhere near the oaks and the angle in the stone wall where the Sixty-Ninth had held the gap left by the Seventy-First Pennsylvania. Maybe Mississippi would never hear the whole truth about one of their own pushing the Confederacy back to Virginia at Gettysburg. Maybe all they would ever know was whatever Iain had written in his letter to his parents, supposing it had reached the Kilgarlin plantation in one piece.

It took ten days for Iain's fever to break. While Clarissa waited and fretted and prayed and nursed him, Ginnie Wade's painful funeral came and went—killed by a musket ball that pierced the wall of a friend's house where she'd been waiting out the battle. People suspected snipers—they had been dueling one another from the town and the seminary out to Cemetery Ridge and back again. Or maybe it had been a soldier in the street. Or maybe nothing at all that made any sense. It seemed impossible to Clarissa that she should survive General Pickett's assault on the stone wall, with muskets going off all around her, and bayonets stabbing and sabers flashing, then come into town to find her friend dead from one single shot.

Once Iain was sitting up and taking her mother's soups, he and Clarissa were able to talk. She cried often, gripping his hands, because she knew she could have lost him in that maelstrom of gunfire and death that was Friday, July third. He wanted to know everything. She told him all that she could. That Colonel O'Kane was dead and Lieutenant Colonel Martin Tschudy as well. So were Pat O'Shea and more than thirty others, she guessed, including those who had died the day after, or were still dying in various hospitals around town. As far as she'd been able to make out, more than a hundred men of the regiment had become casualties. Lee started his retreat the night of Independence Day and was in Virginia now. Vicksburg had surrendered to General Grant the same day Lee withdrew, so the South had lost use of the Mississippi River as well as losing the fight at Gettysburg. Plum Run had survived, and so had Stranorlar; both horses were in the stable by the house. Herself? Oh, she was all right. She had not been detrimentally harmed, but yes, war had proven far more horrific than she had bargained for.

"You've seen the elephant," he said.

She nodded. "It's very big and very dangerous."

"When I can. . .I need to visit the wounded from the Sixty-Ninth. . .whether they're at the seminary. . .or at a field hospital. . .or in one of the churches."

"Of course, Iain, but not yet. You have to regain your strength."

He lay back. Clarissa could see he was taking it all in, everything she'd told him, running it through his mind. She placed her head on his chest and listened to his heart beating, and she was grateful the two of them still had life when so many others did not.

She laundered her corporal's uniform and mailed it to the address in New York City Sam Rutgers had sewn into his pocket—she presumed Dr. and Mrs. Robert Rutgers were Sam's parents. Her father bought Iain a sturdy cane of polished blackthorn, with a silver head and tip, and eventually he began to make his way around Gettysburg with Clarissa at his side. The surgeons declared him unfit for duty, and the word got around, so citizens expected to see him and doffed their hats, considering Iain their very own hometown hero of a battle the newspapers had made famous overnight.

The two of them walked everywhere, farther and farther each day. But she hated to go to the seminary with him, where the halls were still slippery with blood and men of both armies still gasped their last. And she would not go to her beautiful field between the ridges the papers were calling the Valley of Death, or to her stone wall. Or her chestnut oaks, where so many had been slain in one side's desperate fight to preserve the Old South and another's desperate fight to end it, restore the Union, and set four million slaves free. They called the part of the wall where she and Iain and the Sixty-Ninth had fought—and where she had played as a young girl—the Bloody Angle. The name repulsed her.

Her mother had trimmed Clarissa's hair to get rid of the frayed ends and the jagged line the bayonet had cut. Over her head she wore a white cotton cap close to her skull. On top of that, a sunbonnet of blue. She never took either off in public. It would take at least half a year to have any hair worth showing anyone. Or more than that. But Iain caressed her head in the evenings, when the bonnet and cap lay on her dresser, and kissed her hair and her face and told her she was the bravest and most beautiful woman in Gettysburg and the Union. No one could match her. No one. She cried.

Was it normal to be haunted by three days of rough battle? she asked Iain. Did it happen to soldiers the way it was happening to her? Did the gun flashes repeat in their minds day and night? Could they still smell the smoke from the muskets? Still hear the cannons? Was the cry of dying horses and dying men never quite out of earshot? The way a person fell once they were hit never quite out of mind? And, if they killed, what then? How often did they have to watch those death scenes of those they slew replay themselves? Would her thoughts ever be free again? Ever be free of blood and pain?

He listened but hardly spoke whenever she went on like that.

However, one Friday evening in August, when they were sitting alone in the Ross family pew at Christ's Church, she demanded an answer from him. "I need to know something, Iain. A big something. I need to know if it was worth it. The battle in Gettysburg was so terrible. It went on and on. So much death. So much slaughter. I need to know."

Her hands were knotted in her lap and turning white as she squeezed them together.

"I had many high notions before I ever saw a battle," she continued when Iain did not immediately respond. "But now I realize the war has changed everything—it has changed my town, it has changed my soul, it has changed my nation, it has changed you—and not always for the better. The pain and suffering it brings are great. Perhaps too great. What I experienced on Cemetery Ridge cuts and chops away at me inside."

After a few more moments of silence, Iain finally put his arm around her shoulders and drew her close. "Some soldiers feel just as you feel, Avery. Perhaps the majority. But they will never show it or talk about it. They will bury it deep, so deep they count on it never rising to the surface. Others will shrug it off. If you asked them, they would say in war it's kill or be killed. That you can't dwell on it. Only survive and carry on and do your duty. I suppose there are a few that truly don't feel a thing, who wouldn't understand your pain. But most, if they were honest, could see themselves in your shoes. They would admit war is ugly and gruesome. But then they would ask, what is the alternative? Leave the nation divided and broken? Leave four million in slavery? So I guess only you can answer what you ask—are the slaves worth what you've gone through? Is the Republic? Is the town of Gettysburg?"

She could not think of anything to say in response.

He gently squeezed her shoulder. "You told me William was killed at Fort Wagner in July. With the Fifty-Forth Massachusetts."

"Yes. We saw his name in the Boston papers. In the casualty lists."

"Tell me—would he say his life was worth the fight for freedom? That he was glad to pay the price? That he'd do it all over again? You know William better than I do."

"I know what he'd say. I know." She did not bother trying to stop the tears that burned her face. "He believed heaven was on our side. That God was on our side. That's what he felt in his heart. He kept quoting two verses from the Bible, from the book of Judges—'They fought from heaven; the stars in their courses fought against Sisera. The river of Kishon swept them away, that ancient river, the river Kishon. O my soul, thou hast trodden down strength.' He was thinking about it as the defeat of General Lee."

She knotted and unknotted her hands.

"It is difficult. . .but I. . .I must side with William," she went on. "Despite war's terrors, which leave a bitter taste of bile at the back of my throat, I would rather have it and end slavery than not have it and see slavery perpetuated with no end in sight. For it would, I know it would. I have no illusions about the capacity for wickedness of the human heart. I've read the Confederate constitution. They mean to enshrine bondage in their nation and take it west wherever the Confederacy grows. They mean to clasp it to their bosom indefinitely. We must end slavery, Iain. It's worth the pain and sacrifice to end it. But the price is hard. It's so very hard."

Yet even after she was able to resolve this, weeping in the church in Iain's arms, she couldn't return to the ridges or the valley or the hills. It was still too much. But refusing to go to the peach orchard or the Round Tops or up to the stone wall on Cemetery Ridge didn't spare Clarissa the rack and ruin of war, for many buildings in town and a good number of houses had bullet holes in them, which she couldn't fail to notice. Now and then she saw the stain of blood too, black and dried and hard—it was on picket fences, in alleys, on walkways, on the roads, on the stones. So every day the battle she'd witnessed was before her. It was not only in her mind. She could still touch it with her hand. She saw it in Iain's limp. War was in the mirror that showed hair that stubbornly refused to grow back and return, in any appreciable way, to the deep crimson hue she'd been born with.

When people talked about Gettysburg in the papers now, they talked about the Battle of Gettysburg. The town had become the battle; it no longer had any life of its own. The three-day fight that took so many lives was the reason people came to visit. The valley was not just the valley anymore—it was Pickett's Charge. Little Round Top was the bayonet attack of the Twentieth Maine. Cemetery Ridge was the stand of the Sixty-Ninth Pennsylvania. The stone wall was the Bloody Angle. The chestnut oaks were the trees Confederate troops marched toward and used as a marker for their assault—nothing more. It was up to her to come to terms with all of that. It was up to her to make sense of her town, and its farms and fields and hills, and of the great battle.

In the midst of her ongoing struggle, another visitor came to Gettysburg because of the battle. Only because of the battle. And he brought thousands with him. Only because of the battle. And he had something to say. Only because of the battle.

It was Abraham Lincoln.

At first she had made up her mind that she would not go to hear him speak.

Because now they had turned her town into a graveyard for the burial of the Union dead. The Soldiers' National Cemetery at Gettysburg—that was what they called it. To Clarissa, it was another blow. Her town was reduced to burial plots and monuments. And Lincoln had come to consecrate all this.

Yes, the fight for the Republic was worth it. She had made up her mind about that with William at her shoulder. The fight for abolition and emancipation were worth it. But did the fight and the way it was remembered have to continue to destroy the sweet rustic beauty of the town she'd grown up in?

When the day in November came, when some fifteen thousand people jammed Gettysburg to see Lincoln dedicate the National Cemetery, Iain did not try to persuade her to be part of the occasion. He would go, and her parents would attend the consecration with him. Clarissa must make up her own mind.

Was memorializing the great battle a wrong or a right? Did it make her town more, or did it make her town less? Should Gettysburg become a shrine to a decisive battle against rebellion and slavery, or should the battle be forgotten and Gettysburg forgotten along with it?

Just before Iain and Clarissa's parents pulled out of the yard that morning, Clarissa emerged from the house in a navy dress and cloak with a matching bonnet and sat beside Iain, who was driving the carriage, as if nothing had ever been amiss.

"You changed your mind," he said.

"I didn't change it," she replied, looking straight ahead. "I never made it up in the first place."

"Oh. All right."

"Yes. All right."

Iain was a wounded veteran of the very battle the cemetery had been created to commemorate. A number of his men were already interred there, so he was directed to an area set aside for veterans, where he and his party could sit fairly comfortably. Clarissa endured the band music and ceremony and the two hours of oration by Edward Everett of Harvard College: "Standing beneath this serene sky, overlooking these broad fields now reposing from the labors of the waning year, the mighty Alleghenies dimly towering before us, the graves of our brethren beneath our feet, it is with hesitation that I raise my poor voice to break the eloquent silence of God and Nature. . . ."

And then President Lincoln finally stood up.

He was taller than she had expected and his voice a higher pitch too. His face was pale and he looked ill. Even somewhat haggard and destroyed. The way she looked in the mirror if she had fought the fight at Cemetery Ridge all over again in her mind the night or afternoon before. She stared at Lincoln's craggy face and had no doubt he had fought the battle here, and the one at Antietam, at Vicksburg, at Bull Run, at Chancellorsville. He had fought them all, suffered through every defeat, and died a hundred thousand deaths with the men, both North and South, who had fallen in Virginia and Tennessee and Mississippi and Maryland and Pennsylvania. That, in a way, he too was interred at this cemetery along with the Union soldiers and officers who lay in silence under the earth. Seeing him look like death changed everything for Clarissa in a moment. She sat up and paid attention and prepared to drink in every word he spoke.

But there was not much to drink in. Lincoln only spoke for three or four minutes. She heard every word clearly and tried to absorb each sentence. She had thought he would speak for an hour. But he was no sooner on his feet than he was done and the band was playing a dirge. She continued to stare at what she could see of Lincoln and caught a glimpse of his face a final time. It was the color of ice and snow.

He slept with the Union dead.

She turned to Iain. "I want to go and look now."

Fifteen thousand people were dispersing all around them, and he glanced at her in surprise. "What's that?"

"I want to go everywhere. I want to go where we fought. I want to see the fields and the heights. I want to see the stone wall, where it zigs and zags. I want to see the copse of chestnut oaks. I want to go to the Round Tops where we picnicked." She paused, as if catching her breath. "I want to see the town that saved America."

Iain stood rooted. "You said. . ."

"I know what I said. I've changed my mind."

"Why? Why now? Lincoln didn't give us much of a speech."

"Oh, he gave me enough. True, I could have handled a good deal more. But he gave me enough." She gripped his arm. "We live. We live because of this town and what happened here. And now, because of that, this town shall live forever. You understand that, don't you? This town and America shall live forever."

He stared. "You astonish me. You ought to have done the oratory here instead of Everett."

"Please bring the carriage round. While folks are hobnobbing here, you can take my mother and father and me up to Cemetery Ridge."

"That is truly what you want, Avery?"

She smiled. "That is truly what Avery wants."

And it *was* what she wanted. Standing at the trees and the angle in the wall for the first time since the night of Independence Day, when she'd waited impatiently for Lee and his army to retreat south, she suddenly felt right. She saw where Pat O'Shea had fallen and told the rough-hewn Irishman, *You died for something*. She saw the green flag and the American flag and the boys in blue struck to the ground by musket fire, and she said, *Your lives weren't thrown away for power or politics. You gave America its breath. Now we can live a life again.* The crashing roar of cannons swept over her, just as it had more than four months before, along with storm clouds of dirty smoke, and she saw the blue line bend and then snap back more solid than before, and she watched the red battle flags of the Confederacy fall and fall.

It did not take long for the sun to set in November in Pennsylvania, or for the air to cool once it did. All sorts of people were exploring Cemetery Ridge and Little Round Top, and many of them walked the route Pickett's men had taken from one side of the valley to the other. However, once the stars began to appear that Thursday night and the half-moon rose, the ridges and hills and valley were deserted but for Clarissa and her party, for she had insisted they remain until the four of them were alone.

"Such a change has come over you, my dear," her mother murmured. "What is it?"

"I can memorize quite well," Clarissa replied.

"Yes, dear, I know that. You were quick to pick up your letters and your numbers."

"Mrs. Henry said I had a mind like a series of daguerreotypes. Today, I suppose, she might use the term *photographic* to describe my mind instead."

"I suppose she might. What's this about, darling?"

Clarissa stood at the wall and began to recite, linking her arm through Iain's: " 'It is rather for us to be here dedicated to the great task remaining before us, that from these honored dead, we take increased devotion to that cause for which they gave the last full measure of devotion—that we here highly resolve that these dead shall not have died in vain, that this nation, under God, shall have a new birth of freedom, and that government of the people, by the people, for the people, shall not perish from the earth.' " She smiled at Iain. "I believe I have that down to a T. You can compare it to what the newspapers print in the morning."

He shook his head. "Every day I've spent with you, you never fail to knock me back on my heels."

"Good. So, let me knock you back a little more. It's time for a ceremony the whole world can see. Marry me, Iain."

"Avery. . ."

"God has witnessed our love and devotion to one another. Now let all Gettysburg witness it. Marry me, Iain Kerry Kilgarlin."

"Oh Avery." He laughed. "With all my heart."

"And all of mine too. Every single part. With nothing missing, my love. Absolutely nothing."

Early on the morning of Christmas Day, snow mixed with rain came as slowly and softly as cherry blossoms, as white as daisy petals, as silver as coins. Bells pealed from all the churches in town, not simply because it was Christmas Day, but because the town knew that Iain and Clarissa were getting married—Iain was their war hero, Clarissa one of the brave women who had gone out into the fields at night to save the wounded. Clarissa arrived at Christ's Church by carriage with her two bridesmaids, while Iain and his groomsmen waited patiently by the altar with the Lutheran minister. Although the Lutheran church was not prepared to have its bells ring out until after the ceremony, the other churches filled the air with their strong and beautiful sounds, commencing at eight and carrying through until a quarter after the hour.

"Oh my, that sounds wonderful!" exclaimed Clarissa, as she walked up the steps to the doors of the church, her bridesmaids lifting the long train of her white gown. "A little like heaven."

"I hope your marriage will be a little like heaven," one of her brides-maids said. "From beginning to end."

Clarissa smiled. "Thank you. I get goose bumps when I think about sharing the rest of my life with him."

If Iain grinned with boyish delight—looking down the aisle to the back of the small church and seeing his young bride gleaming in a dress whiter than the snow falling outside, carrying a bouquet of three dozen roses as crimson as her short hair—Clarissa felt herself quiver from head to toe, drinking in the vision of her man, tall and heroic in his blue uniform, his groomsmen equally handsome in theirs, having been granted leave from the Sixty-Ninth Pennsylvania to stand with Major Kilgarlin at his wedding. Their swords glistened in the candlelight, their gold braid sparkled, their polished boots shone. Clarissa started up the aisle, the organ filled the church with its music and its power, and everyone in the packed sanctuary stood.

She scarcely heard the vows she made. After all they had been through on the Underground Railroad and at the Battle of Gettysburg, she was finally marrying the man she cherished, the man whose life she had saved twice. It was like a daydream that she might conjure up while she sat in the porch swing or when she walked past the flower gardens and picket fences of her town. The only sentences that mattered to her were when the minister said, "I now pronounce you man and wife," quickly followed by "You may kiss the bride," and then Iain's own whisper as their lips came together: "You are easily as beautiful as the sun or the moon, Clarissa Avery. I will love you long after this earth has ended for both of us. Before God, my sweet bride, you are my soul mate, and I shall happily love you for all eternity."

There were four other officers among the guests, all hailing from Adams County and from different regiments. They joined the groomsmen in drawing their sabers on the church steps and creating an arch of steel the newly married couple had to duck to walk under.

"One slip and my hair will be even shorter than it already is," Clarissa giggled, hugging her husband's arm. "What will you do with me then?"

"The same I intend to do with you now." Iain was grinning his boyish grin again. "Whisk you away on the most amazing honeymoon God has ever gazed upon since He created our green planet."

"It's not green here today, Major Kilgarlin, sir."

"Pennsylvania has put on white just as you have put on white. It's the most splendid day in the history of the world."

"My, your language is extravagant, sir."

"It is an extravagant day, my dear Avery, and a soldier must keep in step."

The last two officers dropped their sabers, barring the couple from passing through, and one said, "Kiss required to pass."

Clarissa glanced at Iain. "You never told me about this."

"The army has so many traditions I can't remember them all." Iain shrugged and smiled. "Anyways, I like this one. It beats shining my boots or polishing my belt buckle."

She laughed. "I'm certainly glad to hear that." She took her time with the kiss, drawing him in as close as she dared. "Now. Does that satisfy the major?"

"It does. But the sabers haven't lifted yet, Avery. You will have to bless me with another."

"I will, will I?" She grinned and pressed her rose-red lips against his once more. "Anything for an officer and a gentleman."

This kiss was even longer. She loved the combined sensations of snow falling on her head and shoulders, the sting of cold on her cheeks, the wetness of his face where the snow drops were melting, the warmth of his mouth on hers, and the strength of his embrace that made her feel so happy and safe. When the sabers lifted and they finally broke off the kiss, she saw him take a gulp of air, as if he'd been drowning and in desperate need of oxygen, and this made her even happier.

"It's a good thing we have permission to carry on now, Major Kilgarlin," she teased, unable to suppress her most dazzling and mischievous smile. "I fear another kiss from me may kill you."

He shot his boyish grin back at her. "Believe me, it would be a most pleasant and honorable death."

"My, my, such conspicuous gallantry. How bold and fearless an officer you are, sir, braving musket fire and cannon blasts and a Yankee girl's kisses."

"I am a man of audacious courage, aren't I?"

Her smile grew in size and beauty as she gave him a swift and final kiss on the lips. "Indeed, sir, you are most valiant and heroic. There is no man quite like you in the service of either army."

"Amen to that. Because there is no woman like you on the face of the earth. How grateful I am for your love and devotion."

"And I, sir, for yours."

Now the bells of Christ's Church began to ring and sing. True to her spirit, Clarissa stuck out her tongue and caught snowflakes the moment she and Iain stepped out from under the crossed sabers and into a shower of rice and well wishes. He helped her up into the carriage she'd arrived in with her bridesmaids, jumped into the seat beside her, took the reins in his hands, and began to drive them down Chambersburg Street.

"Remember," she said, "we're not leaving the town."

"I know that."

"We're going to go round and round and never leave the town."

"I'm confident I know the way, my love."

Snow and rain and ice continued to come down as the horses pulled them up one street and along another. It swirled and spun upon the carriage and fell shining upon the mares' manes and flanks, the rooftops, the avenues and alleys, the seminary, and the valley between the two great ridges. It was daisy petals on the stone wall and on the angle in the wall, silver coins on the naked branches of the chestnut oaks that reminded Clarissa of hands lifted in prayer, lifted as high as possible. It was cherry blossoms on the graves of civilians and soldiers alike. It made everything dark as bright as heaven, everything that was rough and torn beautiful. It made the land and the town and the nation new.

Author and historian, **Murray Pura** began writing at an early age. He has since published numerous works of both fiction and nonfiction. Murray lives in Canada where he enjoys the frontier landscape and its people. To learn more about Murray, visit his website at www.murraypura.com.